6

Murder

in

D1743870

Notting Hill

Phillip Strang

BOOKS BY PHILLIP STRANG

Copyright Page

Dedication

For Elli and Tais who both had the perseverance to make me sit down and write.

Chapter 1

A smart upmarket terrace house in Holland Park, a council flat in Notting Hill, and they appeared to have nothing in common apart from one significant fact: a murder at each location. In Holland Park, Amelia Brice, a socialite, the young daughter of a well-respected and very white media personality; in Notting Hill, Christine Devon, a forty-year-old domestic cleaner with no money, three children, and black. The deaths were identical: a plastic bag over the head, clearly garrotted.

Detective Chief Inspector Isaac Cook, a man who appreciated the occasional weekend off but rarely seemed to get it, knew that once again the Homicide department at Challis Street Police Station was in for a busy few weeks. Not one murder this time, but two on the same day.

'I'd say they were killed within one hour of each other,' Gordon Windsor, the station's crime scene examiner, said. A man used to death, he expressed neither remorse nor delight. He was a man doing his job, without emotion.

Isaac, a tall, good-looking man, Jamaican by heritage, English by birth, and his colleague, Detective Inspector Larry Hill, a man now in his mid-forties, and putting on weight much to the chagrin of his wife, formed a good team. Their sergeant, Wendy Gladstone, staving off retirement, somehow passing the medicals, even if her arthritis was not getting better, was back at the station.

1

'Any ideas?' Isaac said to Larry. Both men were in Notting Hill, looking at the body of Christine Devon, the black woman. It was clear that she had put up a struggle.

'What ideas? From what I've been able to gather from the youngest son, fifteen, a bit of a tearaway, he came home at four this afternoon and found her dead.'

'Tearaway?'

'Gang member probably. We've got enough around here: poorly educated, chip on their collective shoulders.'

'And dangerous?'

'As a group. Individually they're harmless.'

'The son?'

'Samuel Devon is probably ineffectual. He's a skinny individual, on the tall side. He should be at school, probably isn't most of the time, or if he is, it's only to waste time.'

'And the mother?'

'According to the son, she worked in the area. Domestic most days of the week.'

'A cleaner is what you mean. Is she Jamaican?'

'Trinidadian, according to the son.'

'The father?'

'He's not around, although there's a couple of other children: a daughter of eighteen, another son of nineteen. We're trying to find them now.'

'The other woman?' Isaac asked.

'Grant Meston is over there now,' Gordon Windsor said.

'I went there first. What can you tell us?'

'The same type of murder.'

'How and why?' Isaac said.

'You're the detectives, you tell me,' Windsor said.

'It's not as if you could confuse the two women,' Larry said.

'But why? One of the women is well-known and white; the other is black and unknown.'

'A nobody?'

'You know what I mean,' Isaac said.

'It doesn't make sense,' Larry said.

2

'That's why we're here.'

A young woman walked in through the front door of the flat. 'I want to see my mother,' she said to the uniform on the door.

Isaac saw her from the other room; he came out to talk to her. 'We'll need to conclude our investigation first,' he said. The woman, he could see, was well-dressed and attractive.

'She's my mother, I have every right to see her,' Charisa Devon said.

'That's understood, but your mother's been murdered. It's a criminal matter now. I must do my duty.'

'I'll wait.'

'What can you tell me about your mother?'

'She was a hard worker, always cared about us.'

'We've met Samuel. He looks as if he's about to go off the rails.'

'He is. It's the gangs around here, you must know that.'

'I grew up not far from here, so yes, I know.'

A uniform handed her and Isaac a cup of coffee from a café down below. 'Thanks,' the daughter said. 'You've turned out alright.'

Isaac could see that she was putting on a brave face; the enormity of the situation not yet hitting her. 'It's tough. Not all of my friends made it.'

'In jail?'

'Some are dead. Your brother could become a statistic.'

'Our mother used to lecture him to try harder at school.'

'Any success?'

'No. He thinks that petty thieving and hanging out on a street corner offer more. Although, around here, if you're not a gang member, you're singled out.'

'Ganja?'

'If it stays at that, he may pull through.'

'Have you ever heard of a Amelia Brice?' Isaac asked.

'Not me. Not around here anyway.'

'She lived in Holland Park.'

'Lived?'

'She's dead. At approximately the same time as your mother.'

'And you see it as more than a coincidence?'

'It may be circumstantial, but the odds are not in our favour. Two women murdered at around the same time. We're assuming there's a relationship. Would your mother have known the woman?'

'She used to clean for people in Holland Park, but she never mentioned their names.'

In the other room, Gordon Windsor was wrapping up, although his people would continue to comb the small flat looking for clues as to the perpetrator. The young woman left and went outside to light up a cigarette. Isaac could see her from the window, her hands trembling as she attempted to light it.

'Not much to tell,' Windsor said. 'She put up a fight, but nothing's been taken, from what we can see.'

The last statement did not surprise Isaac; it was the flat of a family with little money, the same as many others that had been built on the periphery of wealth. His parents had made it to the city with its streets paved with gold, as he remembered it from a nursery rhyme about Dick Whittington. He did not know why it came to him as he stood there in that dreary flat in that drab block of flats. His parents had suffered for following the dream of a better life in London than in Jamaica, and no doubt the dead woman had as well. His parents had eventually prospered, but the dead woman had not, and judging by the daughter's accent, she had been in England for a long time.

'Any ideas as to the tie-in with the other body?' Isaac asked. The two men had stepped away from the body and were standing in the hallway on the fifth floor of the twelve-storey block. There was an air of decay about the place. The lift door opened; a man and his wife, and their four children exited it in close formation. Christine Devon was black and dressed in a white blouse with a knee-length skirt. The woman from the lift was in the all-covering black of an Islamic woman, her eyes the only visible part.

'I've not seen the other body yet. I'm off over there now,' Windsor said. 'Are you coming?'

'I'll be right behind you.'

Outside on the street, the daughter was lighting up for the second time. 'They'll do you no good,' Isaac said.

'One or two won't harm me.'

Isaac realised that his offering advice to the young woman was the same as his parents had done to him when he was her age.

'You have another brother?'

'He's working in a shop. Billy's a hard worker, the same as Mum.'

'And you?'

'Once I've finished college, I'm off to university.'

'Where is Billy?'

'It's his day off, I've no idea.'

'But he has a phone?'

'He doesn't always answer.'

'Why's that?'

'You'll need to ask him. He's not in trouble.'

'Gangs?'

'Samuel worried Mum, but not Billy.'

'And you?'

'I've got a regular boyfriend. He's studying to be an accountant. We're thinking of getting engaged.'

'You're still young.'

'Maybe, but Troy, he wants to take me away from all this.'

'And you want to go?'

'You said that you grew up around here, what do you think?'

'You seem very calm,' Isaac said. He was enjoying chatting with the woman; in some ways she reminded him of the woman who had come over to London from Jamaica after a holiday fling he had had there some months earlier. It hadn't amounted to much. One day she was phoning to say she was coming to London on a business trip; two weeks later, she was on his doorstep looking for accommodation. He had put up with the situation for a week before telling her that he was a police officer, and her being in England for an extended period, even working, without a visa was a criminal offence, and he could not be a party to it.

He remembered her hints at him marriage her. The problem had resolved itself when he had dropped her off at the airport for the return flight to Jamaica.

'I'm not calm,' Charisa Devon said. 'She was my mother, but what am I meant to do? I'm responsible for my younger brother now, and he's a handful.'

'Your father?'

'I've no idea. He may be here or in Trinidad. He disappeared when I was five.'

'If you get married, what about your brother?'

'He can come and live with us, at least for short periods of time. My boyfriend is American. Once I get a visa, I'll go there.'

'Difficult?'

'Not too difficult. We just need to convince them that I'm not using marriage as a way of beating their immigration laws.'

'Do you have somewhere to stay tonight?'

'My boyfriend's got a place. I'll be fine. When will you be finished with the flat?'

'It'll be a police scene for some time. Do you want to move back in?'

'Once I've removed my belongings, I'll never go back. Too many memories, and it was a dump anyway. This other woman, what about her?'

'White, rich, house in Holland Park.'

'Instead of a dump in Notting Hill.'

'That's about it.'

'It's still tough in this country.'

'It's tough for everyone. Colour is not the defining criteria,' Isaac said.

'That's what I tell Samuel.'

'And he talks back to you in a Caribbean accent?'

'Born and bred around here, but yes. They think it makes them sound important, not that it does. How did you avoid it, the gangs?' the young woman asked.

'I didn't understand the lifestyle, and certainly not ganja. I preferred to study.'

'The same as me, but Samuel, he's not interested, and Billy, he's honest, although he's not academic. It's up to me to look after them.'

'From America?'

'Not so easy, but I'll try.'

From down the road a television crew approached. 'Please excuse me,' Isaac said to Charisa. 'I need to be at the other house. You see the camera down there?'

'I see it.'

'They'll want to interview you. I suggest that you don't talk to them at this time.'

'Not me. My boyfriend's picking me up in two minutes. He doesn't like it around here.'

'Why's that?'

'His colour stands out.'

'White?'

'Not that it matters to me, but yes, he's white. There are some around here who don't like an educated white man.'

'There are some around here who don't like a black police inspector, as well.'

'Samuel's friends wouldn't. Be careful with them.'

'I will. You've got my details. Just phone me at any time for help, also Bridget Halloran in my office. She'll advise you of the situation and about your mother.'

A car drew up alongside them, and a young man in his twenties opened the passenger door. 'I can't park here,' a voice with an American accent said.

'Don't worry, this is Detective Chief Inspector Cook,' Charisa said.

'Pleased to meet you. I'm Troy Hall.' The two men shook hands. 'Is Charisa okay?'

7

'She will be. It's a shock for her.'

'She's tough. I'll make sure she's okay.'

The young woman got in, buckled her seat belt and went off in her boyfriend's car.

'DCI Cook,' the interviewer from one of the commercial television stations said.

'No comment.'

'The woman, what can you tell us?'

Isaac beat a hasty retreat: too many questions, too early in the investigation.

Chapter 2

The distance from one murder scene to the other was not far. One location was lower socio-economic; the other was at the higher end of wealthy. Isaac parked his car outside the terrace house of Amelia Brice, a uniform removing the bollards on the side of the road to let him in. Inside the house there was apparently plenty of money to spare, judging by the décor. Before he had walked through the house to the murder scene, he was accosted by a man in his sixties.

'What are you doing to find who did this?' the man, dressed in a suit, his grey hair cut short, said. He seemed familiar to Isaac.

'We're investigating both murders.'

'I'm interested in my daughter, not anyone else.'

Isaac remembered where he knew him from. The man was often on television or on the radio, bellyaching. An ardent critic of anything and anyone who didn't pander to his view of the world. Jeremy Brice, Isaac knew, would be well-connected and he was guaranteed to be on the phone to Commissioner Davies, the head of the Met, in no time. After that, there'd be a phone call to Superintendent Goddard, who in turn would arrive in Isaac's office to pass on the complaint, followed by the motivational talk on how his department needed to shape up and he was expecting an early arrest.

'This is a police investigation. Both murders will be investigated thoroughly,' Isaac said.

'My daughter has been murdered. You need to be out there with a team of people combing the streets. If I was in charge...'

Jeremy Brice was not Isaac Cook's type of person. He'd listened to him on a few occasions, only to switch off the radio in his car in disgust, and now the man was going to be a nuisance.

'If you'll excuse me,' Isaac said, 'I've got to be upstairs. Rest assured, we'll be working day and night to solve your daughter's murder.'

'And I'll be behind you, kicking you all the way.'

'We don't need kicking,' Isaac said. He knew that he was talking to a grieving man, but he had suffered enough listening to the man on the radio, and he didn't intend to have him running the investigation into the death of his daughter, Amelia.

Upstairs, once he had shaken free of the father, Isaac walked around the body, careful not to impede the crime scene team and their investigation. He could see what had been an attractive white female, a piece of cord around her neck. Gordon Windsor was at the scene, as was Grant Meston, his deputy.

'What's the verdict?' Isaac asked. 'The same murderer?'

'It's probable. The method is the same, the same type of cord to garrotte her, even the bag over the head. Mind you, different houses, different areas.'

'How long before you can tell us if it's the same person?'

'One hour. We'll see if there's any indication as to who it is.'

'Is that likely?'

'Whoever killed these two women had planned it out. It's ten, fifteen minutes to drive from one location to the other, depending on the traffic, and then he would need to know that both women were at home and alone.'

'An accomplice?'

'It seems likely, but why?'

'Leave that to us, Gordon. You give us the facts; we'll figure out who was responsible.'

***

Back at Challis Street Police Station, the team assembled, this time without Superintendent Goddard, although Isaac was sure they'd not get through the meeting without his head poking around the office door.

'What do we have?' Isaac said.

'Two women who lived close to each other,' Larry Hill said.

'Apart from that?'

An evidence board was set up in the corner, with the first attempts at populating it completed. There was no issue about a photo for Amelia Brice; Bridget had found her on the internet.

Isaac had secured a photo of the other woman at her flat; it had been in a photo frame in the kitchen. Charisa Devon had phoned; Billy, her elder brother, would be in the office within the hour.

'What's the tie-in?' asked Sergeant Wendy Gladstone, the department's best person if you wanted someone found.

'We're not sure, yet,' Isaac said.

'It must be something to do with Amelia Brice,' Larry said.

'That's an assumption. We need to establish the connection between the two women first. Focus on Christine Devon's clients that she cleaned for. Maybe she had cleaned for Amelia Brice.'

'Does the house in Holland Park belong to Amelia Brice?'

'It belongs to her father. He'll be throwing his weight around. He's already tried it once with me,' Isaac said.

'Is he a suspect?' Bridget asked.

'Everyone's a suspect until we've cleared them. Check out Christine Devon's children. Supposedly the youngest son is involved with gangs in the area. Larry, check it out, use your contacts.'

'Don't worry. I'll do that.'

'Bridget, you can start producing a case for the prosecution.'

'I've already started.'

'Larry, Billy Devon, the eldest son, is coming in. We'll interview him in the conference room; no need to subject him to the third degree.'

Isaac's phone rang. 'Samuel, he's missing.'

'Charisa, you'll need to talk slowly. I can't understand you.'

The woman on the other end of the phone was distressed. 'Where are you?' Isaac asked.

'I'm down near Billy's place of work.'

'The address?'

'Notting Hill Gate, number 446. It's an electrical store, Glassop and Son.'

'I know it. We'll be there in ten minutes. Is Billy with you?'

'He's here. We tried to phone Samuel, checked with his school, his best friend. He's gone missing.'

'But he phoned the police when he found your mother.'

'He let them in the door and then took off.'

'Any reason for him to disappear?'

'Not really, but he doesn't always come home at night. We need to find him.'

'I'll put out an all points for him, and my DI, he's friendly with the gangs in the area.'

'We'll be outside the shop. It's difficult pulling off the road, and there's no parking,' Charisa Devon said.

'Don't worry about us. We'll flash our lights if necessary. The traffic will stop for us. Remember, ten minutes, don't move.'

'We won't.'

Isaac turned to Wendy. 'Come with me. Larry, check with your contacts. Samuel Devon, fifteen years of age. You know his address.'

'I'll try, but they normally clam up when anyone comes sticking their nose in.'

'Do your best.'

Nine minutes later, Billy and Charisa Devon were in the back seat of Isaac's car. 'Why the concern?' Isaac asked.

'He always answers his phone,' Charisa said.

'Maybe he's upset over the death of his mother,' Wendy said.

'Not him.'

'I thought you said he wasn't in any serious trouble.'

'There's been a couple of times when he's come home after fighting. Once he had a cut on his face; we had to take him to the hospital.'

'What do you reckon has happened to him?'

'Either he saw someone near our flat, or he saw the person who killed our mother.'

'Any chance he's been near Amelia Brice, the other woman?'

'Who knows? He used to get around to a few strange places,' Billy Devon said. His English was clear, no attempt to affect a Caribbean accent as a gang member would.

'There's no point looking for him ourselves,' Isaac said. 'It's best if we get back to Challis Street. DI Hill's coordinating the search. We'll find him soon enough.'

Back at the station, the two teenagers were calmer after a coffee and a sandwich each. 'What's the deal with your brother, the truth this time?' Isaac said.

'Samuel, he's been with this gang,' Billy said. His sister was telling him to be quiet.

'Charisa, we're investigating the murder of two women, one of them your mother,' Isaac said.

'If your brother's in trouble, we may be able to help him. It's best if you both tell the truth. Is his disappearance related to your mother?' Wendy asked.

'Not that we know of,' Billy said.

'Did your mother know what Samuel was up to?'

'Some of it. We tried to shield her from it.'

'Such as?'

'The drug dealing, the fights, one of them fatal.'

'Who died?'

'Someone from another gang.'

'Which means reprisals. You know that, don't you?' Isaac said.

'We know it, but Samuel, he's full of himself, sees himself as invincible.'

'And you suspect the other gang has him?'

'Yes.'

'Are you sure his disappearance has nothing to do with your mother?'

'We don't know, but we don't think so.'

Isaac phoned Larry, who had met up with some of his contacts. 'What are they telling you?' Isaac said.

'Not a lot. If they know anything, they'll keep quiet.'

'Remember, Samuel Devon is a disappearance; his mother is murder. They may not be related.'

'And how does this tie in with Amelia Brice?'

Bridget knocked on the door of the conference room and came in. 'Christine Devon worked for a home-cleaning company. One of their clients was Jeremy Brice.'

'Is it confirmed that Christine Devon worked at the house?'

'On several occasions. If the regular cleaner was off sick, the dead woman substituted for her.'

'Dates?'

'The last time was one week ago, a Thursday.'

'Can we find out if Amelia Brice was at home?'

'It may be best if you do that,' Bridget said.

Another phone call from Larry. Isaac left the room where Christine Devon's other children were. 'What is it?' Isaac said.

'It appears that our Samuel Devon has been associating with the wrong kind of people.'

'What do you mean?'

'My contact, we helped him out once before…'

'My former classmate at school.'

'That's him, Rasta Joe. He's not willing to talk too much. The gang that Samuel is with are known for their violence. They were using Samuel to transport drugs around the area and throughout London. Apparently, a young man in school uniform is less likely to be picked up by the police.'

'At least his education came in useful,' Isaac said.

'There appears to have been a dispute between his gang and another that he was delivering to. There was a confrontation.'

'According to his brother and sister, one of the other gang was killed.'

'Rasta Joe wasn't going to tell me that.'

'Was it his gang?'

'No. He's a mean individual, but he's small time compared to the others. Anyway, Samuel is being blamed by both sides for lightening the load that he was carrying.'

'Was he?'

'According to Rasta, it's unlikely. The packaging is tight, and a schoolboy wouldn't have the knowledge of how to fiddle the amounts.'

'So why blame him?'

'You know the deal, guv. They need a scapegoat, a sacrificial lamb.'

'And Samuel may have been offered up?'

'It's possible.'

'Any chance of finding him?'

'Not alive. Rasta Joe's given me as much as he's got, and he's not going to stick his neck out. I can't blame him.'

'Too many questions and he's dead as well.'

'Something like that.'

'Is this related to the murders of Christine Devon and Amelia Brice?'

'It's unlikely.'

'And Samuel Devon?'

'If he's been taken, then he's probably dead.'

'And when will we know?'

'When we find his body.'

'You'd better come back to the station. We need to maintain our focus on the two women,' Isaac said.

'According to Rasta Joe, Amelia Brice was using cocaine.'

'Did he know her?'

'Sometimes she'd take off her fancy clothes, put on a pair of jeans and a tee-shirt and mix it up with the locals. It seems she liked the occasional Rastaman.'

'Rasta Joe?'

'Not him. She liked them young and virile.'
'Not the image she portrayed in the social pages.'
'They've all got skeletons, the rich and famous.'
'How about her father?'
'We'll need to check him out.'

***

Two days passed, and there was no sign of Samuel Devon. It was not the prime interest for Homicide, and while Isaac could be sympathetic to Charisa and Billy Devon, there was not a lot more that he could do. It seemed that virtually every hour Charisa was on the phone, and even though he referred her to another department, she kept coming back to him. And it still wasn't clear whether her brother's disappearance was related, although probably not if the information coming back to Larry Hill was correct. The man had his ear to the ground in places where it wasn't safe to do so, and the begrudging relationship between a detective inspector and a gang leader was unusual. Typically, two such men would keep their distance, but DI Hill had helped Rasta Joe out on a couple of occasions, and the English-born Jamaican had helped him out in return. Isaac knew Rasta from their schooldays; he did not like what he represented and was not good at disguising the fact, whereas Larry could take the man at face value and not attempt to delve into his dubious background.

The word on the street was that the two rival gangs had resolved their differences, which meant that retribution had been made. Rasta Joe had assumed that meant that Samuel Devon was dead, but as yet there was no proof.

Meanwhile, an interview with Jeremy Brice, the father of one of the dead women, had revealed a man full of invective and not much else. It was his house where his daughter had been found, but he did not see her too often. She went her way, he went his. The relationship between the two of them was not good, although he paid all her bills, and yes, he knew that she was snorting cocaine. He didn't approve, but he wasn't going to throw her out of the house, not like he had wanted to do to her mother

16

when he had caught her in bed with a younger man. The last piece of information did not come from Brice, but from Wendy Gladstone, who had been asking questions around the area. A neighbour two doors down, old and embittered, had been happy to dish the dirt on the sanctimonious and argumentative Jeremy Brice.

Wendy had thought the woman like a crab, with her sideways glances down the road, trying to see what was going on.

'She was a one, that Amelia Brice,' the old lady had said.

'What do you mean?'

'Her men friends, all the time.'

'How many?'

'All the time.'

'Specifically.'

'I saw her there once with a man on the doorstep; they were kissing.'

Wendy checked it out, found no verification, only that the mother of the dead woman had died five years before her daughter in a car accident in Greece, apparently drunk according to the police report.

Chapter 3

The pathologist, Graham Pickett, a tall, thin man in his late fifties, confirmed that the two women had died in the same manner. The amount of pressure applied to the neck, the securing of the plastic bag over the head, administered first to confuse and then to prevent screaming, had all the hallmarks of a professional. Isaac knew that whatever the motive, it was not minor.

The fact that the two women were almost certainly killed by the same person offered some clues as to who it was. The murders didn't, nor the manner in which they were committed, but whoever it was, that person would have had to be able to move freely in upmarket Holland Park and in a council tower block in Notting Hill. An Anglo-Saxon, white male in a suit would have been out of place in the vicinity of Christine Devon's residence and would have raised suspicion.

'Why these two women?' Isaac asked at the department meeting. It was early, six in the morning. Larry was still struggling to wake up, Bridget was wide awake, as was Wendy. Isaac was the senior investigating officer. His idea of a well-managed investigation came with long hours, early starts, and professional policing.

The early starts did not concern him as back at his flat in Willesden, it was just him and his pillow. The would-be wife from Jamaica, looking for a husband or at least residency in the UK was gone. He had enjoyed the nights with her, but the bond between them wasn't there. She was looking for a better life than in Jamaica, and with a police inspector in London, she wasn't going to get it. She had turned up her nose when she had first seen his flat, smaller than the room he had rented at the hotel in Montego Bay. He had tried to explain before she arrived on his doorstep that rainy evening in London that a holiday fling in

Montego Bay was not the same as his usual life, the life of a police officer on a salary.

'If it's the same person who committed both murders, that means at least a time difference of thirty-five to forty minutes,' Wendy said.

'How long to drive from one to the other?' Larry asked. He was slouching in his chair, the result of his burgeoning weight. Isaac looked at him, realised that it was up to him to have a word about it. Larry's wife, an advocate for healthy eating and a healthy mind, always ensured that he had a balanced diet for his lunch, carefully packed in a plastic container, though he didn't eat it with relish, and most days it would lie discarded on his desk until the cleaning staff came and took it away.

'Twenty minutes, give or take a few minutes either way,' Isaac said. 'And then there's the time to park a vehicle.'

'Not if there's another person.'

'Are we agreed that these murders are the work of a professional?'

'According to Gordon Windsor.'

'Then why? What's the information on the two women? Bridget, what do you have?'

Bridget, a woman who loved computers and being in the office, had prepared summations on the two women. 'Amelia Brice, thirty-one years of age, the daughter of Jeremy and Sue Brice. The father is the well-known social commentator. Amelia, educated privately, travelled extensively, fluent in French and English. Her occupation on her passport is listed as a model, but there's little evidence of that. However, I did find some articles in various magazines that show her at Ascot, the opening of a fashion show. As you can see from the attached photos to my summary, she was an attractive woman. We also know, evidence at the murder scene, that she was using cocaine.'

'And we know that Samuel Devon, the son of the other murdered woman, was involved with a gang that traded drugs,' Isaac said.

Bridget continued. 'Amelia Brice, one of the idle rich, not a person that Wendy would admire…'

'You're right there,' Wendy said. All of the team in Isaac's office knew of the sergeant's disdain for those who took what life gave them and did nothing more, and in the case of the dead woman she had been given plenty.

'As I was saying,' Bridget continued. 'Amelia Brice has no history of working, other than on a couple of occasions as a model, once or twice for a fashion magazine.'

Larry had drawn himself up on his chair, the first pangs of early morning hunger setting in. He knew where to go once the meeting concluded to get a full English breakfast.

'We know about the cocaine use from the crime scene examiners, and also I've found that the woman has been remanded for illegal drug use on a couple of occasions.'

'What type of drugs?'

'Cocaine. On both occasions, she got off with a hefty fine and community service.'

'The penalty, at least for a second offence, would be custodial,' Isaac said.

'She put up an ardent defence: the death of her mother, break-up of a long-term romance.'

'True?'

'The mother had died, that much was correct. As for the romance, that's unknown. Anyway, she had a Queen's Counsel defending her.'

'The father's money?'

'Probably.'

'Bridget, what do we have on the father?' Isaac asked, although he knew of the man, everyone did.

'Jeremy Brice, social commentator. He's on the television every night from 6 p.m. to 7 p.m. He's not so controversial there. From 10 a.m. to midday, his programme on the radio is the highest rating in that timeslot. The man is known for his critical views of the police force in this city, its inability to deal with terrorism, and the government's current immigration policy. Not only that, he'll get on the bandwagon of any cause that will get him ratings.'

'He's the only one who can get the politicians to give a straight answer,' Wendy said.

'Is there any more on Amelia Brice?' Isaac asked.

'There's more in my report, but I'll let you all read that on your own.'

'What can you tell us about Christine Devon?'

'Christine Devon, forty years of age, born in Trinidad, arrived in this country twenty-one years ago. A British citizen, she has no criminal record. Her occupation is listed as a housewife, although she's been working as a cleaner for the last ten. She paid her taxes on time. Three children: Billy, nineteen. Charisa, eighteen, and Samuel, fifteen.

'Billy had a couple of run-ins with the law three years ago, petty hooliganism. Apart from that, the children are clean. The two eldest children have been in the station, so we know them. Samuel is missing, presumed dead.'

'Any luck with him?' Isaac asked.

'We're still looking,' Wendy said. 'We know where he was one day ago, but since then, nothing.'

***

Jeremy Brice, known to millions, was not the sort of person to sit quietly on any issue, and being told by a police officer that the investigation was progressing along established lines did not satisfy him. Isaac had tried to be diplomatic with him on the two occasions they had met, but each time the conversation had degenerated into Brice wanting to take control. Isaac, as the SIO, did not intend to give it to him, and now the man was bending the ear of Commissioner Davies, the belligerent leader of the Met, and well-known antagonist of DCI Isaac Cook and his senior.

Even though his daughter had only been dead for a short period of time, and not yet buried, Brice had been on the airwaves berating the police and their incompetence, revealing more than he should have about how his daughter had died. Isaac had listened a few times, realised that he was subjective with the truth. There was no mention of his daughter's predilection for cocaine and the dubious company that she sometimes kept.

'The man's a bore,' Commissioner Davies had said on the phone to Goddard. The superintendent thought that made two, but kept the observation to himself. 'Deal with Brice, and get Cook involved. You're a wet fish in dealing with the public. At least Cook, not that he's much good as a police officer, knows how to communicate.'

Richard Goddard thought the man's comments were offensive, but all he needed to do was to bide his time, and the commissioner would be out on his ear, due to his poor record of achievement.

'Look here, Superintendent,' Brice said as he sat in Goddard's office, 'my daughter's been killed, then cut up by your pathologist, and your man here is refusing to give me her body to bury. What right does he have?'

'This is a criminal investigation,' Goddard said. He was sitting in his high-backed leather chair behind his desk. Brice and Isaac were seated on the other side.

'Your daughter's body is to be released in two days,' Isaac said.

'Why was I not told?'

'Your office was informed.'

'No one told me.'

'You would have received notification according to the procedure. I suggest you contact your office to confirm it.'

'If they've failed to tell me, then they're for the high jump, I can tell you that.'

'Mr Brice, why have you felt the need to contact Commissioner Davies and to insist on a meeting here in Superintendent Goddard's office?' Isaac asked. Goddard cringed, knowing they'd get negative criticism on Brice's radio show if Isaac put the man on the spot.

'You weren't available.'

'My phone is on twenty-four hours a day. I put it to you again, why did you not phone me?'

'You've got some nerve, questioning me. Don't you know who I am? Don't you realise that I could destroy your career?'

'DCI, I suggest you desist. Mr Brice is an important man. It is not for you to put him on the spot,' Goddard said.

Isaac thought that his senior was wrong in taking the soft approach, so did Brice. He leant over, gave Isaac a hearty pat on the back. 'Good man, someone who's willing to stand up and be counted.'

Isaac wasn't sure what to say; his senior was equally confused. 'Our best officer,' Goddard said, the only words he could think of.

'DCI, what can you tell me about my daughter's death?'

'Probably not a lot more than you already know. We believe it was professional, the same as the other woman.'

'The black woman? Sorry, if that sounded racist,' Brice said.

'That's our description of her,' Isaac conceded.

'Are the deaths related?'

'We know they are. There's clear evidence that both murders were committed by the same person, which raises other questions.'

'Such as?'

'Where Christine Devon lived is not the most salubrious area.'

'A slum?'

'Not technically, but it's where the most deprived congregate.'

'Violent?'

'It can be, which means that a person who could walk freely in Holland Park could not necessarily do so where she lived. We've thought of a tradesman, although we've discounted that.'

'Any reason why?'

'We've checked the CCTV cameras in the area of your house. There's a camera mounted on a traffic light not more than thirty feet away from your house. There is no sign of a handyman's vehicle, no sign of a handyman. That's not conclusive, and we've tried to correlate this with the movement around Christine Devon's home, and yet again, no handyman.'

'Amelia wouldn't have let in a handyman.'

'Why?'

'If she were in the house on her own, she wouldn't have felt safe.'

'We've checked her friends. None of them claims to have visited her that day.'

'Not a friend.'

'Then who?'

'Amelia had a problem. We're all aware of that,' Brice said.

'Drugs?'

'Cocaine, and the occasional rough man.'

'We know about both.'

'Maybe someone was coming around to sell her some drugs, or maybe it was one of her men.'

'A black man?'

'It's possible.'

'There's no sign that she was with a man in the house.'

'No signs of sexual congress, is that what you're saying?'

'Exactly.'

'Then say it for what it is. No point beating around the bush here. My daughter was the indulged daughter of a rich man; she did little other than sleep around and take drugs.'

'Disappointing?' Goddard said.

'Catch 22. I'm either out there making money for her to abuse, or I'm at home acting as nursemaid to her.'

'Your wife?'

'Goddard, I suggest you read up or ask your DCI,' Brice said. 'My wife died five years ago, and before that, she had not been in her daughter's life for some time. Amelia inherited her bad habits from her.'

'My apologies.'

'Accepted. After that, it was just Amelia and me. She was fine until a few years back, and then the drugs, and the highs and lows. I hired staff, but they never lasted long. For the past six months, there's been no one permanent in the house, only people on an occasional basis to clean and look after the garden.'

'Christine Devon had cleaned at your house.'

'There were a few different women. I remember someone from Italy, but I wasn't there often.'

'Any reason why?'

'I maintain a flat in Mayfair. I'm there most of the time.'

'And you have the house in Holland Park?'

'My daughter's there on her own. And besides, I need my space.'

'Space?' Isaac asked.

'A woman. Clear enough?'

'If your daughter's there on her own, we've didn't see any evidence of wild parties, drugs, apart from your daughter's cocaine.'

'Amelia could be antisocial, likely to throw tantrums. In the house, she'd be in her own little world. Outside, she'd be extroverted and game for anything.'

'It must have been difficult for you.'

'Emotionally, sometimes. And as for my woman, she's a university lecturer. We keep our relationship secret, or at least, we don't go to awards nights or film premieres together. At home, we're just a boring couple doing our own things.'

'Your friend and Amelia?'

'Fireworks. Amelia's spoilt. She's never had to work a day in her life. My friend grew up on a council estate, worked three jobs to get through university, the same as me. We've both known poverty, Amelia never did. Maybe, if she had…'

'It doesn't pay to dwell on such matters,' Isaac said.

'I know, and I've no regrets about what has happened. She had a destructive streak, the same as her mother. Amelia had attempted suicide on a couple of occasions, so I'm not as upset as you would expect. Sad, of course, but her life was unusual, and she wasn't a happy person.'

'Any ideas as to why she was killed?'

'We've been through this before.'

'Last time, you weren't on our side,' Isaac said.

'True. I'll go easier on you from now on.'

'You haven't answered the original question.'

'I don't know anyone who'd want her dead. Some of the men she entertained would have been regarded as dubious, but murder: that's something else.'

'The dilemma we have is that if your daughter and the cleaner have been murdered for the same reason, then what is it?'

'I'm an open book. I suggest you talk to the men she went around with.'

'We have. The murders were professional, more like assassinations. The gangs around here are mainly poorly educated individuals. This seems too complex for them.'

Chapter 4

It wasn't expected that Isaac would attend the funeral of Christine Devon, but for some reason, he felt the need to. His parents had experienced grinding poverty when they had first arrived in England, and there seemed to be an empathy between him and the two eldest children of the murdered woman. The church was full to overflowing. There were a few faces from his earlier years; some recognised him, some didn't. Others avoided him because he was a police officer, but he wasn't there to conduct an investigation; he was there to support the family. Charisa, the daughter, was being consoled by her elder brother. Samuel, the youngest, had still not been seen.

The priest led the congregation in prayer and praise of the woman. Charisa said a few words, interspersed with tears, as did Billy, her brother, even mentioning Samuel's name. At the end, a typical Caribbean religious service, the congregation burst into song, the type of song that made Isaac proud be a West Indian. Even he joined in, and it had been some time since he had been in a church.

'I didn't expect to see you,' a familiar voice said. Isaac looked behind him.

'Rasta Joe,' he said. The man was a school friend, but they were friends no more after one had embraced the police, the other, gangs and drugs.

'I thought you had embraced the white man's world,' the dreadlocked man said.

'I still remember where my parents came from. Christine Devon deserves a proper send-off.'

Rasta Joe, flanked on either side by two of his gang members, turned to them. 'This man is cool. He'll not trouble us today.'

27

Isaac knew of the antipathy towards anyone who represented the police, and the church was in the centre of the gang's heartland. 'Samuel Devon?'

'He's not been seen.'

'Killing of a fifteen-year-old youth seems extreme.'

'There are some who wouldn't have a problem. And don't come snooping around here at any other time.'

'Not good for my health, is that it?'

'Not from us.'

Isaac could see that Rasta Joe had cleaned himself up for the ceremony.

'You know the family? Isaac asked.

'They were not involved in anything wrong if that's what you're fishing for.'

'What about Samuel Devon? You owe that to his brother and sister, to Christine Devon.'

'We don't owe anyone anything. We do what we want.'

'Where can I find someone that will talk?'

'Not around here.'

'Who murdered his mother? Do you know that? And how about Amelia Brice? Someone was supplying her with cocaine.'

'Isaac, drop it. We didn't kill Christine Devon; and as for Amelia, we knew her. If she was taking drugs, she didn't get them from us.'

Isaac knew that Rasta Joe was not usually a man to be trusted, but this time he did. After the service he went to talk to the daughter of the woman they had congregated for. Charisa Devon was pleased to see him. 'Samuel, we've not heard from him.'

'We've had no leads either, other than the word on the street.'

'That he's dead.'

'Is he?' Isaac asked.

'We think so. We pray every night, hope that he'll come home, but it's only wishful thinking.'

'His disappearance, your mother's death, are they related?'

'Why would someone kill her? She minded her own business.'

'It's tied in with Amelia Brice.'

'Then maybe you should ask there. We had nothing worth stealing, no great secrets. Mum was a battler, Billy's a hard worker, and I'm a student.'

'Any strange occurrences since?'

'We've not been back to look, other than to take our personal belongings.'

'Where are you staying?'

'With my boyfriend.'

'And Billy?'

'He's sharing a flat with some of his friends, probably getting up to mischief.'

'Mischief?'

'You've met Billy. He's popular with the girls. He tried to sneak one into the flat one night, Mum went spare. Where he is now, there'll be no issues. At least they keep his mind off what happened.'

'And you?'

'I try, but sometimes I get upset, thinking about what Mum went through.'

'It's best not to dwell on it,' Isaac said.

***

Amelia Brice was buried in the family plot in the local churchyard. Isaac had watched from a distance. He saw Jeremy Brice arrive in the company of a woman.

Nothing was said at the service and in the media about Amelia's issues with rough men and cocaine; Isaac assumed that the father had pulled in favours to keep the disturbing parts of his daughter's life quiet. Jeremy Brice, an abrasive personality on the radio and the television, had been remarkably pleasant after Isaac had broken through his cover. They had met on two other occasions since to discuss Amelia's death. Isaac thought the man to be cold, considering that she had died, or maybe he was stoic, not a man who showed emotion readily.

Isaac had felt a tear at Christine Devon's funeral, but nothing as he stood across from the churchyard at Amelia's. The constable on duty had recognised him, offered to let him through, but Isaac had declined, and besides, there were more pressing issues to deal with.

For once, Commissioner Davies was holding back; Isaac assumed that Brice had had a word in his ear, but the man was pushing hard to find out who had killed his daughter. Isaac knew that he would not have long.

It was straight up to Superintendent Goddard's office on Isaac's return from the church. The man was in a good mood. 'What's the latest? Any breakthroughs?'

Too often Isaac had been called into his senior's office to listen to his invective about why the investigation was going too slowly, or the results were poor, or the budget was being exceeded. This time was different. He wondered why.

'Davies phoned up and congratulated us.'

'For what?'

'The current investigation into the death of the two women.'

'We haven't done anything,' Isaac said. 'Why would he do that?'

'Perceptions, I suppose.'

'Or Brice singing our praises. Our commissioner is easily hoodwinked. Brice could change on the turn of a coin.'

'Enjoy it while you can, Isaac.'

'I can't while one of the women's sons is missing and we haven't got a clue who killed her and why.'

'Brice, could he know something?'

'It seems unlikely. Why would he kill his own daughter? And besides, it would need a third party.'

'Why?'

'Jeremy Brice would not have the strength to kill either of the women.'

'Why do you say that? He seemed fit enough the day he was here.'

'He suffers from a form of upper muscular atrophy, the result of a car accident in his youth. He wouldn't be able to apply sufficient pressure.'

'He told you?'

'I checked with his doctor.'

***

Isaac felt it was his responsibility. He picked up Billy Devon from his work and then swung by Charisa's place of learning. The road was busy, no parking. He displayed his permit on the window and left the car close to a set of traffic lights. Under normal circumstances, he would have driven around the area until he had found somewhere better. 'What is it?' Billy asked when he was picked up.

'It's Samuel.'

'Is he…?'

'It's not confirmed yet, but it's almost certain. I didn't want you two to find out through the grapevine.'

'Where is he?'

'Let's get your sister first.'

The two officers found one of the lecturers who directed them to the correct room. Isaac stuck his head in the door, introduced himself to the lecturer and scanned for Charisa. She was head down, studying. 'Charisa,' Isaac called.

The young woman lifted her head, took one look and burst into tears. 'It's Samuel, isn't it?'

'I've got Billy with me. It would be best if you are both at Challis Street.'

'I want to see him,' Charisa said. Her classmates were hovering close to her, some were in tears, some were placing their hands on her, one had her arm around her.

The three left the college and walked briskly to Isaac's car. Inside the car, Billy and Charisa sat in the back seat. 'Where is he?' she asked.

'The River Thames at Hammersmith.'

'We're going there?'

'It's a crime scene. You won't be able to get close.'

'I want to be there. You can do that at least for us.'

Isaac relented and made the short drive to the river. Out on the mud flats at the side of the river was a team of men. 'Wait here. I'll go and see what the situation is.'

'We want to see him, regardless.'

Isaac kitted up, realised that whatever happened he was going to be covered in mud. At the scene, Grant Meston, Gordon Windsor's colleague, was taking charge.

'Gordon?' Isaac asked.

'Fell down, twisted his ankle. I'm taking charge of this today.'

'What do you have?'

'Male, black, age between twelve and nineteen.'

'What's the cause of death?'

'There's evidence of violence.'

'What do you mean?'

'There's a knife wound in the body.'

'Fatal?'

'Probably not, but he would have been unconscious when he was thrown into the Thames.'

'He's just reappeared?'

'Nothing to do with those who killed him. He's been weighted down, but the low water level revealed the chain above the water. Some local lads out for a lark pulled on it and up came the body.'

'Is he identifiable?'

'It's not a pretty sight but if someone knew him when he was alive, then maybe. Anyone in mind?'

'His brother and sister, nineteen and eighteen.'

'Don't let the sister see the body.'

'I'll not be able to keep her away. How long before you take it from here?'

'Twenty minutes. I'll try and clean it up first.'

'Thanks.'

Isaac returned to Billy and Charisa. 'Twenty minutes and they'll bring the body up here.'

'Is it?'

'Billy, are you up to identifying the body?'

'I'll do it.'

'So will I,' Charisa said.

'The body's been in the water for some time. It would be best if you don't.'

'He's my brother. I want to see him.'

***

The crime scene team brought the body up from the river bank. An attempt had been made by them to improve its appearance, especially the face. A vehicle was there to take it to Pathology, for the autopsy. Isaac stood with Billy and Charisa Devon, holding the young woman back. 'I want to see him,' she said.

Isaac could understand the sentiment, but knew full well that most people's reaction, if they were not used to it, would be to stare at the body before vomiting. It had happened to him a few times, but now he was impervious to it, although he could emote with the two who were to be confronted with the reality of a dead sibling, and only just after their mother had died.

'Are you sure about this?' Isaac said.

'Yes,' came the reply in unison.

Grant Meston positioned himself close to the head of the body, the two teenagers nearer to its waist. Meston unzipped the body bag at the top and peeled it open enough for the face to be visible. Billy stared, transfixed by the scene; Charisa grabbed hold of Isaac's hand and held it hard. 'It's Samuel,' she said. Billy, the colour in his face drained, ran from the site and vomited in the gutter beside the road. Charisa stayed where she was as

Meston rezipped the bag. Isaac made a phone call to Challis Street.

Isaac had to admit that he had been surprised by the reaction of the dead man's sister, although he had noticed that she was the stronger of the remaining children of the murdered woman. One hour later, and after drinking some tea, both of them were better. 'It was going to happen one day,' Charisa said.

'It's all too common,' Isaac said, by way of consolation. The young man had run with a gang. He'd apparently cheated on one of them, either out of sheer stupidity or because he thought he was smarter than them, and they had dealt with him. It wasn't the first gang-related death in London, and sometimes a person would disappear, never to be seen again.

'At least you know. You'll have closure,' Isaac said when Billy Devon commented on what he had seen.

'Do you get used to it?'

'You become immune to the sight of death. You can never get used to the reaction of loved ones of the deceased, of telling them that there's been an accident, or that someone's been murdered.'

'But you were emotionless back there.'

'I'm trained to deal with it, and I've seen much worse. In time, you'll be able to deal with what has happened in your lives.'

'Our mother?' Billy said. The colour had returned to his face.

'We're still working on that. Is there any more that you can tell me?'

'Our mother always taught us right from wrong, and she was at church every Sunday.'

'We know that she cleaned Amelia Brice's house.'

'First she was murdered, and now Samuel,' Charisa said.

Isaac, sadder than he should be, left Billy and Charisa at the house of an aunt. 'We'll be fine,' they said. He knew they would be. They had grown up in an area of London where violent death was not uncommon, and time was a great healer.

Back at the station, Bridget had pinned up a photo of the dead youth. 'Is his death related to the women?' she asked Isaac as he walked in the door.

'We'll treat them as unrelated for the time being. You'll need to open another case file.'

'I've already started. There's not much in it at present.'

Isaac grabbed himself a coffee from the machine in the corner. It looked good, but he knew good coffee when he drank it, and this was far from excellent. 'Where's the team?'

'Wendy's out checking on Christine Devon's movements. Larry's over at the Brice house.'

'With the father?'

'No. He wanted to spend a few hours going through the place.'

'Okay. Set up a meeting for 2 p.m. We'll discuss what we have so far.'

'And what do we have, sir?'

'Three dead bodies. One's gangland, may not be so easy to solve.'

'Why's that?'

'The people that Samuel Devon associated with regard life as expendable. Instead of roughing him up, they kill him.'

'You grew up with them. You must understand them.'

Isaac did not feel inclined to talk more. He moved away to his office. Bridget returned to her desk and her computer. Above the monitor a picture of two cats, the cats that Wendy had rescued from a dead woman in another case. She entered the password on her computer, the file of Samuel Devon was visible, and she inputted what they had so far, noted that the body had been identified.

In his office, Isaac sat back in his chair. For him, no photos of cats, no pictures of loved ones. He picked up his phone and dialled. 'Jess, are you free this Friday?' he said.

'Not this Friday, maybe next. I'm too busy,' was Jess O'Neill's reply.

He knew that the romance that had gone on for too long was dead, and that busy had been an excuse. He would phone her again some time, but for now he was lonely, and all he had was a Homicide department, his team, and three bodies. Somehow, to him, it did not seem sufficient. He got up from his chair and went out to see Bridget. For some reason, the sadness of the day had got to him. 'Bridget, do we have the reports back from Pathology for the two women?'

'They're on the shared drive.'

He realised that he was making idle conversation.

Another phone call, this time for him. 'Isaac Cook,' he answered.

'I'm at the Brices,' Larry said. 'Are you free?'

'Do you want me there?'

'If you could.'

Chapter 5

Isaac arrived at the Brice house in Holland Park within twelve minutes. He was glad to be out of the office.

'Samuel Devon, unpleasant sight?' Larry said on meeting him at the front door.

'Not the worst I've seen.'

'And the siblings?'

'They handled it well enough. When you get a chance, you'd better use your contact to find out who killed Samuel Devon.'

'He's your contact as well. You went to school with him.'

'Rasta Joe's playing a dangerous game. He could end up dead as well.'

'He knows that, but his love for me buying him pints of beer keeps drawing him back.'

'One day, they'll be fishing him out of the river. What do you have here?' Isaac asked.

The two men walked through the house and up the stairs to the first floor. They were wearing foot protectors and gloves, even though the house had been handed back to Jeremy Brice. He was moving back in, this time with his girlfriend, although he wanted the room where his daughter had been killed to be redecorated and changed into a walk-in wardrobe. 'I don't want to be forced to remember,' he had said.

'In here,' Larry said. Isaac could see that the man was starting to waddle, the result of too much food, not enough exercise. Isaac took stock of himself, noticed that he had put on a couple of extra pounds. He resolved to get out of the office once a day and to take a stroll around the area, or maybe join the gym not far from the police station.

'What have you found?'

'It was hidden.' Larry pushed his way down the side of a wardrobe in one corner of the murdered woman's room, and extending his arm, he took hold of a book tucked away behind it. 'She kept a diary.'

'And this was missed before?'

'The others were not as thorough as me. Nobody thought that she did anything other than spend money, snort cocaine, and get herself laid by the occasional criminal.'

'Have you looked inside?'

'The first few pages. She was articulate.'

'No one's ever doubted her education.'

'It goes back to the beginning of this year. There may be other diaries for earlier years, but I've not found them yet.'

'What does this one say?'

The two men had relocated downstairs to the kitchen and were sitting at a table, the diary opened in front of them.

'The usual,' Larry said. 'Details of her trips into town, the clothes she bought. It's not until she's been writing in it for two months that I found something.'

'I thought you hadn't studied it in detail.'

'I hadn't. I was just skimming through, random pages.'

'Get to the point,' Isaac said. He had become annoyed with the slovenly appearance of his DI, even after he had given him a reprimand about maintaining standards in the department. At the time, Larry had been apologetic, promising to turn over a new leaf, but to date it was only thought, no action.

Isaac knew that Larry's relationship with his wife was suffering as well, because of the ever-present curse of the modern police officer: the unsociable working hours, missing the children's school open days, the inability to be there to help with their homework.

'Here it is,' Larry said. He put on a pair of glasses, the first time that Isaac had seen his DI wearing them. "February 2nd Q came over".'

'Q?'

'No idea. I'll continue. "My life is a living hell; I'm not sure if I want to continue".'

'The date of one of her attempted suicides,' Isaac said.

'Her father said that she had medical reasons for her suicide attempts. This would indicate that there was another reason.'

'So why did the father tell us it was medical?'

'We'll ask him in due course. It may not be important, although this Q is.'

'Does this tie in Christine Devon?'

'It depends if she saw the diary and understood its significance. It's more likely she knew who this Q was, and what Amelia was doing with the man.'

'Man?' Isaac said.

'It could be a woman, I suppose.'

'We'll need the diary checking.'

'Bridget can go through it,' Larry said.

'The woman's loaded up as it is.'

'We're all loaded up. And what are we going to do about the murder of Samuel Devon?'

'Attempt to see if his death and that of his mother are related. All three murders are important, although it's Amelia Brice who garners all the attention.'

'I'll go back to the office,' Larry said.

'Give Bridget the diary, ask her to start work on it. We'll then meet up at Brice's radio station. You know which one?'

'At this time of the day, he'll have another fifty-five minutes to go. We need to ask him about Q.'

'He's likely to clam up.'

'And we're likely to bring him into the station and put on the pressure.'

'It's getting murky.'

'What's different from our other cases?' Isaac said.

'There may be some other diaries in here. I'll come back later, maybe bring Wendy with me.'

'You'll need to do something about your weight, you know that,' Isaac said, trying not to sound too authoritative.

'I know, only these diets of my wife leave me starving. I've tried telling her, but it's in one ear and out the other.'

'You'll need to take control.'

'Not so easy. If I lay the law down too strongly, she's likely to walk.'

'Anyway, I've said my piece. I don't want to make it official, but there's a compulsory medical coming up soon. If you want a promotion, you'll need to be fit.'

'Point taken. Give me three weeks, and you'll not recognise me.'

'Okay, let's go. Brice is not going to like us turning up on his doorstep.'

'Do you care?'

'Not me,' Isaac said.

***

Isaac arrived at the radio station as Jeremy Brice was wrapping up. He had listened to him on the car radio as he was driving over. Something to do with the pitiful condition of the hospitals in the country, and what was the government doing to resolve the problem. He had even had the prime minister on the line.

'I never expected you to be here,' Brice said. The man was standing outside the studio where he had just been broadcasting. There were others present, and he was pleasant. 'We'll go into another room.'

'Mr Brice, we've found a diary belonging to your daughter.'

'She always had one. Have you found out who killed her?'

Larry walked in and took a seat next to Isaac.

'The diary mentioned February 2nd. It's a significant day.'

'Yes. I know what day it is. Another one of her episodes.'

'Have there been many?' Larry asked.

'Two in the last year. Is this important? My daughter had a medical issue. She did not die by her hand, but by someone else's.'

'In the diary, it mentioned a Q,' Larry said. 'We assume it to be a man, although it could be a woman.'

40

'And? I'm a busy man. I need to be in makeup within the hour. A television programme tonight.'

'According to your daughter's diary, she had met with Q, and she was contemplating suicide.'

'Who knows what goes through the minds of someone who's suicidal.'

'Did you have her checked out?'

'What kind of father do you think I was? Of course she was checked out. The best medical treatment, the best psychiatric help, but it needed discipline, hard work on her part.'

'And as long as you supplied the money, the hard work was not necessary.'

'Don't lecture me on raising a child. If I had not given her the money, she would have been on the street. I couldn't let her do that, and if the money meant that she took drugs and screwed black men, then so be it. At least she was still alive.' Brice looked at Isaac. 'Sorry about that, but she enjoyed the seedy side of life.'

'No offence was taken. We know the type of men she enjoyed,' Isaac said.

'Are there any other diaries?' Larry asked.

'She was always secretive with them. As a child, there'd be a lock on them, but now, I don't know. I never read them, my wife would sometimes, even though I told her not to.'

'We're concerned about the reference to Q. We're also checking other dates that your daughter may have attempted suicide.'

'Don't put any credence on what she wrote.'

'Unfortunately, we must.'

'The other woman's murder? Did you find out who killed her?'

'It's the same person that killed your daughter. We solve one, we solve the other, and now the other woman, Christine Devon, her son has been murdered.'

'Are they related?'

'We don't think so. We'll pursue your daughter's and Christine Devon's murders as separate to Mrs Devon's son. If we make a connection, we'll let you know.'

***

Samuel Devon's death had been confirmed by Pathology as drowning, although the youth had been knifed a couple of times before being weighted down with chains and thrown off a bridge. Charisa and Billy Devon were holding up well, coordinating with Wendy Gladstone who was attempting to retrace their mother's movements, trying to understand why she had been murdered as well as Amelia Brice.

Wendy had known one thing when she entered the office of the ABC Cleaning Company, Christine Devon's last known employer: they weren't as clean as she would have expected. Inside the main door were some brooms, a bucket of dirty water. The place also smelt of bleach. 'What can I do for you, luv?' a red-faced woman asked. Wendy guessed her age as close to hers, and whereas she would admit to not being in the best physical shape, she was certainly better than the woman who sat behind the computer monitor, a haze of smoke rising into the air. Wendy could only look longingly at the cigarette in the woman's mouth. She had not smoked for nearly a year, but even now she could take one with ease.

Not so long ago, she had weakened, put one in her mouth, only to spit it out. Not because she didn't want to continue, but because she knew it was not good for her. The woman behind the computer looked as though she'd never realised that it was affecting her health, not that she seemed to be the sort of person to care.

'Detective Sergeant Gladstone,' Wendy said. 'I'm from Homicide. I've a few questions.'

'Christine Devon?'

'Yes.'

'There's not much I can tell you. She only worked here a few weeks. No complaints, though.'

42

'Do you get complaints?'

'Some of my employees regard stealing as acceptable.'

'And you pay the minimum wage?'

'I need cleaners. Someone who's cheap and reliable, nothing more.'

'And the alternative to the low pay is the thieving?'

'I get those I employ to sign that they are responsible for damages and theft.'

'Waste of time?'

'What do you think? At some of the houses, the cash is left on display, the mobile phone is lying on the table, they can't help themselves. Not that I can blame them, but I'm the one dealing with the owner.'

'Christine Devon, any problems with her?'

'No, but she'd only been here for a few weeks. They're normally okay for a few months until the owners start to trust them.'

'How do you deal with it?'

'Most of those working for me don't last that long.'

'You sack them?'

'If they're not up to scratch.'

Wendy saw no reason to discuss the woman's approach to her staff. She was there investigating two murders. 'What do you remember about Christine Devon?'

The woman behind the desk shifted uncomfortably in her seat; she leaned forward and took another cigarette from a packet. 'Do you want one?' she asked.

'Not for me,' Wendy replied. 'Christine Devon?'

'There's a steady stream of women like her in this office. She did her job, I paid her. Apart from that, we didn't talk.'

'And you sent her to the Brices' house?'

'Their regular cleaner was ill. They needed someone for a few days. I sent Christine. There were no complaints from anyone else that I sent her to.'

'Which means you'd keep her until she asked for more money?'

'She'd ask eventually, they always do.'

Wendy realised that the owner was a mean-spirited woman who was willing to take advantage of those less fortunate. 'Did you meet Amelia Brice?' she asked.

'I met the father once when we negotiated the contract to clean the house. Apart from that, I never saw the daughter, not at the house anyway.'

'Elsewhere?'

'She used to get around. I'd see her sometimes, high as a kite or drunk. Attractive, though.'

'Anyone in particular that she was with?'

'She liked her men to be dark.'

'You mean those from the Caribbean.'

'That's it, not that I'd fancy them.'

'Where did you see her?'

'She used to go to the Westbourne pub in Bayswater.'

Wendy thanked the woman and left. The Westbourne had already been visited by Larry, and some of the men that Amelia Brice had gone around with had been noted.

Chapter 6

Bridget studied the diary that Larry had given her. As usual, it was shaping up to be a late night.

Isaac had brought back a couple of pizzas with him, and judging by Larry's exuberance, he wasn't going to lose weight that night. Isaac kept to one slice, however.

Bridget and Wendy had no such problems, and they finished off the pizzas.

'Q is mentioned on three separate occasions in the diary,' Bridget said. 'You know about the February 2nd entry, which correlates with one of the woman's suicide attempts. There's another in January, similar, in that Q was being difficult. No mention that she was contemplating suicide. And the final entry, May 3rd. Yet again, Q was difficult.'

'On the one hand she complains, attempts suicide, and then, on the other, she's up at the pub with the men. What is it with this woman?' Isaac said.

'Maybe the father was correct,' Larry said.

'He knew who Q was.'

'You noticed his reaction when we mentioned it?'

'We need to know who it refers to. We'll assume it's a person's initial, first or last. Anyone that fits the bill, Bridget?'

'I've got you a name.'

'You have? You kept that quiet,' Isaac said.

'I needed to go through what the diary had to say first.'

'Who is it?'

'I can't be one hundred per cent certain on this, but Amelia Brice was involved with a man by the name of Quentin Waverley some years ago. I looked through the social pages, found a picture for you.' Bridget handed each of those present a folder containing, amongst other things, several photos of the man, one with his arm around the dead woman.

'Was this a long-term relationship?'

'Apparently, they were living together.'

'Where?'

'The same place she was murdered.'

'Her father told us that Q meant nothing,' Larry said.

'The man lied,' Isaac said.

'Where can we find Quentin Waverley?' Wendy asked.

'Canary Wharf. He's a merchant banker.'

'Any more on the relationship?'

'He married money, the daughter of another merchant banker. After that, his fortunes improved dramatically.'

'What else do we know about the man?' Isaac asked.

'Quentin Alistair Waverley, thirty-nine, school captain, academically gifted, Master's degree in economics.'

'Smart man. Amelia wouldn't fit in with where he was heading – the daughter of an outspoken social commentator, into drugs and bad men.'

'The drugs came about after she had separated from Waverley. The man's "butter wouldn't melt in his mouth" clean,' Bridget said.

'Which means he's got skeletons in the cupboard,' Isaac said.

'Bridget, a full dossier for tomorrow. Larry and I will go and see Waverley. Wendy, keep up the pressure on the cleaning company. Check if there's any dirt, any attempt to use the access to the houses of the affluent to steal or embezzle.'

'And to blackmail,' Wendy said.

'It's possible. We need to tie the two women together. Waverley's one option, the cleaning company is another, and now we have Jeremy Brice lying to us.'

'We could visit him tonight,' Larry said.

'He'll be defensive.'

'That's up to him.'

Isaac made a phone call. Brice answered the phone, reluctantly agreed to a late night visit. The two police officers left Challis Street. It was already ten in the evening. Larry knew he'd not be home before 2 a.m. and his wife would be livid.

Isaac had no one to go home to, and for once, seeing how Larry suffered, he didn't mind.

Brice let the two officers into his flat in Mayfair. His girlfriend, who looked to be in her fifties, introduced herself.

The three men excused themselves and went to the study. 'Now what is so important?' Brice said.

'Quentin Waverley,' Isaac said.

'That's a few years back.'

'But you knew him?'

'Of course I did. I thought he was going to marry Amelia. If he had, she'd still be alive.'

'You approved of the man?'

'Yes, I did. He was a good influence on Amelia.'

'Why did you deny on our last visit knowing anyone who could have been Q?'

'They were not on good terms. As far as Amelia was concerned, the man was dead.'

'It's still not a good enough reason to deny his existence.'

'It is for me.'

'According to your daughter's diary, she had some contact with him. Were they having an affair?'

'My daughter sometimes had trouble distinguishing fiction from fact. Quentin Waverley, in my estimation, is a thoroughly decent man. I'm only sad that he turned her over for the other woman.'

'Gwen Happold. What can you tell us about her?'

'She was a friend of Amelia's. They used to go around together. Her father was successful, and she was attractive.'

'As attractive as your daughter?'

'It's hard to say, but she was a good-looking woman. Anyway, she had her eyes on Quentin.'

'How, if he was with your daughter?'

'She made sure that Amelia caught the two of them in bed.'

'Devious?'

'An excellent woman to have on your side.'

'You still admire her?'

'Not for what she did to my daughter, but she was, still is, a driven woman. I can admire people who know what they want and will do anything to get it.'

'Even sleeping with someone else's partner?'

'Life's a bitch, DCI. You must know that.'

'I do, but I don't go sleeping with my friends' partners.'

'She did, and now Quentin's living well, in line to take over his father-in-law's chairmanship of the bank.'

'Amelia's diary implied that she was still in contact with the man. Are you?'

'I see him from time to time.'

'And his wife?'

'Yes. There's nothing wrong with that, is there?'

'Not in itself. Did Amelia know?'

'We never spoke about it, but yes, she would have known. And besides, she broke up with Quentin some time ago. People move on with their lives.'

'Not according to Amelia. She was in fear of the man.'

'I don't see why. Quentin is perfectly charming.'

'Don't tell me that he wouldn't harm a fly.'

'He's an ambitious man, he would have trodden on a few toes in his time. No doubt you'll find others out there who didn't appreciate him. You'll find plenty who don't like me, not that it bothers me.'

Isaac could not be sure whether the man was telling the truth or lying through his teeth. On the radio, Brice would fluctuate between aggressive and passive, charitable and hard-nosed. He'd suck up to one politician, belittle another. If he could do that, then the pretence of helping a murder investigation would not be difficult, and it was his daughter who had died. He had shown no concern over the death of Christine Devon, yet on the radio he would be sympathetic to a woman whose husband needed medical treatment that they couldn't afford or he would be organising delivery of much-needed help to a pensioner in trouble. Yet a black woman who had cleaned his house had not caused the man to do anything. Not even an offer of help or concern for her children.

Larry's wife always listened to Brice, was one of his most avid fans, and he knew she'd be jealous that he was meeting him. Behind the face of wisdom were an artificial suntan and a hairpiece. Larry had to admit they were both very professional, but as with the man's demeanour, they were as fake as he was. He wasn't sure why he did not like him; maybe it was because of his wife droning on about what he had said or done that day, or because instinctively he did not believe a word the man was saying. He wasn't even sure that Waverley knew when he was contradicting himself.

'Mr Brice, we intend to talk to Quentin Waverley and his wife,' Larry said. 'We need to understand the references in your daughter's diary to him. If we find any disparity in his account and yours we will need to question you again.'

'If you've no more questions, you'll need to excuse me,' Brice said. 'It's late, and I have had a busy day.'

Isaac and Larry realised that Brice had been careful in what he said, not always answering the question posed. For the time being, he could wait. They knew they would be meeting him again.

***

Samuel Devon's funeral was at the same church as his mother. Isaac had attended, not only as a police officer, but also as a friend of the family. It was clear that his sister admired the DCI, a feeling that was reciprocated. Isaac could see himself in the young woman: articulate, educated, aiming to better herself.

Charisa Devon was in the front pew of the church, her boyfriend on one side, Billy Devon on the other. The boyfriend had his arm around Charisa, pulling her in closer to him when the woman faltered due to the emotion of the ceremony. She had read a passage from the Bible, and then, unexpectedly, eulogised her dead brother, and how it was a life wasted, a light extinguished.

Isaac could recognise the passion behind what Charisa said, not the truth. He had seen too many take the same road that Samuel Devon had. The gangs were seductive, he remembered that. The chance to do what you want, to indulge in what you could not afford. If you wanted an expensive car, you took one. If you wanted a Rolex watch, the same solution, and if you wanted money and women, then they were available in equal measure. Of the twenty-eight students that had been in his final class at school, four had succeeded, himself included, another fifteen were still in the area battling away at mediocre jobs, six were either in jail or dead.

'It's a good send-off,' Rasta Joe said, one of three remaining from that class who should be in jail. The man had taken a seat next to Isaac on his arrival though neither man liked the other.

'Did you know Samuel?' Isaac asked.

'In passing. He was always polite. I knew his mother, that's all.'

'How?'

'I took her out a few times when we were younger.'

'She was a few years older than us,' Isaac said.

'It didn't last long, and besides, she was uptight.'

'What do you mean?'

'Not receptive to my charms.'

'You didn't sleep with her?'

'She was into religion and how it was a sin to indulge in sexual relations outside of marriage.'

'It's a good enough sentiment,' Isaac said.

'Maybe it is, not that I'd know. It certainly didn't stop her husband putting it around.'

'What happened to him?'

'I've no idea, and that's the honest truth.'

'We're still focussing on the death of Amelia Brice. You knew her?'

'Not really. We all knew who she was, but she'd come into the pub, line up a likely candidate and take him outside.'

'Sex?'

'That's a polite word for it. Once she was finished with him, she'd either have a few drinks or disappear.'

'If she had chosen you?'

'I'd have gone outside, but I've got more than I can handle.'

Billy Devon, the eldest child, gave a eulogy as well: long on praise, short on his brother's failings. In fact, the young man's death and the reason for it were glossed over.

Isaac did a scan of the church, and after the ceremony he stood close to the door, trying to see who he knew, who he didn't. In there, he supposed, might be a murderer.

Charisa approached him as he stood to one side. 'Thank you for coming. Samuel would have appreciated it.' Isaac doubted that the dead man would have welcomed him there, but he understood that it was politeness on her part.

'How are you and Billy going?'

'We manage from day to day. Have you found out who killed Samuel?'

'Not yet.'

'And our mother?"

'We're working on it. We've some possibilities, nothing concrete. Just one question.'

'Yes, of course.'

'Was your mother an honest woman?'

'Too honest for her own good.'

'What do you mean?'

'That dump we lived in. It belongs to the council, but if it had been me, I'd have refused to pay and taken them to court for their failure to fix it up, but not our mother. She paid the rent every month without complaint.'

It sounded litigious to Isaac, the sort of thing that an American boyfriend would come up with. He knew that the council was not the problem; it was the wasted effort that in most cases they would fix it up one day, only for it to be vandalised the next.

'What are your plans?'

'I've told you before. As soon as I have my visa for America, I'll be going there with Troy.'

'A complicated process?'

'It is wasn't for Troy, I'd stay here. Billy would prefer it if I stayed.'

'He could always go to America.'

'Not him. They'll only let him in if he has a degree, something to offer. His working in a shop is not a skill they're in desperate need of.'

Charisa Devon excused herself and went to speak to the other mourners. Isaac took a step back from where he was to allow himself a more unobstructed view. Over to one side, Rasta Joe was talking to some other men. He was sure that they were bartering the price of drugs, judging by the gesticulating of their fingers. Billy Devon was standing on his own. Isaac went over to him. 'A good send-off,' Isaac said.

'I suppose so, but he shouldn't have died.'

'Have you been tempted to take up crime?'

'Sometimes.'

'Don't go there,' Isaac said. 'I don't want to be pulling you out of the river.'

'I won't. Our mother brought us up well, taught us right from wrong.'

'It didn't help Samuel.'

'Not him. It's a shame, but there it is.'

Isaac realised that he was not likely to get much more out of the man. He excused himself and saw no one else of interest. The funeral procession to the cemetery left. Isaac did not attend the get-together later that day. Instead, he returned to Challis Street.

Chapter 7

Shirley O'Rourke cursed Christine Devon. ABC Cleaning, a byword for excellence, or at least that was what it said on the door, did not need the police inside its office, and now they'd been twice in as many days.

'Mrs O'Rourke, is it possible that your employees were stealing?'

'We spoke about this yesterday. They've got nothing, and then they're in Aladdin's Cave.' The owner sat back in her chair. Wendy Gladstone could see that it was an attempt to be nonchalant, although she had been around enough villains to know the woman was unnerved.

'It would be easy for someone in your company to coordinate these activities. It's a viable theory for the death of Christine Devon.'

'How, what do you mean?'

'The cleaners take photos on their phone. Someone else with the necessary knowledge makes a judgement call on what should be taken and when. Nothing too obvious, but the rich tend to leave money and jewellery around the house. A lot of the people would not even register the missing item and then claim insurance. Is that what's happened here?'

'Are you accusing me?' Shirley O'Rourke said.

'Not you directly, but it's a hypothesis.'

'I vet my people.'

'But you take advantage of desperate people, pay them a pittance, cream off plenty.'

'That's slanderous. I'm a businesswoman. I've done nothing to be ashamed of.'

'Christine Devon was an honest woman. If she had not done anything wrong, you would have sacked her within a few months.'

53

'I've told you this once.'

'I can't prove it yet, but you've been stealing from these houses and fencing the goods. The people who clean for you don't have the contacts. They may help themselves to some money lying around, take food from the fridge to feed their families, but the big money is in the jewellery, the antiques. Maybe you're in collusion with some of the house owners.'

Shirley O'Rourke raised her bulk from her chair and steadied herself with one hand on her desk. 'How dare you come in here with such accusations. I will report this matter to the relevant authorities.'

'I'll give you the number,' Wendy said. 'And besides, I have a warrant to seize all of your accounts and employee records.'

'How, why?'

'A court order. We've done some research into you and this company. Also, we know about your time in jail for fraud.'

'That was a long time ago. You could have asked for my records.'

'And allowed you time to shred or delete them? I'll also need the password for your computer.'

'I'll have my lawyer onto you.'

'Mrs O'Rourke, please take whatever steps that you feel appropriate.' Wendy made a phone call. Soon after, two men, one woman came into the office. 'These people are from Fraud. They will take all that they require. You can either assist them or not.'

***

Isaac had been told that Quentin Waverley was an agreeable man. That was not the impression that he and Larry formed on meeting the man.

Isaac had made the appointment earlier in the day, received a brusque reply when he mentioned what it was about. Waverley had attempted to suggest that the bank's legal team would look into the validity of Isaac's request to meet that day. Isaac had to inform him that he was possibly implicated in the death of Amelia Brice and if he wanted his legal team to assist, he'd better tell them that fact first.

After Isaac had held his ground, two in the afternoon was agreed on.

Both the police officers had to admit that Waverley had an excellent office: fifteenth floor, panoramic vista of the city of London, personal assistant in the other room. 'My time's limited,' Waverley said.

'Amelia Brice?'

'What about her?' Waverley replied. Isaac could see that he was a confident man by the way he sat in his chair. The man's office was expensively decorated, original oil paintings on the wall, plush carpet on the floor, in contrast to the central area of the merchant bank: functional and businesslike with tiled floors and open-plan offices.

'You were in a relationship with her.'

'For some time. We even lived together, but that's in the past.'

'We have reason to believe that you were still in contact with her up to the time of her death.'

'I wasn't and why do you believe that?'

'In her diary, it mentions a Q on several occasions.'

'Is that it?'

'It is clearly you.'

'Why? I'm not the only person with a Q in their name, and even then, it may mean something else.'

'A type of code?' Larry said.

'Amelia liked to play games. I suggest that you both leave and come back here when you've done your research. For your record, we broke up some years ago. Since then I have married. I have no wish to relive the past.'

'Not the part where Amelia caught you in bed with her friend?'

'Not that part or any other part.'

'Are you saying that she did catch you?'

'Who have you been talking to, her father?'

'Yes.'

'Jeremy's fine. We keep in contact.'

'Why, if your relationship with his daughter was fractured?'

'Fractured? I'm not sure I understand the word. Our relationship came to an end, that's all.'

'And you've not spoken to her since.'

'Not by choice. I saw her in a restaurant once. We acknowledged each other.'

'Was your wife with you?'

'Not that time.'

'Have there been other times?'

'There may have been, but none come to mind. How do you deal with old lovers?'

'We need to establish your relationship with Amelia Brice,' Isaac said.

'There was no relationship. She caught me with another woman. We were virtually separated by that time. Amelia made a scene, stormed out of the place. After that, I have not spoken to her.'

***

The strongest motive for the murders of Amelia Brice and Christine Devon lay with the cleaning company. Isaac knew, as did his team, that most people tend to overvalue their assets, mainly for insurance purposes. Even Isaac believed that his flat was worth more than the current property market would pay, and those with wealth would have no difficulty overvaluing their jewellery, the most likely items to be stolen. But that would require a police report of theft. Bridget was assisting Fraud to make some checks. Fraud was also going through the records of Shirley O'Rourke's cleaning company. The woman had instructed her lawyer to take action for their return.

So far, the employees were known and the addresses recorded. It was not thought likely than any ill-gotten gains would be registered, and they would probably have been deposited into an offshore account or would be in cash. With the addresses of the premises that had been cleaned, they'd be able to compare them with the insurance company claims. If they found any that matched, Mrs O'Rourke would be called in for further questioning.

Even so, Isaac knew it was a long stretch from theft and insurance fraud to a professional assassination.

Superintendent Goddard was looking for a result, yet the only possibilities seemed weak. Amelia's diary had revealed nothing more of interest, other than the usual day-to-day activities of a woman who was sometimes a little too direct about which man she had slept with, and their score out of one to ten. Further checking of the house had failed to find any more diaries, which concerned Isaac and Larry. An exhaustive check of all of the woman's acquaintances had not discovered another Q, although after their meeting with Quentin Waverley, they had come away uncertain about him. Checks into his background, his banking expertise, had revealed a competent man. There had even been a picture of him in a magazine with the blushing bride on the day they got married. Isaac had studied the image and had to agree with Jeremy Brice that Gwen Waverley was an attractive woman, although not as appealing as Amelia had been. And now the Waverleys had a child, another on the way.

In Homicide, it was time for the regular early morning meeting. Bridget had organised the coffee, Larry was working his way through one of his wife's healthy snacks, saying little, just pulling a strange face as he took a bite. None of the others commented although they all enjoyed the entertainment. Wendy could empathise as she had managed to lose some weight in the last few months; it had piled on after she had quit smoking, and the walks around the block before breakfast were doing her good.

Bridget, not subject to the strenuous medical that Wendy would have, and not troubled by arthritis, remarkable considering that she was a heavier-set woman than her friend, felt no need to diet, no need to exercise. Each morning she'd be into the bacon and eggs, while Wendy would be on muesli.

'What have we got?' Isaac asked the team. He was sitting back, pleased that he had found himself a potential new girlfriend. They had been out for a meal the night before, but it was early days, and they hadn't gone back to his flat afterwards. He had liked the woman, did not want to ruin it with an ill-timed move, and besides, she had made it clear that she took her relationships seriously and she was not into one-night stands.

'Is it possible that it is Christine Devon who was the primary target?' Wendy asked.

'We've considered this before,' Isaac said, 'but the woman has no history. Apart from a few friends at her church, she kept to herself.'

'She cleaned in other houses. Maybe she had seen something, mentioned it to Amelia Brice. And then Brice attempted to use it to her advantage. The woman's morals were suspect.'

'Sleeping with men she picks up at the pub is not analogous to bribery and extortion.'

'Agreed, although she may have mentioned it to someone else who had no issues with extortion.'

'Bridget, what do we know about where Christine Devon worked?' Isaac asked.

'She had been cleaning houses for nine years. Before that, she had worked in a clothing factory.'

'The clothing factory, is it still there?'

'It's located in China now.'

'Okay, so she's a casualty of the need to produce somewhere cheaper. After that, cleaning?'

'We have copies of her tax returns with details. Since the clothing factory, only cleaning.'

Chapter 8

Two people remained worried: Billy Devon and his sister, Charisa. Their mother was dead at the hands of persons unknown and their brother, Samuel, at the hands of one of the gangs in the area. Both of them knew that Billy had almost fallen under a gang's influence a few years earlier, but his mother had firmly taken control of him, clipping him around the ears a few times when he came in late or was abusive. It had worked with him, but then he was as strong-willed as his mother, and the idea of petty crime and ganja had never attracted him. His brother, he assumed, took after their father, although neither he nor his brother remembered him. Charisa, his sister, was also strong and wanting to leave England, and Billy knew he would then be alone.

Charisa had had trouble with the gangs in the past, with their attempts to accost her as she walked down the road to the place that had been home, although it was never cosy, more utilitarian. It was a depressing building, its communal areas graffitied, its attempt at a garden outside littered with dog faeces and old syringes. On some nights, if it was dark, Charisa had stayed with a friend, or in more recent times with her boyfriend. Her mother hadn't approved, but as the young woman had said, 'What's worse? My being mugged, even raped, or sleeping with the man I love?'

Christine Devon had told them of some of the places where she cleaned – their beauty, their affluence, their ease with which the owners left their valuables on display.

Billy knew that his mother had never touched anything, although Samuel had thought her crazy, and was none too subtle in his comments. Billy reflected on Samuel, four years younger than him, yet he had been taller. At fifteen, he had already been in a couple of gang fights: a group on one side hurling insults and brandishing knives at the other; the other gang following suit, the occasional miscreant coming forward, the opposite side pushing one of theirs to take up the challenge. Then the taunting, the thrusting of the knives, the contact, the blood, the retreat. And in the confrontation, the tempo increasing, fuelled by drugs and drink, giving them Dutch courage. Eventually, according to Samuel, someone would get hurt, and on one of the two occasions that he had been there, one of the gang members had been killed. That was the time for all of those so-called brave men to vanish into the ether, the body left where it was, usually in an area where the police did not venture too often.

Afterwards came the taunting, across the street, by graffiti, or by phone, about when revenge would be exacted. Billy had seen it as pointless; Samuel thought it made sense, even told his mother so once, and she had sent him to his room. Not that it did much good; the young man was physically stronger than the mother, stronger than anyone in the household. He did what he wanted, even though his mother, their mother, loved him.

'What am I to do?' his mother had said after he had walked out of the door the last time.

It had been Charisa who replied. 'Don't you remember Billy? He grew out of it. I'm sure Samuel will soon.'

Billy had known that Charisa was saying it for their mother's sake. His involvement with the gang culture had been minor. He had not indulged in fighting, not even in their use of ganja. He had met up with one of the more harmless gangs once or twice and the most they did was to talk big.

One gang member had been persistent with Charisa, even following her home from college, driving past the block of flats where she lived late at night. But he had died in a fight, his body thrown into a rubbish bin.

And then Samuel had embraced the gangs, even after all that his family had experienced.

Billy had known that no good would come of Samuel's death, and now the gang that he had cheated would be looking for someone in the Devon family to make up for their financial loss. They had made this clear one evening as he walked home from work. He had been close to where he was staying when a

60

BMW had pulled up alongside him, a couple of gang members in the back, another two in the front. 'We need to talk,' the front passenger said.

Even though there were other people on the street, it was dark, and it had just started to rain. Billy was dragged into the back seat, face down in the crotch of one of the men, an unsavoury character by the name of Bruce Lee. Billy knew who he was, knew that he made out to be a martial arts expert, even though he carried too much weight and he did not have the gentle manner of his namesake, nor the svelte body. Another man was prodding his backside, making suggestive comments in an attempt to frighten Billy, and succeeding. 'Almost as good an arse as your sister's. If she doesn't want to play, we can use you instead. What do you reckon, Billy Devon? You or your sister?'

He had protested, he knew he had, but a car full of gang members, him face down, one man pushing his head into his crotch, the other caressing his rear, did not help. He wanted to grab each and every one of them and to pummel them, but he could do nothing, except to act subserviently. 'Whatever you say,' he had replied instead.

After five minutes, the car had stopped on a derelict piece of land, and he was roughly pushed out onto the ground.

'Billy Devon, your brother stole from us. We want it back.'

Billy was leaning on the car, his legs feeling unstable. 'Did you kill him?'

'We're not here to answer questions, only to tell you what to do.'

'What do you expect from me? I only work in a shop.'

'That's not our problem. Your brother stole twenty-two thousand pounds. We want it back, with interest.'

'I never saw him with any money.'

'Then he gave it to someone. Maybe his gang.'

'Then why don't you ask them?'

'They have honoured their part of the agreement. Now it is time for you to do your part.'

'They killed him for you?'

'Why not? We want that money. And remember, each day the interest will increase by one thousand pounds. If we don't have all the money in five days, we will grab your sister, and she can work off the interest.'

'You bastards.'

'Such language. Bruce Lee, teach him some manners.'

Roughly pulled from where he had been leaning, Billy was thrown to the ground. Bruce Lee then started putting his boot in, as well as leaning down to hit Billy's body with a karate chop.

'Okay, that's enough,' the leader said. 'I don't want Isaac Cook to see that he's been roughed up.'

The gang members got into the car, pushing Billy Devon away. 'Don't forget. Five days, or we'll pick up your sister,' the front passenger said. Billy looked around him. In the distance, he could see the main road. He walked hesitantly, slowing regaining his strength. It was nine in the evening before he finally made it home. The others in the house saw him come in and head up to the bathroom.

***

Gwen Waverley was not pleased to be interviewed in her house by two police officers.

The Waverley house, fifty-five minutes from London, was in a pretty village where a few celebrities lived as well. The house, Victorian and substantial, occupied a position set well back from the road. Upon arriving at the front gate, Isaac had wound down the window of his car and spoken into the intercom located outside it. Once the formalities had been dealt with, the gate swung open. Two hundred yards ahead, the house came into view.

At the door, a woman waited for them. 'Mrs Waverley will receive you in the library. Would you like tea or coffee?'

'Tea, please,' Isaac said. Larry chose coffee.

The two men waited for five minutes before the housekeeper returned with their drinks, as well as some biscuits on a plate. Another six minutes and Gwen Waverley, clearly very pregnant, appeared. 'What can I do for you?' she said.

'We're investigating the death of Amelia Brice. We understand that you were good friends with her.'

'We were, thick as thieves, but time moves on.'

'We need to know about her.'

'Then why do you need me? I have not spoken to her for quite some time.'

'Mrs Waverley, we have yet to establish a reason for Amelia's death. We are hoping that you may be able to help.'

'I don't see how. We ceased to be friends a long time ago. Quentin, my husband, was with her for some years. Eventually, their relationship dulled and he transferred his affections to me.'

'Dulled?' Larry asked.

'They were not involved at that time, or they weren't as far as Quentin was concerned. Amelia, obviously, had different ideas.'

'There was a scene?'

'Amelia caught us in a compromising situation. You don't want me to elaborate, do you?'

'That will not be necessary. After that?' Isaac said.

'She pestered Quentin for some time, and occasionally phoned me to call me a bitch.'

'What was your reaction?'

'I was upset. We had been great friends, and there she is, calling me all the names under the sun, but then, she could be unstable, emotional.'

'Drugs?'

'Not when I was with her, although we'd smoke the occasional joint together. More as a lark than anything else, pretending to be sophisticated and grown up.'

'Not very sophisticated,' Larry said.

'I know that now, but her father used to have parties at the house.'

'Anyone famous?'

'Some of them, and they were out to enjoy themselves.'

'How old were you two?'

'Eighteen, nineteen. Old enough to do what we wanted, silly enough to do it.'

'Apart from the drugs and the drinks?'

'Okay, we were both a little easy. I grew up, found myself a good man; she didn't.'

'Any reason as to why anyone would want her dead?'

'Not really. She could be strange at times, abrasive, but not enough to kill her. Although she started to find rough men after she broke up with Quentin. I'm not sure if it was as a result of Quentin, or whether that was her inclination.'

'Her father?'

'He treated her well, indulged her. He's not the same as he portrays himself.'

'We're aware of that,' Isaac said.

'In a recent diary that she kept, there is a reference to a Q,' Larry said.

'It wouldn't be Quentin. He's not spoken to her for years, although he would sometimes meet up with her father.'

'Any reason why?'

'Quentin admired the man, and as for Jeremy, I think that Quentin was the son-in-law he never had.'

'Is there any reason why she would write Q in her diary?' Isaac asked.

'As I've already said, it's not Quentin. Amelia could become fixated on people, situations, a dress in a shop window, but apart from that, I've no explanation.'

Chapter 9

Before the influx of immigrants who were willing to do anything for half the price of the English, Shirley O'Rourke had been an ideal employer with a motivated staff. She was a woman who had never had much in her life, apart from a farm that her parents had called home in Northern Ireland, and now there were cheap staff and plenty of money.

The companies that they had initially cleaned for had wanted to pay only minimal money, but the wealthy with their luxury houses were willing to pay plenty, and so, with cheap staff, she knew she could make a tidy sum for herself.

In the early days of dealing with the wealthy, random checks on her staff's quality of work had been expected, but the business had expanded. The random checks had ended, the money was flowing in, the complaints were moderate and quickly dispensed with, as Shirley O'Rourke had a disarming manner when it was required.

And now, when she was living almost as well as those that her company cleaned for, the police were snooping around, and all because two women had been killed. She regretted employing Christine Devon, had even known she would be trouble, but the woman was cheap, even if she didn't respond to the gentle hints about a little extra on the side.

Shirley O'Rourke could not understand people such as the Devon woman. A woman who had lived in England all of her adult life; a woman who should have known how the system worked. The address that she had given when applying for the job showed that she lived poorly in a rundown area. And there she was, willing to clean for those who had plenty, those who had cheated on their taxes, enjoyed overseas holidays and drove expensive cars.

And now, the police had her records and her business was at a virtual standstill. Somehow, those clients that she had garnered over the years were gone. The word had got out that ABC Cleaning had been involved in nefarious activities.

Although innocent until proven guilty, not that she would be able to prove her innocence, the police investigation had destroyed her business, due to one sanctimonious woman.

At Challis Street, the records of ABC Cleaning were being checked by Fraud and Bridget Halloran, the Homicide department's best person with numbers. Her preliminary work had shown anomalies: understated income, exaggerated expenditure. Not necessarily criminal, although the extent was enough to raise suspicion. Then there were the woman's bank accounts. Accessed following the approved procedures, they showed more money than the business had generated, yet according to the owner, it was her sole income. There was also a house in Bayswater, not as expensive as some of the homes that the company cleaned, but valuable nonetheless.

***

It was early in the morning, Isaac Cook's preferred time, not Wendy Gladstone's, and definitely not Larry Hill's. Wendy was more of an evening person, Larry was suffering the pangs of hunger. At home it was his wife feeding him healthily; in the office it was his DCI, who had been firm that his DI needed to shed weight. Larry would have to admit that the two of them, a formidable team, were having an effect. So far, he was down two inches on the waist, and he thought if it continued, he'd need to wear braces or buy clothes more suited to his thinner frame. And now, his house, adequate for him, had become too small for his wife, and there was an extension planned, more encumbrance on his mortgage. He didn't want it, his wife did, and he knew who would win.

It was strange, Larry thought, that he had no trouble dealing with a villain, showing him who was in control, but with his wife, he was a total wimp. But then, he didn't love the villain, he loved his wife, and even if they fought sometimes, there was still the making up, and the reduced weight had done wonders for his libido.

If his DCI and his wife continued to push him to control his weight, he'd endure it, and he had even started to go for walks whenever he could, but there were still two murders to solve, and working from early in the morning until late at night required more than small portions. It was alright for his DCI, he knew. The man was well over six feet, could eat as much as he liked, and the weight never went on. Even though his DCI would complain about the extra pounds, it was nothing. For Larry, he knew, it was that extra pint of beer, that full English breakfast, and the next day the difference would be noticeable, and he'd get the cold shoulder from his wife.

He'd avoided the full English breakfast as much as possible for the last month, even missed the waitress who would ask for details of their latest murder investigation, only to be shocked when he told her. But most of all he missed the pub and its beer. The last time he had met with Rasta Joe, attempting to unravel why a fifteen-year youth by the name of Samuel Devon had needed to die, he had kept his consumption down to three pints, though it hadn't stopped Rasta Joe drinking six. Larry had not been satisfied with the gang leader's replies, either. The man continued to act ignorant about who had killed the youth. Larry had tried to pin him down but had not succeeded. Either the dreadlocked man did not know, which seemed unlikely, or he was scared or involved. Larry did not discount either of the last two options, although hoped it was the first.

Rasta Joe, who had been a school friend, even a fellow choirboy, of DCI Cook, was charismatic, and Larry would admit to liking the man, even if his activities were illegal.

In fact, all of Larry's contacts were reluctant to talk about Samuel Devon, which was disturbing. If his death concerned the gangs, then something was going on, and that something could get worse.

***

Shirley O'Rourke sat in the kitchen of her house. On a table in the corner she laid out her papers, the ones the police had not taken. There in front of her was the evidence the police wanted. The evidence that would convict her of criminal activity, namely, the theft of artefacts from the houses her company had cleaned, the fake jewellery that had been substituted for the genuine article, the occasional insurance fraud with the owner of the house over an over-insured antique.

Once, one of her cleaners had knocked over a Ming vase, shattered it into pieces. It had already been insured for ten times its value after it had developed a large crack six months after the insurance company had valued it. Shirley O'Rourke, an honest woman, expected the owner to be livid, but on the contrary, he had suggested that if the cleaner said it was an accident, then he would claim the full value from the insurance company, and divide the profit. Shirley had needed time to consider the proposal.

'Five thousand pounds if you agree,' he had said. Back then, two hundred pounds a week after expenses was a decent return.

'Agreed,' she had said, and since then she had not looked back, not until now, and it was time to protect herself.

Along the way, she had gathered a couple of husbands, both dispensed with, a child, now thirty-one and married, and an offshore bank account. The next day she would put into place her exit strategy, but first, she needed to waylay the police investigation.

It was two in the afternoon when she arrived at Challis Street. She had brought her lawyer with her, an imperious little man with horn-rimmed spectacles. Isaac thought that he would not have looked out of place as a character with a monocle in a P.G. Wodehouse farce.

The interview room had been booked, ready for the woman's arrival. Wendy, with Isaac, represented the police; Shirley O'Rourke and Peregrine Woodley sat on the other side of the table. Isaac went through the formalities, advised the woman of her rights.

'Mrs O'Rourke, you are here of your own free will to make a statement,' Isaac said.

'I thought it was best to clear the air.'

'There are anomalies in your accounts,' Wendy said.

'It is clear that I have taken advantage of tax loopholes, as any person in business is entitled to do. The fact that I have probably been more aggressive than others does not in itself constitute a crime. No doubt Inland Revenue will want to conduct a full audit of my financial records after you have seized them.'

'Does that concern you?' Isaac asked.

'Of course it does. A tax audit is always unpleasant.'

'Have you committed any criminal wrongdoing in your tax avoidance?'

'Not criminal, but they'll find something, they always do. The deaths of these women are going to cost me plenty.'

'Is your financial well-being more important than us bringing their murderer to justice?'

'Don't go putting words into my mouth. That's not what I said.'

'My client is here to assist, not to be accused of a crime,' Woodley said.

'The question was valid.'

'Christine Devon worked for me for a short period of time. I did not know the woman other than in a professional capacity. I knew Amelia Brice's father, and I had met his daughter once. Her death is disturbing, as is Christine Devon's, but I was not involved. A tax audit will result in a fine at most, and a time to pay any outstanding monies. As you can see, their deaths have inconvenienced me. I do not have any motive to want them dead.'

'A complete check of your records, your bank statements, will continue,' Wendy said.

'It appears that your interest in me has permeated through to my clientele.'

'What do you mean?'

'Most of them have cancelled my contract with them.'

'We would not have told anyone.'

'I realise that, but someone has.'

'Any ideas?'

Wendy looked at the woman, unsure why she had come voluntarily to the station. She had said nothing other than admitting to irregularities in her financial records. Shirley O'Rourke, it was assumed, was talking about thousands of pounds over the years.

This was the first time that Isaac had met the woman. He knew her to be fifty-eight, although she looked older. She dressed well enough, the sort of clothes that could be bought in a high street clothing store. For a woman who had supposedly made herself rich, she did not show it. Isaac assumed it was the woman's nature, her frugality.

'Mrs O'Rourke, we are confused as to why you have come here today,' Wendy said. 'If you have cheated on your taxes, that is either fraud or not.'

'I needed to clear the air, to explain my innocence. I am a hard-nosed businesswoman, that's all.'

'Let us come back to Christine Devon,' Isaac said.

'The woman applied for a job; she had the necessary qualifications and suitable references.'

'You checked?'

'Always. And besides, it's becoming increasingly hard to get good staff. Most would rather scrounge off the government than work. Mrs Devon never gave any trouble. She did the job, and I paid her on time.'

'Minimum wage?' Wendy asked.

'I run a business, not a charity. No doubt some of the homeowners would have given her tips.'

'One avenue of enquiry is that Amelia Brice and Christine Devon shared some common knowledge. We've assumed that it was gang-related, or possibly politically-related, given Amelia's father's friendship with those in power.'

'What's this got to do with me?'

'Do you have any ideas as to what it might have been?'

'Not me. I didn't speak to Mrs Devon often, and Amelia, never.'

'But her father? You'd speak to him.'

'Sometimes. We understood each other.'

'What do you mean?'

'We'd both come from nothing. We could speak to each other without any pretence.'

'Is what we're seeing from you today, a pretence?'

'Not at all. I grew up in Ireland. We were dirt poor. Do you know what that means?'

'Yes, I do,' Wendy said. 'Subsistence farming.'

'Then you'll understand the need to better yourself.'

'I can understand, but I've remained honest, whereas you haven't.'

'Insults are not appropriate,' Peregrine Woodley said.

'My apologies.'

'Mrs O'Rourke, I put it to you that you are worried that we will find more,' Isaac said. 'That we will find fraudulent insurance claims from homeowners that tie in with your cleaning of their houses. It will be a criminal offence if you have knowingly received stolen goods and then sold them, sometimes with the homeowner's permission, sometimes without. How do you plead, Mrs O'Rourke, guilty or not guilty? We will uncover the truth.'

'This is unacceptable,' Woodley said. Isaac ignored him.

'Did Amelia offer you a deal?'

'I must protest,' Woodley said. Yet again, Isaac ignored him.

'Or maybe her father was starting to tighten up on her lifestyle. We know he did not approve of the drugs or the men, angry with her for letting Quentin Waverley get away from her. Amelia Brice is desperate; the word is around that you can help out. You approach Christine Devon: knock over that vase, destroy that painting accidentally, steal some jewellery, replace it with a fake, and there is this good woman, this good dead woman, refusing. What did you do? Call someone you knew? You've lived around here long enough. You know someone who can rid you of two troublesome women: one desperate that the plan has gone awry, angry, wanting to lash out, tell the police, and another woman, honest and decent, refusing to go along with it. You're cornered. Your business and your reputation are compromised. You take the only option possible.'

'That's lies, scurrilous lies. Woodley, do something. Don't sit there like a lemon,' Shirley O'Rourke said.

'I'll be making a formal complaint,' Woodley said.

'That's your prerogative,' Isaac said. He had shaken up the case. He knew that Shirley O'Rourke, if she were guilty, would react with more urgency. Wendy could keep a watch on her.

'I'll need a full transcript and copies of this interview,' Woodley said.

'They will be supplied.'

The interview ended, and Shirley O'Rourke and her lawyer left.

'You were tough there,' Wendy said.

'Just keep an eye on her. See what she does,' Isaac said.

Chapter 10

There was nothing that Isaac Cook disliked more than an investigation that was going nowhere. And whereas Shirley O'Rourke had felt the heat from him, he was not sure of her guilt. To him, she was a woman who skirted around the boundary between right and wrong. She may well have acted in collusion with some of the homeowners to allow fraudulent insurance claims; she may have been responsible for the theft of money and valuables. A conviction for receiving stolen goods was one thing, but murder was different altogether.

Wendy, Isaac's dependable sergeant, was not as convinced, although proof would be difficult. She had not liked the woman from first meeting her, and after the interview she liked her even less. She had met people like her before; the type of people who gave capitalism and free enterprise a bad name.

Isaac met with Charisa, the daughter of one of the murdered women. They had arranged to meet in a café in the centre of London, some distance from Challis Street. The DCI saw a worried young woman. Inside the café, she relaxed a little but remained tense. Isaac purchased two caffè lattes; they sat towards the back of the café, away from the view of the street.

'What is it?' Isaac asked.

'It's Billy,' Charisa said.

'What about him?'

'They threatened him.'

'Who?'

'One of the gangs.'

'Tell me the full story.'

'They made it clear that if you were told, it would be worse.'

'They always say that. When was he told?'

'Three days ago.'

'How long have you known?'

'He told me this morning.'

'What did he tell you?'

'He was on his way home from work, close to where he lives. A car pulled up, he was bundled into the back, and it took off with him inside. They said that Samuel owed them twenty-two thousand pounds and the interest was accumulating – one thousand pounds a day.'

'Which Billy doesn't have.'

'He's been stealing from where he works to get the money.'

'How much has he?'

'Eight thousand.'

'What else?'

'They told him that if he didn't give them the money within five days, they'd take me.'

'Did they say why?'

'Inspector, you know what they meant.'

'Sex, prostitution.'

'Exactly.'

'And Billy's been trying to get the money to protect you?'

'I told him that he was crazy and that he should have told you straight away.'

'If he gets them the money, they'll only want more. Their claim against Samuel may be bogus anyway. Did they have names, this gang?'

'Billy said that one of the gang is known as Negril Bob.'

'I've heard of him,' Isaac said. 'He's been in trouble over the years, although I don't think there are any convictions against him.'

'I'm frightened for Billy.'

'It's you that I'm frightened for,' Isaac said. 'Where is your boyfriend?'

'He's gone to America for a couple of weeks.'

'Are you staying at his place?'

'Yes. But it's not far from where we used to live. They'll find me soon enough.'

'In that case, you need to move out. Is there anywhere that you could go?'

'Not really. Anyone we know lives in the area.'

Isaac could see the dilemma. If they protected Billy and Charisa Devon, a uniform assigned to each, then those that had threatened Billy would realise that he had spoken to the police, and that would be a death sentence for him. If the police did nothing, then Billy would be squeezed more, and they would take Charisa as a way of ensuring his compliance. Once Billy was in their control, they'd be after more money, all the while using his sister as leverage.

Isaac phoned Larry and gave him the address of the café where they were sitting. The young woman did not like the idea, but Larry had better contacts with the gangs than Isaac ever would. To them, he was a traitor to the brotherhood, a man who had deserted his race and had become a token white.

Larry arrived after fifteen minutes and made his way to the back of the café. Isaac ordered him a cappuccino. Larry would have liked a slice of cheesecake as well, but desisted. 'Negril Bob, I've heard of him. He runs with a bad crowd. If they make a threat, they'll carry it out.'

'Then what do you suggest?' Isaac asked. 'We can't let Charisa be taken.'

'Agreed, but if she's not around, they'll go for Billy. These people don't make idle threats. How long have we got?' Isaac asked.

'Two days maximum.'

Isaac could see the fear on the woman's face, understandable under the circumstances. He wondered how many more were under threat from the gangs; how many more who did not have the nerve to stand up to them and to contact the police. Probably a lot, he reasoned, and if their mother and their brother had not been murdered, would she have come forward, or would Billy have been relegated to stealing and the selling of drugs, even coerced into joining the gang that had changed his life?

'We'll do nothing for now,' Larry said. 'I'll meet with my contact first. Charisa, if there are any more threats, people loitering around, following you, then you are to call us straight away.'

'And?'

'We'll pick the two of you up and make sure you're both safe for a few days.'

'What are you thinking?' Isaac said.

'It's a loose plan, but if we have to, we'll hide them for a couple of days. That should give us enough time to round up the gang and to bring them in for questioning.'

It seemed unsatisfactory to Isaac, but there wasn't a lot more the police could do officially. The two Devon children were not witnesses to a crime and did not justify protected witness status. He was worried for Charisa, not so much for Billy, although another beating for failing to pay the money could result in his death, and the young man was about to lose his job for theft. If he had so far managed to acquire eight thousand pounds by offloading merchandise from the shop on the black market, there was no way that theft of that magnitude would stay hidden for long.

The three left the café at intervals, Charisa first. Larry briefly caught sight of her as she slipped down the steps not far away to the London Underground. After a few minutes, Larry left, but not before phoning Rasta Joe to meet up for lunch. Isaac waited for another twenty minutes.

***

Wendy kept a close watch on Shirley O'Rourke. Her money was on the woman being involved somehow, even if indirectly, in the two murders. Isaac thought she was chasing a red herring. If the woman was guilty of criminal activity, the fact remained that the murders of the two women had all the hallmarks of a professional.

Apart from the occasional visit to her business premises, Shirley O'Rourke stayed in her house in Bayswater, and the ABC

Cleaning Company appeared to be no longer in operation. Wendy realised that she would need to talk to the woman again shortly, although this time woman-to-woman and away from the police station and the woman's lawyer.

Inside the house, unbeknownst to Wendy, Shirley O'Rourke was fully occupied planning her future. She knew that Peregrine Woodley was the best there was, but even his legal skills could not prevent her receiving a custodial sentence. It had been a good life, but she did not intend to spend time in prison, and it wasn't as if the Brice home had given her much. The previous cleaner had been there for three years, and the arrangement had been fine. Any cash lying around, and Amelia Brice had been too spaced out on a few occasions to notice the loss, and the jewellery, she had plenty, so it had been easy to take, sometimes just removing it, other times substituting with a fake.

Shirley had felt no pang of regret over fleecing the woman: a woman who had been born with a silver spoon and nothing else, apart from being attractive. Shirley O'Rourke knew that she had never been able to rely on her looks to get by, and no man would ever have been swayed by her wiggling her arse, flashing her assets.

Wendy could see the smoke in the woman's backyard, realised that she couldn't do anything about it. It was compromising evidence, not old leaves, that was burning.

Bridget Halloran had been busy in the office at Challis Street checking insurance claims against the records taken from the ABC Cleaning Company.

Wendy left from outside the O'Rourke house and went to the first of the homes that concerned Homicide. At the house, not far from the Brices', a cheerful young boy of no more than six answered the door. 'Is your Mummy or Daddy in?' Wendy asked.

'Mummy's here.'

A woman in her forties came to the door. She was dressed in a top and jeans, an apron tied around her waist. 'Sergeant Wendy Gladstone, Challis Street Police Station.'

'Is it bad news?'

'Not at all. I've just got a few questions for you.'

'Then come in. I'm busy in the kitchen. If you don't mind me continuing, we can talk.'

'That's fine.'

In the kitchen, the marble-topped worktop, the gadgets, were all of the best quality. 'Do you want a cup of tea?' Emily Cardiff said.

'Yes, please.'

Two minutes later, a cup of tea was put down in front of her. 'What can I do for you?'

'Eighteen months ago, you made an insurance claim for a vase that had broken. How did it break?'

'The cleaner knocked it over.'

'How much did you claim for?'

'You've got the figures, I assume?'

'Twenty-five thousand pounds,' Wendy said. 'That's a lot of money for a vase.'

'It was antique, a family heirloom.'

'It couldn't be repaired?'

'No. It was smashed beyond repair.'

'ABC Cleaning, what can you tell me about them?'

'Reliable, do a decent job. I've no complaints.'

'We're investigating the deaths of Amelia Brice and Christine Devon. Did you know either of the women.'

'I knew Christine Devon. She used to clean here.'

'What can you tell me about her?'

'Not a lot really. She'd do her job and leave.'

'Was she here when the vase broke?'

'Not then. That was another cleaner.'

'Her name?'

'Victoria Neville.'

'Do you know where she was from?'

'I never asked. I don't make a point of becoming too friendly with the staff.'

'And the vase that was broken?'

'We used the money to buy another.'

'Where can I find Victoria Neville?'

'I've no idea. She used to live locally, that's all I know. She was Jamaican, or at least, she was born there.'

'Do you have any problems with the immigrants here?'

'If they cause no trouble, I don't.'

Wendy left the house, not sure that she had achieved much. A vase broken by a cleaner did not seem an impossibility. She'd ask Bridget to find Victoria Neville for her.

***

Isaac entered Billy Devon's workplace to find the man hard at work. 'We need to talk,' he said.

'Ten minutes and it'll be my lunch time. You've been speaking to Charisa?'

'She's a worried woman, and you're in trouble.'

'I'll do anything to protect her.'

'Admirable, no doubt, but you've broken the law.'

'There's a place down the road. They make a decent sandwich. Do you fancy one?'

'I'll treat,' Isaac said. He could see that the young man was worried. In the far corner of the store, the manager kept an eagle eye on his employee and the man in the suit he was speaking to.

'Can I help you?' the manager asked, moving quickly to waylay Isaac before he left the store.

'DCI Cook, Homicide.'

'And what do you want with Billy?'

'It's confidential.'

'I don't want my people involved in murder.'

'How long have you been the manager?'

'Two weeks.'

'Then you are not aware of your employee's history.'

'His history is not my concern; his ability to do his job is,' the manager said. Isaac looked at the man: white, dark-hair parted in the middle, a surly disposition. Isaac did not like the man. If he

79

knew what Billy had been up to, he'd have him out of the shop within the hour, but not before informing the police to let them know that he had apprehended a thief.

'Mr Devon's mother and brother were murdered.'

'He's a suspect?'

'No. As far as I am concerned, I would take it as an affront on your part if you question Billy on the matter, or use your influence to remove him from this store.'

'I don't hold with his sort,' the manager said.

'What sort is that? The black sort?'

'His involvement with murders.'

'He has not been involved; he is an honest, law-abiding citizen. Any attempts by yourself and others to remove him from this store will be met with a strong rebuke from me and further investigation into you.'

'Is that a threat?'

'It is not. Society is multicultural, and if you've looked, I'm black, as well.'

'You're different.'

'Is it because I carry a badge?'

'You're educated, a police officer.'

'I grew up around here. I know where you're coming from.; I've experienced it all my life.'

Isaac knew that he should not pass judgement on people, but he wanted the manager to back off. If he did a detailed audit of the stock in the shop, of sales made, he'd no doubt find anomalies.

'I'm ready,' Billy said.

'Okay. The sandwiches are on me.'

The two men left the shop and walked down the street. 'He's a bastard, that one,' Billy said.

'And you're a fool for not contacting me.'

The two men ordered their sandwiches and coffees, take away. Not far from the sandwich shop was a small park. One of the benches was vacant. 'I don't want anything to happen to Charisa,' Billy said.

'And how about you?'

'I can handle myself.'

'No you can't, and you know it. Level with me,' Isaac said. 'You've been stealing from the shop, trying to find the money.'

'I'll pay it back.'

'No you won't. That's money stolen, not earned. It'll take you years to make it back by honest graft. Your best hope is to tell me the truth of what happened.'

'Okay. They picked me up not far from the shop and took me to a vacant block of land.'

'Where?'

'Not far. I can show you if it's important.'

'It's not. What happened?'

'Negril Bob, he was the one who told them to work on me.'

'Work?'

'Beat me up, make remarks about Charisa.'

'What sort of remarks?'

'You know what sort.'

'How they were going to let her pay the money back.'

'That's it. They were crude though. It's not the language I intend to repeat.'

'Billy, you're too gentle. These are violent men. They'll have no issues with bleeding you dry and doing whatever they want with Charisa. How did you think you could protect her without the police?'

'I wasn't thinking, just doing what I had to.'

'And that manager at your shop, he's a hater. You can't keep stealing.'

'I need to protect Charisa.'

'You'll not protect her this way.'

'Then what do I do?'

'I need the two of you to keep me informed.'

'But how will you stop them taking her,'

'And killing you.'

'I'm not important.'

'Stop acting the hero, you're not the type. It's you and Charisa now.'

'She's got Troy.'

'You're still family.'

'Did Negril Bob and his gang kill Samuel?'

'We don't know. They may just be trying to cash in on your grief, or they could be acting under instructions. These men are garbage, don't try to make out that they're not.'

'I know what they are. Once Charisa's out of the country, I'll try and make something of myself, maybe get an education.'

'Maybe you will, maybe you won't. The future's up to you. I need to know what you've taken from the store, itemised, and I need it today.'

'Why?'

'I'm going to get you out of trouble.'

'You're a friend.'

'Don't say that. I'm doing what is right. If the manager reports you to the police, it's a criminal case, and I can't help you.'

Chapter 11

Quentin Waverley had been found out. His denials in the past about his relationship with Amelia Brice had come to nought. Gwen, his pregnant wife, had found out the truth, not through her husband or her former best friend, but through the police. 'You bastard. You've been screwing Amelia, even after we were married. What kind of man does that?' she said.

'The type of man that's not married to you.'

'Wait till my father hears about this. He'll have you out of the company.'

'And then what will you do? You're the wife of a merchant banker, one of the social elite. You'll do nothing, and you'll do it with a smile. Do I make myself clear?' Waverley said.

Gwen Waverley knew that he was right; she had married him, not out of an overriding love, but out of practicality. She wanted a man and children; her father's merchant bank had needed someone to succeed him, and Quentin Waverley had fitted the bill. The fact that he was Amelia's man had not come into it. Her father had agreed to the match, even helped plan her approach to the man, almost a hostile takeover.

It had been planned that she and Quentin were naked in bed when Amelia had walked in. Quentin had not known; he had thought they had two hours, but Gwen had received a message: fifteen minutes.

She had acted fast, touching him up and down his body, ensuring that he was salivating in anticipation, before hauling him up the stairs and removing all his clothes and hers just in time.

When they had first moved in together after his bust-up with Amelia, they had made love every night, and he had had no time for any other, but then the first child came along, and now the second, and he was back to his old ways.

'Did you kill her?' Gwen asked. She knew that he hadn't, but she could be argumentative, she knew that, and he needed to be brought to heel. After one child, with another on the way, she realised that she was not as firm as she had once been, not as tender to the touch, and her husband was a man who appreciated the beauty of a younger woman. If he was to take over the merchant bank, then he needed to respect that it was her who had put him there.

Quentin Waverley reacted in the only way possible; he became angry for not having chosen Amelia over Gwen. But, all Amelia could offer was a famous father, whereas Gwen offered the chairmanship of a bank and a substantial fortune once her father died, and that would be only a few years in the future.

'How dare you make such a scurrilous statement. I've a mind to…'

'Mind to what? Hit me, give me a tongue lashing? You're a weak excuse for a man. If only I had known.'

'What do you mean? It was you who seduced me, inveigled me into your bed. Amelia was a better proposition than you. Why would I have killed her? After your father dies I could have had the bank and her, and now she's gone. As for you, you can go to hell.'

Gwen knew bluster, and her husband's spouting was just that. The man was fiercely ambitious, and he did not intend to let anyone or anybody get in his way until he had full control. Gwen had never told him that there was an irrevocable clause, legally binding, that on the event of her father's death the majority holding would be in her name, leaving her husband with forty-nine per cent. And if her husband left her or died, then full ownership reverted to the daughter.

'But why Amelia? You know how I feel about her,' Gwen said. The two of them were sitting down calmly. It was not the first time they had argued, and would not be the last, but Quentin knew why he was with Gwen. In part it was because she was the way to a fortune, but also because she was the same as him.

'And why not Amelia? Her father remains a friend, so had she. You might not understand, but I was with her for some time.
84

The relationship never ended in the correct manner; it was unfinished business.'

'Unfinished screwing, is that it?'

'If you say so. I was still fond of the woman.'

'But you preferred my father's money.'

'And you saw me as the father of your children. You used me; I used you. We're very much alike, you and me,' Waverley said.

'Maybe we are, but Amelia's dead and the police will not give up on who Q is. My denial will not hold them off for long.'

'If it is becoming an issue, I'll own up to it.'

'You know what she thought of you at the end? What she may have written in her diary.'

'I can deal with it.'

'You're a bastard for becoming involved with her again. You know what my father would say if he knew.'

'Then it's for us to never let him know. Agreed?'

'Agreed, but no more screwing.'

'You know me better than that,' Waverley said.

'Unfortunately I do. I chose you, faults and all. I've no intention of letting you leave me.'

'And I've no intention of leaving, but a man's got to have a hobby.'

'You could always take up model aeroplanes,' Gwen said.

'I'd need more than one model,' Waverley said. His wife knew it to be true. Regardless of what had occurred, what would occur again, she'd stay by her husband's side.

***

Larry met up with Rasta Joe. Begrudgingly, they had to admit they liked each other.

'Negril Bob, what can you tell me about him?' Larry said. It was the Westbourne pub again, Rasta Joe's favourite.

'You don't want to mess with him,' Rasta Joe said. Two of his gang were outside, keeping a watch. Larry couldn't understand the life the man chose. It was clear that he was educated, even his former schoolmate Isaac Cook had said that, but the man wanted the life of a gang leader, making his money from selling drugs, running some women. There was a buoyant economy and a charismatic man such as the Jamaican could have made lawful money, no looking over the shoulder, no fear of a knife or a bullet.

'Why?' Larry asked. He'd ordered two pub lunches. In the three weeks since he had agreed to curb his eating and drinking, more on his DCI's insistence than his wife's, he had kept to her food, had even come to enjoy it, but today he was reverting to old habits. He knew that if he wanted Rasta Joe to talk, he'd need to prime him, and the man would take it as an insult if he kept to one beer and a salad.

'He's a violent man.'

'Could he had killed Samuel Devon?'

'It's possible, but I doubt it.'

'Why's that?'

'Devon was not involved with Negril Bob's gang. The man is a standover merchant: extortion, stolen cars, that sort of thing. He doesn't get involved with drugs.'

'Any reason?'

'No reason. He's just found a more profitable way of making money, and it's easier to stay out of sight of the police.'

'It's still illegal.'

'Maybe it is, but how can it be proved?' Those he's extorting from will not go to the police or give evidence. And he's focussed on high-end cars: Bentleys, Rollers, Porsches, the occasional Ferrari. As soon as they're stolen, they're in a shipping container, the tracking device immobilised. The next time those cars appear, it's a long way from England, no questions asked.'

'Why are you telling me this?' Larry said.

'I'm trusting you.'

'And you're expecting me to turn a blind eye to what you're up to.'

'If you want me to talk.'

'Negril Bob is threatening Samuel Devon's brother. Is he working for someone?'

'Probably, but not so easy to find out.'

'What do you mean, difficult or dangerous?'

'Both. You know how it works.'

Larry could see himself going home drunk. A shame as he saw it, as his relations with his wife had been much improved for the last few weeks, but he had a job to do.

'Very well,' Rasta Joe said as he finished off his glass of beer, looking for another to be ordered. 'The word is that Samuel Devon was killed by Negril Bob, on the order of Samuel's gang.'

'Harsh.'

'They're not the Boy Scouts. Devon had become smart, creaming off the drugs and the money.'

'How much?'

'A few thousand pounds.'

'Negril Bob mentioned twenty-two thousand pounds.'

'He wants his commission.'

'Anyway, what's the deal?'

'Devon's gang or Negril Bob kills him, and then the other gang use Negril Bob to get back the lost money.'

'Would he take Devon's sister as payment in lieu?'

'The man would take his own sister. Of course he will. I've seen her, she's attractive.'

'What do you suggest we do?' Larry asked.

'You're asking me? I'm not the police.'

'You know how these people think.'

'Get her out of the area.'

'And her brother?'

'If he doesn't pay, they'll continue to pressure him. He's easier to deal with.'

'What do you mean?'

'They can force him into crime. He can always burgle a shop or a house.'

'The sister?'

'You know what she can offer.'

'Unfortunately, I do.'

It was past ten in the evening. Larry ordered the two men another pint each.

***

Jeremy Brice, the father of a murdered daughter, had been hesitant to use his position to disparage the efforts of the police. The first that Isaac and his team heard of a change was when Bridget came into the office. 'It's the father. He's on the radio, and he's complaining about us.'

'What is he saying?' Isaac asked. The man had been pleasant enough in the dealings that the department had had with him, although his on-radio manner was full of pontificating and putting politicians and senior government officials on the spot, even the prime minister. None of them would refuse to talk to him, such was his ability to sway public opinion.

The prime minister could hold his own, and some of his ministers could too, but most came away from a Brice debate chastened and feeling as though the world was about to cave in, which in the case of a few, it had. The man had a team of ten people behind him sourcing the stories, checking the facts, as well as a couple of sharp lawyers who would instruct him as to how far he could go.

Bridget turned up the volume on the small radio she carried in her hand.

The voice of Jeremy Brice was loud and clear. 'Commissioner Davies, you've come in for a lot of criticism for the handling of the latest terrorist attacks in London.'

'We've a team of highly-competent professionals at the Met,' Davies replied.

'Is it true that you have replaced the head of Counter Terrorism Command with someone that you personally knew.'

'I have the utmost confidence in the man.'

'Unfortunately, the public does not. There have been calls for you to resign, the previous head of Counter Terrorism

Command to be given your job, and a new man assigned to deal with terrorism.'

'I am unable to comment on the Met's operations.'

'That's nonsense. You are aware that it has been mentioned in the Houses of Parliament on more than one occasion.'

'Yes, I am.'

'Commissioner, your first truthful answer. Let me be the first to congratulate you, at least on that.'

'I do not appreciate your sarcasm,' Davies said.

Isaac could see trouble up ahead. Davies would feel the need to react, and it was clear that Brice was being fed inside information.

Brice chose to ignore Davies's comment. 'The previous commissioner had placed his faith in the leadership of Counter Terrorism, and the first thing that you did was to start bringing in your people. Why is this? Were you attempting to shore up your position, surround yourself with lackeys? And what about the death of my daughter, Amelia? I've been reluctant to talk about this before, out of sorrow for her death and that of the other woman, Christine Devon.'

'We have a competent team working hard to solve the tragic death of your daughter,' Davies said.

'No doubt they're hardworking, but my daughter's death is still unsolved. How long will you allow this to continue? How long will you reward sycophancy? You've been given a job to do, that of the senior police officer in this city, and my listeners are asking questions, as are our political masters. Commissioner Davies, I have decided to speak at this time for the good of all of us, and for my daughter. It is time for you to stand up.'

On the other end of the phone line, an inwardly seething man spoke calmly. 'Mr Brice, your aspersions are ill-founded. Terrorism is not an easy issue to address, you must know that. Our activities are reducing the numbers of attacks, the recent changes in the law have given us more powers to act. Believe me, we will deal decisively with those who wish to undermine the values of this country; who believe that they have a right to murder.'

'My daughter, what are you going to do there? It is my right as a grieving father to ask. And don't tell me that you're going to bring in someone to take over the investigation. I know what happened the last time. In the end, it was Detective Chief Inspector Cook, the man that you replaced, who brought the woman to justice, not your man.'

Isaac sat back in his seat at the conclusion of Brice's interview with Commissioner Alwyn Davies.

'Hell,' Larry said. 'What's next?'

'Detective Chief Superintendent Richard Goddard,' Isaac mumbled.

Chapter 12

After Jeremy Brice's on-air interview with Commissioner Davies, the atmosphere inside Homicide was tense, as if they were waiting for the sword of Damocles to appear above their heads. Bridget, the least disturbed, made coffee for everyone. Larry took his black, the result of the night before with Rasta Joe. Wendy attempted to make conversation, although there were no takers.

After ten minutes, they heard the melodious tones of DCS Goddard. The man had made the trip from his office to Homicide. Isaac, for once, was pleased to see him.

'DCI, what do you make of all this?' Goddard asked. He had closed the door to Isaac's office on entering. Larry was still there. Outside, Wendy and Bridget attempted to make sense of the muffled sounds coming from the room.

'At the end, he gave me an oblique compliment,' Isaac said.

'Brice wants his daughter's murder to be solved.'

'So do we. We've no motive for either of the women to be killed. We have our suspicions but nothing solid.'

'Davies is going to go crazy. Be prepared for anything,' Goddard said.

'We'll continue with the investigation. Any reason for Brice taking on Davies?'

'Political, I assume.'

'Assume or know?'

'DI Hill, Larry, could you leave, please. I need to talk to DCI Cook in private.'

Larry got up from his seat and went outside. He realised that politics, national and internal, were at play.

'Isaac,' Goddard said, 'Brice was fed the information.'

'Why?'

'He wants his daughter's death solved, that's certain, and he also wants to get in with the senior politicians.'

'Who fed him the information?'

'There's a move to shake up the Met. The prime minister wants Davies out; sees him as incompetent.'

'But he doesn't want to be seen to be openly against the man as it would undermine confidence in our police service,' Isaac said.

'Exactly. So Brice's been fed certain information on the authority of someone senior; someone who must be seen to be impartial.'

'Clothed in ermine, answers to the title of Lord?'

'I can't answer that question.'

'The previous commissioner, Charles Shaw,' Isaac said.

'As you say,' Goddard replied, a wry smile on his face. 'They've been trying for the last year, but the man's slippery. He keeps putting his people in authority, sidelining any who can cause him trouble.'

'That would include you,' Isaac said.

'If he removes me, then I'll sit it out.'

'It doesn't help with our investigations. I've still got three murders to solve.'

'It does help. Hopefully, Davies will be too scared to bring his own people in now. The focus is on him and his supporters. His interview with Brice may bring you some protection, but you still need to wrap this up.'

***

Billy Devon continued to work at the shop. The manager continued to keep the young man in his sight. It was clear that the situation was coming to a head. On the one hand, Billy was receiving the occasional phone call about the money he owed – 'It's now at twenty-six thousand. One more day and your sister will be paying off the interest.' – and on the other hand was a man who expressed racist sentiments. Billy phoned Issac.

'What about Charisa?' Billy asked.

'What about you?' Isaac asked in reply.

'They still intend to take Charisa.'

'We're aware of that. You'll need to stall them when they want their money.'

'But how? I've given you the money I had for them.'

'I can attempt to protect you from criminal prosecution. I can't protect you if you continue to go to work.'

'I need to work. If they don't see me here, they'll take Charisa.'

Isaac could see the truth of the situation. It was not possible to protect the two of them if one continued to work in a shop and the other continued to attend college. He phoned Charisa. 'We need to protect you,' he said.

'But how? I can't hide, not around here, and I'm not leaving.'

'You're aware of the situation.'

'We're trusting you,' Charisa said.

'That's the problem. Officially, I can't offer you protection. When's Troy back from America?'

'Not for another week.'

Isaac knew that the situation was dangerous and the protection of two people was not his priority, not even his responsibility, but it was clear enough from Rasta Joe that Negril Bob would carry out his threat. Isaac took an unexpected action and phoned his former school friend. 'Joe, we need to protect Billy and Charisa Devon,' he said.

Rasta Joe, pleased to hear from Isaac, said, 'Negril Bob's not a person to mess with.'

'You'd have a better chance to protect them than we will.'

'It'll cost you,' Rasta Joe said.

'What's the price?'

'Your friendship.'

'You know I can't do that. You're a gang leader; I'm a police officer.'

'Then your trust in me to do the right thing.'

'I wouldn't phone you if I didn't trust you. I want Billy and Charisa safe, and I know you won't let me down.'

'We'll try, but you'd better be prepared in case it gets nasty.'

'We'll be there.'

'What about Billy? He's been stealing.'

'I'll deal with it,' Isaac said. The two men ended the phone call.

Isaac then phoned the owner of the shop where Billy worked. They arranged to meet later that day.

***

Quentin Waverley met Jeremy Brice. The two men had been friends from the first time Amelia had brought her latest boyfriend home. 'I heard you on the radio,' Waverley said.

'Were you still seeing Amelia?' Brice asked.

'Sometimes.'

'You should have married her.'

'I know,' Waverley admitted. 'She would have made a good wife.'

'Yet you went and married her friend. You've been a bastard, you know that.'

'I know that, but you've been one in your time.'

'I still am. You heard how I spoke to the Met's commissioner?'

'You were tough.'

'Did you kill my daughter?' Brice asked.

'Why would I do that?'

'Because she would have told Gwen that you were still sleeping with her.'

'Are you shocked?'

'Why should I be? Amelia was a reflection of her parents; fidelity never meant very much to either of us, and with you, she would have been safe. You would have loved her, but you would have strayed. Does Gwen know?'

'She does now. The police gave her a hint.'

'How?'

'That damn diary she kept. She referred to a Q. Gwen denied it was me to the police, but she confronted me. I told her the truth.'

'A major mistake, Quentin. Never tell the truth until it can no longer be denied.'

'I know, but I needed to make my peace with Gwen. There was no Amelia to confuse me.'

'If Gwen had known, it would have been a motive for murder.'

'Gwen could not have committed the murder, and besides, she's pregnant. She'd not be capable.'

'Then someone else might be.'

'She has a cousin she is fond of.'

'His background?'

'The best schools, British Army.'

'Capable of murder?'

'I'd say so.'

'If he could have killed Amelia and the other woman, he could kill you as well. Is he a close cousin?'

'First cousin. You don't think…?'

'I don't think anything. If you didn't kill Amelia…'

'I didn't. I loved the woman for all her faults; she loved me. It was Gwen who ensured I married her.'

'You'd better check your claim on the bank and your father-in-law's fortune. Make sure it comes to you, and not to her cousin.'

And why was Amelia frightened of you, and why were you threatening her?'

'You know the truth. Why ask me?'

***

Even though it was still early and the weather was cold, Wendy found herself outside Shirley O'Rourke's door. Inside the house, silence. Wendy knocked on the front door. After five minutes, it opened. Two suitcases stood in the hallway. 'What do you want?'

'Are you leaving?' Wendy said.

'With you and your investigation, there's not much for me to do here.'

'Where are you going?'

'Greece.'

'And if we need to contact you?'

'My phone will be on roaming.'

'Are you attempting to leave the country on a permanent basis?'

'Why? I've done nothing wrong. I'll be gone for two weeks, that's all.'

Wendy could not trust the woman. She phoned Isaac for advice. 'You'll need to tell her that her leaving the country at this time would not be advisable,' he said.

'Mrs O'Rourke, it would be preferable for you to stay in this country,' Wendy said. 'There are further questions relating to the deaths of Amelia Brice and Christine Devon. Also, the issue of bogus insurance claims, thefts from the houses where your staff worked, is ongoing.'

'None of which applies to me. I had a good business, and then your snooping destroys it. Nearly twenty years down the drain. I should sue the police for maligning my good name.'

'Your inability to keep your business viable is not our concern and was certainly not caused by us. You are welcome to lodge a complaint, but you'll need to be in this country. There still remains the possibility that you are implicated in the murders, that somehow you had obtained knowledge about Amelia, were bribing her, or she knew something about you. The woman was not always stable, but maybe she saw you at the pub, or she saw one of your cleaners helping themselves to valuables in her house.'

'Don't you dare come into my house and accuse me of murder. I'm just a sharp businesswoman, that's all. I've heard the scurrilous rumours before, by some of my neighbours included. How could such a woman, common as muck, make so much

96

money. I'll tell you: hard work, long hours, and watching every penny. There's no inheritance for me. I made it myself, and if you think I'm going to lose it by murdering two women, one rich and lazy, the other as poor as a church mouse, then you're sadly mistaken. Now, am I going on this holiday or not?'

'It would be better if you stay,' Wendy said, aware that the process to legally stop her would take time, probably more than it would take for Shirley O'Rourke to drive to Heathrow Airport.

'Very well. You'd better come in for a cup of tea.'

Apart from the suitcases, the state of the house gave the impression that the woman intended to come back. Wendy did not like the décor of the home, too dull for her. Nowhere were there photos of loved ones, a sign of an animal. It was a cold house, Wendy thought. Not the temperature, as it was warm enough, but it lacked what it was that made a house into a home.

'Do you live here on your own?' Wendy asked.

'Nowadays. There was a Mr O'Rourke, but he took off. No great loss either.'

'Why's that?'

'I was the driving force, not him. His idea of fun was sitting in front of the television, a beer in one hand, a cigarette in the other.'

'You were not close?' Wendy asked. It had been some time since her husband had passed away, and whereas sharing the house with Bridget had been a suitable arrangement, she still missed him occasionally.

'We were at first, but you know what happens with time.'

'You tell me.'

'When you're young, it's the love that seems more important, but with time, and a lessening of the passion, it's material assets that take over, a secure roof over your head.'

'And you didn't have those feelings.'

'I did, but he didn't. He was an eight-to-five man, five days a week. Sometimes, I'd be out cleaning all day, and then dealing with the paperwork until two or three in the morning.'

'How long since he left?'

'Nine, maybe ten years.'

'And you've been on your own since then?'

'The occasional man has found his way into the house, but only on a casual basis.'

'What do you mean?'

'What do you think I mean? They can spend the night and then out the next day before breakfast. I don't want any of them thinking that I'm an easy touch.'

'You're a hard woman,' Wendy said. They were both seated in the kitchen. Wendy knew that Shirley O'Rourke cheated on her taxes, paid her staff the minimum, almost certainly was involved in insurance fraud, theft if she could get away with it. However, the woman had a disarming honesty about her. For the first time, Wendy found her company amenable, and as for the lazy husband, both women had something in common.

'I'm not hard. I was involved in a cut-throat business. There's always someone trying to undercut you.'

Chapter 13

A man notoriously difficult to get hold of, Phillip Loeb made himself available when he was informed that a Detective Chief Inspector Isaac Cook from Homicide was outside his office.

'Come in, Inspector,' Loeb said, his hand extended. 'What can I do for you?'

It was not often that Isaac left the confines of London, but Loeb ran his shopping empire from Brighton, a seaside resort to the south of London. The man, not unknown to Isaac, not unknown to the majority of the population, had built up a chain of electrical goods stores throughout the country, thirty-five in total. Isaac had checked him out on the internet. How he had arrived in the country, a penniless refugee, a child, seventy years previously, and with time and an education, he had built up an impressive portfolio of real estate and stores. He was also known to be semi-reclusive, and not willing to venture far from his home if it could be avoided.

'We're investigating the murder of three persons.'

'Is it anything to do with me?'

'Indirectly.'

'You'd better explain. Do I need my lawyer for this?'

'I don't think so. You're not implicated, other than through one of your employees.'

Both of the men were seated in comfortable leather chairs in Loeb's office, a view out towards the sea and the pier. Out on the water, someone was windsurfing. Loeb's personal assistant brought in a pot of tea with two cups and some biscuits. The PA gave Isaac a smile as she left, which he returned. He had been too long on his own, and the woman was attractive. He wanted to talk to her further, but first he had to deal with the reason he had driven down to Brighton.

'You are aware of the murder of Jeremy Brice's daughter, Amelia?' Isaac said.

'Brice, I've met the man, and yes, I'm aware. Tragic.'

'Another woman was murdered at the same time.'

'A cleaner at the house.'

'Yes, that's correct. You are more aware than most of the facts.'

'I like to keep in touch with current affairs. How does this affect me?'

'The other woman, Christine Devon. She came from Trinidad, and she was doing it tough: three children, one running with a gang, the other two hardworking and honest.'

'No money?'

'Not a lot.'

'You've still not explained what this has to do with me.'

'The woman has been murdered; her youngest son has subsequently died.'

'How?'

'He was killed by one of the gangs in the area.'

'And he was a gang member?'

'He was, but he cheated them. He was only fifteen.'

'The other children?'

'The eldest son, Billy, is nineteen. The daughter, Charisa, is eighteen. Both of them are honest. Billy works for you, and Charisa, the more educated, is still in college.'

'What do you want from me?'

'The youngest son, Samuel, stole money from his gang, or maybe it's a made-up story. The truth is not important. Billy is being threatened to reimburse the stolen money. He's already been severely beaten, and they've threatened to take his sister as payment in lieu.'

'As a hostage, or something worse?'

'Something worse. These are dangerous men.'

'I've experienced dangerous men, but that was a long time ago.'

'These men will take the young woman, no doubt abuse her.'

100

'And you want me to make up the money owing?'

'That wasn't my reason for coming to see you.'

'What do you want then?'

'Billy, he works in your store in Bayswater; he has been attempting to get the money they want. Please remember that Billy is not a thief, and he is a man with a good moral base.'

'Has he been stealing from me?'

'Yes.'

'You're a police officer, why are you concerned about him?'

'I don't want another murder.'

'It's more than that.'

'I grew up near to where they lived. I know the lure of the gangs. Some of my friends became involved, some of them still are, and some are dead. I just don't want Billy Devon to end up the same way, and Charisa, the daughter, needs to be protected.'

'You've taken a risk coming here today, haven't you? I could have him charged with theft.'

'I checked on the internet. You're known for your charitable causes. I believed that I was on safe ground with you.'

'You are. What do you want from me?'

'Billy's manager will soon find out about the thefts. He needs to be pulled out of the store. Charisa needs protection.'

'And the money that's been stolen?'

'It's about eight thousand pounds,' Isaac said.

'And how much more does he need to pay off this gang?'

'Twenty-two pounds and accumulating, but I'm not suggesting that it's paid. Once they know they can get that much money, they'll increase the pressure on Billy Devon to give more.'

'I came across these types of people when I first went into business in this country.'

'I'm not advocating violence,' Isaac said.

'Nor am I, not at this time.'

'In the past?'

'It was before your time.'

Phillip Loeb called in his personal assistant. 'Ann, DCI Cook will give you some details and a plan of action. You are to act on them immediately, is that understood?'

'Yes, Mr Loeb.'

'Inspector, you were right in coming here today. Courageous even.'

'I don't think so, sir. I knew that you were an honourable man.'

'Billy Devon, where is he now?'

'He's at work.'

'Good. We'll get him out of this trouble and then consider him for managerial training.'

'He'll not let you down.'

'And the mother's murderer?'

'We're still working on that.'

Isaac left Loeb's office and went next door to where the PA sat. The two of them went through the details of what was required. Ann, in her mid-thirties, dark-haired, interested Isaac. Forty-five minutes later, he left the office. In that time, the money needed to pay off Negril Bob had been organised, the troublesome manager at Billy's store had been immediately transferred to another, and Billy was running the store as acting manager. Isaac spoke to Billy briefly to let him know what was happening. He also tried to phone Charisa, but her phone was not answering.

That weekend, if his work permitted, Isaac and Ann were meeting in Brighton for a meal. All in all, Isaac considered that his trip to Brighton had been successful.

***

Larry Hill felt guilt, Isaac felt a degree of sadness, and Wendy had shed a tear. All because a gang leader by the name of Rasta Joe had been found dead in an alleyway not far from Paddington Station. He wasn't the first member of a gang to meet a violent death, for that had already happened to Samuel Devon, but Rasta Joe was different. Isaac had gone to school with him, even sang in the church choir every Sunday with him, and whereas one had chosen crime and the other had decided on the law, there was a bond that time could not diminish.

Larry assumed that he had died as a result of his association with him. They had become infrequent drinking buddies, and even if nothing was said that was controversial, the idea of a police officer and a gang leader was anathema to many. Wendy had shed a tear, not because she had known the man, but because her DCI and her DI had, and both of them were upset by his sudden death.

Goddard, their chief superintendent, was in the office on first hearing of the death, which was as well, as Isaac and Larry were heading off to the crime scene. 'You knew this man?' he said.

'I went to school with him.'

'Is this going to be the start of a gang war?'

'We don't know. We'll have a clearer idea later today.'

'Okay. Keep me posted, and Davies is on the warpath again.'

'I thought that Jeremy Brice had clipped his wings,' Isaac said. Both he and Larry were halfway out of the door, only hesitating at the name of their nemesis.

'He had, but Davies is a fighter. He'll go for broke, bring in whoever, and see where it all lands. If his timing is right, you'll solve the current investigations just in time for his man to take your seat and claim the success.'

'That's not fair,' Larry said.

'What's fair got to do with it. This is the real world. That fool that Davies is no doubt phoning up right now will be packing his bags in the next day or so, and getting ready to take your position.'

'We need to go to the crime scene, sir,' Isaac said.

'What's holding you?'

'Thank you,' Isaac said. 'We'll talk when we return.'

***

Neither of the two men was prepared for the savagery of Rasta Joe's death. Seeing him lying there, covered in blood, the knife wounds clearly visible on his semi-naked body, Isaac could only think back to the cherubic little black boy that had been his childhood friend. Larry could just see the man who was willing to talk as long as he was primed with beer.

The two men approached the body, remembering to put on shoe protectors and gloves. Gordon Windsor, the CSE, was due on the scene within the next twenty minutes. A group of onlookers were being kept at a distance by a couple of uniforms.

'Did he die here?' Larry asked.

'I'd say so, judging by the blood.'

One of the uniforms came over. 'I've got a witness,' he said.

Isaac and Larry left the dead man lying on the ground and walked over to the witness. Isaac could see that the man was dishevelled, probably homeless, almost certainly drunk. Not the ideal witness, he'd have to admit, but it was better than none.

'What did you see?' Larry asked.

'I was walking up here last night. It was late, close to midnight. I saw the car pull up.'

'Did they see you?'

'Not me. I know how to stay hidden.'

'Why were you up here?'

'Sometimes I spend the night here.'

Isaac asked one of the uniforms to organise the man a coffee and something to eat.

The three men sat down on some old wooden crates stacked in a corner.

'What did you see?' Isaac asked.

'I was up past that bin.'

Isaac and Larry looked; there was a bin thirty feet away.

'It was dark, could you see anything?'

'I could hear them arguing. The dead man was pleading for his life, the other men attacking him.'

'You could have called for help?'

104

'Not me, and besides, the only way out was past them. If I had moved, they would have killed me as well.'

'What was said? Do you remember anything?'

'They called the man Rasta Joe, the others, I don't know what their names were.'

'Was there a leader?'

'There was one, the others called him Negro.'

'Negril Bob?'

'That's it. It's an odd name.'

'It's the name of a place in Jamaica.'

'That's why I couldn't understand everything they said.'

'What do you mean?'

'They spoke with a strange accent.'

Isaac mimicked the Jamaican style of speech.

'You're not one of them, are you?'

'Not me, but we know who they are. Did they say why they killed him?'

'Not that I could understand. They were vicious.'

'If we need to contact you again?'

'Just wander around the area, ask for Gappy, you'll find me.'

***

An alley around the back of Paddington Station was not the most salubrious place at any time. The crime scene investigators were at the scene, the uniforms were out at the entrance to the alley, organising the barriers, trying to move on those heading to the railway station and those leaving, and, as always, there was someone from the media.

Isaac, intentionally polite with the media and an accomplished performer whenever a camera was placed in front of him, not like his chief superintendent who fluffed it every time, was not willing to indulge the reporter this time; he had more important things to do.

Firstly, there was Negril Bob to deal with, not so easy unless the CSIs came up with some evidence, which seemed possible. A gang killing was not usually the most subtle, and not professional. Neither Isaac nor Larry could imagine that they would have been wearing gloves or attempting to conceal their faces from the CCTV cameras located all around the railway station. Initially they were put there to control the movement of passengers, but now they had increased in numbers to assist with terrorism.

Larry made a phone call as he and his DCI drove towards their first destination. His wife had expected him home at a reasonable hour that night; her parents were coming over, and he was required. He had to tell her way in advance that it was unlikely would make it on time. The death of a gang leader, not the only gang in the area, was bound to have recriminations. Tit for tat, you kill one of mine, I'll kill one of yours, and now, Negril Bob, one of the most violent leaders, had killed one of the more passive ones.

Isaac could see trouble with a capital T, and this time Commissioner Alwyn Davies would be interceding. A gang war in London was bound to be a media event, and Isaac was not sure how to proceed.

And if Negril Bob could kill Rasta Joe, he could also kill Billy Devon and take his sister at any time. The two police officers pulled up outside Billy's shop. The man was busy inside. He finished with the customer and came over. 'Takings are up. Thanks for what you did. I had a phone call from Mr Loeb.'

'What did he say?'

'He said that you had seen him and that I was on probation. If I did a good job, he'd see me right. It's not what I expected.'

'There's a bigger problem,' Larry said. Time was of the essence, and self-congratulatory pats on the back could wait for later. 'Negril Bob's killed another gang leader, Rasta Joe.'

'I don't know him,' Billy said. Another customer had come into the shop; he was anxious to get to him before he walked out.

'We do,' Isaac said. 'I went to school with him, Larry's been in contact with him.'

'I need to deal with this customer.'

'Billy, this is serious. Negril Bob is acting irrationally. He could come for you.'

'I'm not leaving here. Mr Loeb's placed his trust in me. I don't intend to let him down.'

'Very well,' Isaac said. 'Phone us if he shows up. Where's your sister?'

'At college.'

Isaac drove to the college, passing by Challis Street to drop off Larry, and parked close to the administration office. He knew that he had parked across the rear of two cars; he put a police sign on the dashboard and a number to contact. Time was critical, and he needed to see that Charisa was secure.

Isaac had to show his ID to the woman in admin, and three minutes later Charisa entered the room. 'DCI Cook, what is it?' Her face showed alarm.

'We needed to check that you were okay.'

'I am. Troy's coming back tonight.'

'I need you to phone my office every hour on the hour, is that understood?'

'If you want me to. What's happened?'

'Negril Bob has killed another gang leader. We're preparing for trouble.'

'He'll leave us alone, won't he?'

'We don't know. Don't leave here without phoning us first, and if you move from one place to the next, you must inform us. Is that clear?'

'What are you going to do?'

'We'll try and find those responsible for the murder. If they're charged, and in custody, then we can all sleep easy.'

'Until then?' Charisa asked.

'We will all worry.'

***

Phillip Strang

Gwen Waverley paced around her home. The father of her children, the man she had loved, still did to some extent, had been leading a double life. The devoted family man, the senior partner in her father's merchant bank, had also been seeing Amelia Brice, his former lover. And now, she couldn't be sure of him; was he playing around with the woman in his office, or maybe it was someone else? Whoever and whatever it was, she would not tolerate anything other than total devotion to her. And as for Amelia's father, the man who had tried to get her husband and his daughter back together after she, the daughter of a merchant banker, had snared the man from the daughter of a minor celebrity, she'd deal with him in time.

Quentin, she knew, had been ambitious back then, though a little rough around the edges, edges she had been smoothing, and now he was playing the field, seeing what piece of fluff was susceptible to his charm. She had been receptive to it; she had seen the potential, and now she had no intention of letting anyone else, Amelia or no Amelia, take him away from her. In her anger, she picked up a plate that had just been removed from the dishwasher and flung it down on the tiled floor, smashing it into pieces. It felt good. She picked up another and broke it.

I'll leave the plates there, she thought. *Let Quentin see the extent of my anger.*

She moved to the other room, closer to the drinks cabinet, and poured herself a gin. She gulped it down in one. For a moment, she remembered that the doctor had told her to go easy on the alcohol while she was pregnant.

'To hell with him and his damn advice,' she said out loud, although the house was empty and no one would hear. She then poured herself another drink and went and sat down in her favourite chair. On the television, an American soap opera.

What has my life come to, she thought. *If Quentin wants to enjoy the good life, it's not happening at the expense of my carrying his children, and not as a result of my father's generosity.*

108

Chapter 14

Shirley O'Rourke was back in business, the door to her office open. She was welcoming as Wendy entered through the front door. 'We've got a special rate for today,' she said.

'Not for me,' Wendy said. 'Once a week I clean the house. I don't have the money your clients do.'

'There are not many left that do. You've frightened them off.'

'The Brices?'

'We're back there. Jeremy's moved in, with his girlfriend.'

'You've met her?'

'Oh, yes. I've been over there. She's an educated woman, not like me.'

'You're smarter than you think. You certainly did a good job with your financial records, your attempts at not paying tax.'

'I did nothing illegal. When can I have them back?'

'I'll arrange it. Just one thing, there was an insurance claim, a house in Bayswater. Supposedly, a painting was damaged beyond repair. One of your cleaning team went crazy and put a knife through it.'

'The woman had marital problems. She took her anger out on the painting.'

'Any reason why?'

'It was modern art. For whatever reason, the woman flipped. The owner had it insured; I had insurance. Is there a problem?'

'Apart from the fact that further testing six months later it was found to be fake.'

'So?'

'Did you know that the owners, who've since disappeared, knew that?'

'Not me. The claim was settled with the owners by the insurance company, and I paid an excess for my insurance, as well.'

'The claim was for three hundred and fifty thousand pounds.'

'I know that.'

Wendy looked at the woman, attempting to see if there were any tell-tale signs of lying: the beads of sweat on the forehead, the fidgeting, the avoidance of eye contact. She could see none.

'The cleaner?'

'I kept her on for a couple of months. After that, she left and went back to her home country.'

'She went back with money in her pocket; we've checked,' Wendy said. 'Once back there, she bought a small house, not expensive by English standards. And you paid fifty-five thousand pounds off your mortgage, and the painting's owners left the country.'

'I acted correctly.'

'The only issue is whether you knew it was fraud on the owner's part.'

'I did not. I've told you, I play it tough but fair.'

'Then where did the fifty-five thousand pounds come from?'

'Are you accusing me?'

'Not at this time. We are attempting to make contact with the painting's owners. If there is a case to answer, then I will return.'

'There is no case. I have told you the truth,' Shirley O'Rourke said. Wendy knew that she had not. It was only one of several cases of potential fraud that had been uncovered and the Fraud team at Challis Street were working with the insurance companies.

'Insurance fraud, purposely damaging property for financial gain, are criminal offences. They are subject to a custodial sentence, you do realise this?'

'I understand the law. That is why I vet my employees.'

110

'If you admit to your guilt it will go in your favour,' Wendy said.

'There is no guilt.'

'Insurance fraud is a possible motive for the murders of the two women.'

'Unless you have any more accusations, I suggest that you leave, or we'll meet again with my legal representative.'

'I've no more questions, but remember, your confession will help you later. If the two women were murdered as a result of fraud at the Brice house, then you could become an accessory to murder. That could be a long term in prison. You were leaving the country once before. I'd suggest that you do not attempt to leave now.'

'I will not leave.'

***

Gordon Windsor confirmed that the death of Rasta Joe had been as a result of multiple knife wounds. There was also evidence that he had been beaten severely and that his hands had been tied. Also, that four people had been at the crime scene: three inflicting the violence, the fourth on the receiving end.

Isaac and Larry had not needed the CSE's report. The witness at the scene had given them enough information to bring Negril Bob into the station, not that he would come quietly. Even in the area there were small pockets where the police did not enter unless in numbers, and two police inspectors would have no chance.

Larry had made a few phone calls. Rasta Joe had been his primary contact, but he still knew two other members of his gang. 'What's the deal with Rasta Joe?' Larry said over the phone after it was eventually answered.

'We're not around,' Jimmy said. Larry remembered him as the skinny man who always kept in the shadows whenever he had met with Rasta Joe.

'Why did they kill him?'

'He was too friendly with you. You're poison.'

'I'm your only hope now.'

'We can look after ourselves.'

'Is that why you're not answering the phone? Where are you, hiding out, under your bed? Great real, Jimmy, we need each other.'

'There's going to be trouble. Some of the other gangs want to unite to take down Negril Bob. He had no right to kill Rasta Joe.'

'Jimmy, don't take the law into your own hands. If you kill someone in revenge, it's still murder. We can deal with him, and whoever else was there. Tell us where the man is, and we'll arrest him,' Larry said.

'79 Wellington Street. If he finds out that I told you, you know what will happen?'

'Jimmy, you'd better hide under your bed until I call you again,' Larry said.

***

'What's this I hear about a gang war down in your neck of the woods?' Commissioner Davies said. It was the phone call that DCS Goddard had dreaded.

'There's no war yet. DCI Cook has the situation under control. They have an address for those who murdered Rasta Joe.'

'What kind of stupid name in that?'

'Joe Brown, but they prefer to use their street names.'

'What do you know about the man who was killed?'

'Isaac Cook went to school with him. We know a lot about him. He's helped us before.'

'Very well. It's strange bedfellows you keep down there. What about those that killed him? It sounds as though he needs help down there, or maybe your DCI's compromised. He's not related, is he? A lot of them are.'

'There's no relationship,' Goddard said. He was tired of the phone conversation, anxious to get down to Homicide. A police raid, set up according to the book, was something to be involved in; dealing with an unpleasant commissioner of the Met was not.

'I'll be keeping a watch on what you're up to. If this escalates, and I'm asked questions, I intend to have the right answers,' Davies said.

'There'll be no gang war.'

'That's what you said with the serial-killer woman, and she still kept killing. I've met your DCI, and believe me, he doesn't do much for me. Sure, he scrubs up clean, puts on a good show, no doubt loved by his team, but where are the results? The man's all smoke and mirrors.'

'I'll resist any attempts to move him out,' Goddard said, in defence of his DCI.

'He's yours for the time being and don't stuff up. And if there's a press conference, make sure that Cook is there; you're a wet blanket in front of a camera.'

The phone line went dead. Richard Goddard was pleased that the conversation had been short. He left his office and headed downstairs.

'Isaac, are you sure about this?' Goddard asked. He was sitting in the chair closest to the door in his DCI's office.

We've set up roadblocks in the vicinity. No one's leaving.'

'And the house?'

'A nondescript terrace house.'

'Is your man inside?'

'According to our information, he is. We're staking out the house from a block of flats opposite. There are three inhabitants.'

'Negril Bob is one of them?'

'Unconfirmed.'

Bridget came in with two coffees. She gave one to Isaac, the other to their senior.

'I've had the commissioner on the phone.'

'The usual?'

'He was remarkably calm. He had a go at you though.'

'Derogatory?'

'Smoke and mirrors, that's his description.'

'It's an improvement. Any sign of his man coming back to claim my seat?'

'Not yet, and I suspect never.'

The two men had known each other long enough for Isaac to ask more. 'What does that mean?'

'The pressure for Davies to resign is mounting.'

'Confirmed?'

'If my contact is correct.'

'And you're for Counter Terrorism Command?'

'That's the idea. I'll need good men.'

'I've got enough to deal with here.'

'We'll talk about it another time. What's the agenda for the raid?'

'At 6 p.m. we'll commence the operation.'

'It's a busy time of day.'

'It can't be avoided. Ten minutes later, we'll send in our specialist firearms command to secure the place. We can't rule out those inside not having weapons.'

'After that?'

'Once the place is secured and we have the occupants in custody, we'll return to the station. If it's Negril Bob, and we can identify the others from finger and shoe prints at Rasta Joe's murder, we'll charge them all with premeditated murder.'

'They'll claim they were provoked.'

'Three against one, and besides Rasta Joe's hands were tied.'

'What about the other murders?'

'We believe that Samuel Devon was killed by Negril Bob.'

'Proof?'

'Only from Rasta Joe. If we can prove Negril Bob is guilty of one murder, he may confess to the other. Although we don't think that it was his gang that the young boy cheated. Negril Bob is there for extreme violence. The gangs in the area, their rank and file are not too bright, and most are cowards on their own. Negril Bob isn't.'

Larry came into the office. 'It's time.'

'Are you coming, sir?' Isaac asked his senior.

114

'Not this time. I've got to protect our positions in case it goes wrong.'

***

On the drive over to Wellington Street, Isaac's phone rang. 'Are we still okay for this weekend?' It was Ann, Phillip Loeb's personal assistant.

Her phone call brought a smile to Isaac's face. 'I've booked a place,' he said.

The phone call ended. Larry looked over at his DCI. 'It's looking up for you, guv. Pretty, is she?'

'Aren't they always?' Isaac replied. 'How about you and your wife?'

'She's fine. I've lost ten pounds since I've cut back on the food and the beer, feel much better for it, as well.'

On arrival at the end of the street, Isaac showed his ID. To either side of the house, armed officers wearing body armour waited. It was a well-rehearsed team; there was not a lot of conversation. Around the back of the house, by a brick wall with a small gate out into a common walkway, another group of armed men waited. As the residents in the street had left, they had not been allowed to return. Some had complained, most had agreed. Inside the house, all was quiet.

'They know we're here,' the lead armed response officer said.

'Any sign of weapons?'

'We'll not know until we break the door down.'

'A frontal assault?'

'This time. There's not a lot of space around the back.'

Isaac and Larry stood back, about forty feet from the front door of the house. A voice, amplified by a megaphone, could be heard. 'This is the police. Lay down your weapons and exit the house.' No response. One more time. 'This is the police. Please lay down your weapons and exit the house.'

After sixty seconds, the front door of the house was knocked open with an enforcer, a specially designed battering ram. From in the house, a shot. 'Back off,' the lead officer ordered. The police retreated out of the line of fire.

'Throw out your weapons,' the lead officer shouted. Inside the house, no noise, bar a door banging on its hinges.

'We can't use tear gas,' the lead officer said as he came over to Isaac and Larry. 'If there's someone old and infirm or with breathing difficulties in an adjacent house, it could do them harm. We'll just have to rush the house.'

'You're the experts. Just let us know when it's clear, and we'll come and take charge of them.'

Twelve minutes later, watches coordinated, one team entered at the front, another held firm at the rear. A brief flurry of gunfire, and then the all clear. Isaac and Larry moved forward once the signal had been given. Three men came out of the building, securely wedged between the police officers, their hands cable-tied.

'Where's Negril Bob?' Isaac asked as he looked at the three men.

'He's not here,' one of the three replied. Isaac had seen him around before. The man had a scar on the left-hand side of his face and a surly manner.

'Which two of you were with Negril Bob when Rasta Joe was killed?'

'None of us,' one of the other three said.

'Samuel Devon? What can you tell me about him?'

'Never heard of him. What are you doing here, arresting us? We were watching the television, having a few drinks. We were going to get a few women over tonight, as well.'

'They can visit you in the cells at Challis Street,' Larry said.

'Very funny,' the first of the three said, 'a regular comedian. Our lawyer will deal with this false arrest. He'll haul your sorry arses through the courts.'

'There's nothing false here,' Larry said.

Isaac made a phone call to Wendy. 'Get over to Charisa Devon's place with some uniforms, check that she's alright.'

'Problems?'

'We've not found Negril Bob.'

Chapter 15

Jeremy Brice's radio programme was enjoying record ratings, his contacts within the political arena were firm, and his biting invective was at its very best. It had been some time since his daughter's death; enough time to get over the initial sorrow and to move back into the house where she had died, nevertheless he had a sense of foreboding.

That day, he had had the prime minister in his studio; the man was floundering in the polls, and another scandal was about to engulf him, and he had let him off. There would be criticism from the other political commentators, aspersions about why Jeremy Brice, the most vexatious interviewer, had let the prime minister off when he had him on the ropes. The chancellor of the exchequer had fudged the figures on unemployment to portray the state of the economy in a better light than it was. It was a lie given in Westminster; a lie that should ensure a resignation, but the numbers were tight between the governing party and those on the opposition side, and the prime minister could not afford to lose an experienced debater, let alone someone who supported him in the party room.

Brice knew this, having regarded the PM and his chancellor as personal friends, though it wouldn't stop him laying into them when the situation demanded, and it certainly did that day, and he had let the man off the hook.

'What is it, Brice?' the owner of the radio station asked. 'Have you lost it? You had the man where you wanted him.'

Brice did not like the man, regarded him as charmless and uncouth, but he knew that he was right. On the one hand, he was in the studio with a microphone in front of him and on the other, he was reading the messages on his phone, checking the latest news on the internet: a shootout in London, not far from where he lived.

He knew that his daughter, knowingly or otherwise, would remain a thorn in his side and he cursed her. He had loved her as a father loves a daughter, but she had grown from a sweet young child who would sit on his knees while he read her a nursery rhyme into a mature woman who couldn't keep the one man she should have married. And then there were the men she spent time with: gangsters, hustlers, pimps. He never knew if Amelia had sold herself, but why the men? The scum of society, lacking in finesse and class, a world laterally opposed to the upbringing that she had had. The best of schools, trips to the continent, skiing in Switzerland in winter, the Caribbean in summer. And in the end, after Quentin Waverley had moved on to Gwen Happold, she had found love and lust in the arms of the criminal classes, downing drinks in the pub, no more than a serving wench, no more than a whore.

It had been the same with her mother; as beautiful as the daughter. Jeremy Brice remembered when they had met; he, the up-and-coming political reporter, she, a fashion designer. They had instantly been attracted to each other, made love that first day, and had been inseparable, their lives blessed with a beautiful daughter. And now, mother and daughter were both dead.

The love for his wife had faded after ten, or maybe it was eleven, years. Her need to stay young, to take young lovers; his need to focus on his career, to put a roof over their heads. Then, one day, he found a note attached to the fridge with a magnet. The marriage was over, and she was going to the south of France with her latest paramour, a younger man.

He had never forgiven her: not for leaving, or the young lover, but for discarding their daughter.

He had brought her up, and she had been a joy until her late teens, and then, the drinking, and the parties, and the men. He had tried his best, but he came to realise that she was her mother's daughter, not his. The behaviour that he had attempted to steer her away from was not acquired through example; it came through DNA, the mother's DNA, and even though she was a thousand miles away, with one or another lover, her influence was there with Amelia.

And now, a lecture on how he had lost it from a man who was crude and obnoxious, a man he detested. Brice left the radio station and headed home. For once, he would seek salvation in a bottle of whisky.

***

It was known that Rasta Joe had a wife and a family and that they were not living with him. Larry was aware that not a lot would be gained from the wife, but there was still a formal identification of the man's body to be arranged.

Larry pulled up outside the wife's house, a small, neat bungalow a twenty-minute drive from Challis Street. The garden was tended, the area looked clean. All in all, Larry had to admit, it was not what he expected. He knocked on the door, a small child opened it.

From the back of the house, a voice said, 'I've told you not to open the door to strangers.'

'Detective Inspector Larry Hill,' Larry shouted, to allay the woman's fears.

The door to the room at the back opened. A woman, neatly dressed, and with rubber gloves on her hands, came through. 'Sorry, I was washing the dishes. I'm always on to Cindy here not to open the door. You never know who might be around.'

'Mrs Brown?'

'I don't use that name, not around here anyway. It's Joe, isn't it?'

'I'm afraid so.'

'I knew he would always end up dead in a gutter somewhere. That's what's happened?'

'I'm sorry,' Larry said. Rasta Joe's wife, Jamaican heritage like her husband, did not have the affected Jamaican accent; she was pure Cockney.

'I'll make us a cup of tea.'

'You seem remarkably calm.'

'I'm not, but Cindy's here, and I've another two home from school soon.'

'They'll need to be told.'

'Eventually. We haven't seen Joe for nearly two years, and we've not been living together for four.'

'Why?'

'Did you know him?'

'We used to meet occasionally.'

'A police inspector and Joe.'

'Symbiotic. He needed me; I needed him. Tell me about your husband,' Larry said, as he looked around the kitchen. It was neat, functional, everything in its place. The woman he was talking to had come as a shock. He had been used to Rasta Joe and the women he went around with. His widow seemed to be a law-abiding person, no attempts at portraying herself as anything other than a respectable middle-class housewife and mother.

'We met at school. He was a good man then.'

'Not into gangs?'

'I knew he was into ganja, but who wasn't?'

'Were you?'

'When you're young, you're foolish, try anything once. I grew out of it; Joe never did, and now he's dead. Tell me about it.'

'He fell foul of another gang. They killed him.'

'Violent?'

'I'm sorry, but yes.'

'That was Joe, always pushing the boundaries. Can I see him?'

'We need someone to conduct a formal identification. Are you up to it?'

'I'll need someone to look after the children. I still loved the man, even after what he had become. He never failed to pay the rent on this place, and he always ensured there was money for the children's school uniforms and anything else they wanted.'

'But they never saw him.'

'That was what we agreed. He knew what was best for us, and he kept away. He'd phone sometimes; I'd send him photos of the children. Did you like him?'

'I did. I know what he was, and I should not have.'

'That's Joe. A good man, not really suited to being a gangster, but then, life takes us down different roads. How's Isaac?'

'He's fine. You know him?'

'I remember when he and Joe were great friends. Isaac turned out alright, Joe didn't.'

'DCI Cook is in charge of the investigation.'

'Do you know who killed him?'

'Yes.'

'Where are they?'

'We've arrested two of them; the third is still evading capture.'

Two children entered through the back door; both were polite and asked who the strange man was. Rasta Joe's wife made an excuse that Larry was a friend of their father's.

After another forty minutes, a friend came around from the house next door. 'Gloria will look after the children. We can go now.'

On the way back to London, and relieved of her children, Rasta Joe's wife cried.

***

Quentin Waverley struck his wife. It had been going on for days – her niggling him about his relationship with Amelia Brice.

He realised soon after he had married, that he did not love Gwen in the same way that he had loved Amelia.

Amelia had an innocence about her, a vulnerability, whereas Gwen was hard and cruel. Amelia was the type of person to take in a neglected dog; Gwen would have fed it meat laced with rat poison.

Waverley knew there'd be fallout from hitting Gwen. Her father, a brilliant man, had made a fortune in London by setting up the merchant bank. He had a reputation as a fearless adversary, a loyal friend, and now the bond of friendship between the man and his son-in-law was irrevocably broken. It had been made clear when he had asked Gwen's father for his daughter's hand in marriage that her father would not tolerate his precious daughter being upset in any way, and now he had hit her, and she'd be sure to tell her father.

Waverley phoned Gwen from his office when he arrived. 'Sorry, the stress of work,' he said.

'I understand,' Gwen said. 'We'll talk later.'

'Your father?'

'I've not told him.'

Waverley breathed a sigh of relief, one less problem to deal with.

***

Larry arrived in the office at Challis Street. It was already past 9 p.m. 'Rasta Joe's wife identified the body.'

'How is she?' Isaac asked.

'Fine. It appears Rasta Joe was supporting his family.'

'I knew Gloria.'

'You never mentioned it.'

'Was it important? I knew that she'd want her privacy respected.'

'How?'

'We were all friends when we were young. She was always a very private person, but she had wanted Joe. They were total opposites, but I had heard that she was fine.'

'And if she wasn't?'

'I would have done something for her.'

'Where are we in our hunt for Negril Bob?' Larry asked.

'Billy and Charisa Devon are fine. They've seen no sign of him.'

'He's not the sort of person to lie low for too long.'

'He'll be around here somewhere. Probably someone's protecting him.'

'He could leave London.'

'Not him, or, at least not for long. His support network is here. Anywhere else, he'll just be another hustler out on the street. He'll be weighing up the options, checking out the case against him, seeing if he can get out of the crime.'

'Can he?'

'It's always possible with a smart lawyer. The evidence at the crime scene is not strong, against him at least. We have fingerprint matches on the other two, although they're not very good, but not his.'

'But the homeless man said he'd heard his name called out and his replying.'

'Reliable witness?'

'In a courtroom, in the witness box? Five minutes of rapid questioning from a smart lawyer and he wouldn't even be able to remember his own name.'

Chapter 16

Gwen Waverley phoned her father. She knew there was a risk that it could backfire, but she could not let Quentin get the upper hand. He had been willing to throw her over for Amelia if he had half a chance, and he was still an attractive man; he'd find another one soon enough to replace her. 'Quentin hit me,' she said. She knew the reaction to expect.

'That man will pay for hitting my little girl.'

Gwen forgot to mention that she had hit her husband on a few occasions, not that her father would be concerned. The relationship between father and daughter was all that was important, not that of the interloper who had married one and ingratiated himself with the other.

'I'm fine. He was angry after I accused him.'

'Of what?'

'That he was seeing Amelia Brice.'

'Was he?'

'I'm certain of it. I could smell her on him sometimes.' Gwen knew she had told a lie. Her father was a man who doted on his daughter, and whatever she told him, he believed. It had been the same when she was young, and even up through puberty and the raging hormones and the boys she had slept with.

Her father had trusted her implicitly, even taken her side when the evidence was overwhelmingly against her. She loved him for it, this blind trust in her. She knew that Quentin was in trouble, and if she handled it well enough, she'd have him back under her control with no legal way to get out, not if he wanted to run the bank.

George Happold was not a fool, and whether it was the truth that he had been told or a fabrication did not concern him. He was a man who supported his family against all others. And now, his daughter's husband was hitting her when she was pregnant. Happold rose from his chair and walked down the corridor of the top floor of the bank's headquarters.

On one of the doors, a sign: Quentin Waverley, Senior Director. George Happold listened at the door, no sound emanating from inside. He knocked with a closed fist and opened the door.

'George, what can I do for you?' Quentin Waverley said, surprised to see the bank's chairman in his office.

'Are you in the habit of hitting Gwen?'

'It's a misunderstanding, nothing more.'

'You bastard, how dare you assault my daughter and call it a misunderstanding. If I were younger, I'd take you out of here and thrash you to within an inch of your life.'

'You? You could barely lift the skin off a rice pudding. Look at you, all skin and bones. You're hardly likely to last until the end of the year.' Waverley knew he was playing a dangerous game. Whatever happened with George Happold, it wasn't going to help to be subservient and allowing the man to get the upper hand. Happold, he knew, was a bully who intimidated if he could.

'I could have you out of here today. And then what will you do?'

'You won't do that. I'm married to your daughter, father to your grandchildren. You'll put up with me, so will Gwen. She accused me of sleeping with Amelia Brice. I'm not guilty of that, at least.'

'I knew you'd be trouble,' Happold said.

'No, you didn't. The two of you thought I could be controlled, and believe me, I have been. Did you put your daughter up to it?'

'Up to what?'

'Did you arrange with her to make sure that I was in bed with her when Amelia walked in?' Are you that devious that you'd allow your daughter to be a whore?'

'I thought you loved my daughter.'

'I did. Now I'm not so sure, but you, dear father-in-law, had better get used to it. I'm taking over this bank from you, and I'm going to make it work.'

126

'You ungrateful bastard.'

'You never answered my question. Am I the prize bull only fit for mating with your daughter or am I going to run this bank as well?'

'You'll run it well, but don't go hitting my daughter.'

'And you tell her to stop phoning daddy every time there's a problem, and tell her to back off accusing me of something I did not do.'

***

Isaac still had an arrangement to meet up with Ann, Phillip Loeb's PA. Their first attempt at getting together had been deferred due to the death of Rasta Joe; their second, scheduled for the weekend coming, looked doubtful as well.

So far, there had been four murders, with one investigation almost wrapped up once Negril Bob was found. One out of four was not good considering the time that had been expended. Isaac had to admit that he was becoming jaundiced by the ongoing investigation; he needed Ann, the attractive and personable PA. He made a phone call. 'How are you?' he asked.

'Fine. Looking forward to the weekend,' Ann replied. She was in Brighton, he was in London. It was an easy commute and ideal for a relationship, and she was giving hints that it would be more than a meal and a couple of drinks.

Isaac would have liked to spend more time talking to her, but Goddard, his DCS, was making his way into the office.

'See you at the weekend, I hope,' Isaac said to Ann and ended the phone call. She was a busy woman, the same as him, she would understand.

'DCS, what can I do for you?'

'Brice has been sounding off again on that damn radio programme of his.'

'The usual?'

127

'Yes,' Goddard said. Isaac could see that he had something on his mind.

'What is it?' Isaac asked.

'Commissioner Davies has had a few wins lately.'

'He'll hang on for a while yet?'

'Until the next terrorist attack, I suppose. It looks as if you and I will be here for a while longer.'

'If Davies is feeling secure, he'll attempt to bring in his people.'

'Be prepared. I'm aware that you and your team are working hard on the current investigations, but I can't hold the man off for too long.'

'Is he pushing?'

'He is. He's on the phone to me every other day. The man never gives up.'

'A political animal,' Isaac said. 'Pushes when he can; holds back to ride out the storm.'

'So am I,' Goddard said. 'You know that the usurper who took your seat for a while, made a right hash of it, is now a detective superintendent?'

'Yes, I've been told. It grated at the time.'

'Don't let it get to you. Incompetency does rise to the top occasionally.'

'Sometimes I feel like taking the easy life,' Isaac said.

'No, you don't. You're just frustrated by a difficult investigation, and the imminent interference of Commissioner Davies.'

'Imminent?'

'He's about to start his visits out to see his empire. He'll be here at some time. It'd be nice if we could head him off at the pass.'

'By wrapping up this investigation?'

'What about Brice's daughter?'

'We're drawing blanks. We know the death was not committed by an amateur, but why? The woman was an open book. She was promiscuous, into drugs, and did very little with her life except for sponging off her father. It's hardly a reason to be killed.'

'Her father?'

'We've not made any connection. He's back in the house with his girlfriend, but we've never found there to be any animosity between father and daughter. If there had been, it would have been in the woman's diary.'

'And the other woman?'

'Christine Devon. If we solve one, we solve the other.'

'And her son, is there a tie-in?'

'We don't think so. Her son was playing with the big boys; he was running the risk of an early death. His mother must have known that.'

'It must be difficult to deal with,' Goddard said. Isaac could see that the man was happy to sit and talk.

'I remember when Joe Brown became involved with a gang.'

'Joe Brown?'

'Rasta Joe.'

Bridget came into the office and gave the two men coffee. Goddard exchanged pleasantries with her; she appreciated his interest in what she was involved with, and how her day was.

'As you were saying,' Goddard said.

'Rasta Joe, he was a good student, good friend, but then the ganja and the lifestyle took over. He enjoyed the life. For a while, his parents tried to bring him back, but it wasn't possible.'

'Where are they now?'

'They've both passed on. Just as well, really. A murdered son would have been hard for them, and his mother was a sensitive woman.'

'The father?'

'Stern, but fair. Rasta Joe was close to both of them, but after he had left school and joined with a gang on a full-time basis, they went back home to Jamaica.'

'They couldn't stand to see what their son had become?'

'That's it,' Isaac said.

'It must be the same with Brice. His daughter's into drugs and men. And then, she's not doing much. Brice, you'd have to admit, is a man with a lot of energy, a lot of drive. I listened to him this morning as he was laying into us. Full of fire and brimstone.'

'But why? We've kept the man informed.'

'Who knows? He's a complex man; you can't rule him out as a potential murderer.'

'He's not the murderer. It needed an agile person. Brice moves slowly, limps on one leg.'

'He could be the organiser.'

***

Charisa Devon was doing fine; she had exams coming up, and Troy, the boyfriend, was back from America. With no sign of Negril Bob, there was the inevitable easing of the security surrounding her.

The Homicide department had been gravely concerned about her for a few days after the raid on the house in Wellington Street, and an assumption that Negril Bob would try to grab her. As he hadn't, and his whereabouts were unknown, even on the street, Charisa had gone back to her regular routine of walking between Troy's place, hers now as well, and the college. Troy would sometimes drive her, but most days she enjoyed the relative solitude of walking down the streets, looking in the shop windows, generally minding her own business.

Billy, her brother, not having given the money that he had stolen to Negril Bob, had repaid Phillip Loeb in person when they met for the second time. As the acting manager of the shop that he had stolen from, he was enthusiastic and rushing from here to there, moving the stock around, making special offers, enticing the customers to buy. Before his descent into hell, he had been enthusiastic, but the shop had only been a means to an end; now, having risen from purgatory, he could see a future in running a store of his own.

Troy had plans for him and Charisa; Billy had plans for his future. The anguish over the deaths of their mother and their brother was lessening with each passing day, although Charisa continued to visit the cemetery every other day to stand over their graves and to say a few words.

As Billy was working in the shop, a man he had not seen before came in. The man, in his forties, was black, spoke in the familiar lingo of the home country, and was well-dressed in a pair of jeans and a white shirt, with a large medallion suspended by a gold chain around his neck. On his fingers were rings, large and expensive.

'You've got yourself a good number here,' the man said. Billy studied the face, did not recognise him.

'We have the best prices in the area. What are you interested in?'

'I'm interested in you, Billy. You still owe us money.'

'Who are you?'

'I'm not important. How much was it before? Twenty-two thousand, plus a thousand a day. How is your sister, she's a pretty little thing? I wouldn't mind her myself.'

Billy knew that the man was dangerous. He was frightened, and he could not tell the man to leave the shop. If he refused to talk to him, or if he phoned the police, then the consequences were too frightening to imagine.

'I don't have the money,' Billy said.

'You do, and plenty more.'

'Not the shop.'

'There's to be a burglary this weekend.'

'This place is alarmed; the police will be here in minutes.'

'That's why we want you to immobilise the alarms when we tell you.'

'Are you with Negril Bob?'

'What does it matter who I'm with? You will do what you are told, or we'll take your sister. She'll be turning tricks for one hundred pounds a time within a week.'

'You bastard.'

'I'm your new best friend if you want your sister to be left alone.'

'Have you harmed her?'

'Not yet, but we will.'

'I'll get you the money, the twenty-two thousand pounds.'

'What about the interest?'

'Very well, whatever you want, but please leave Charisa alone.'

'Until after we empty this place.'

'And then?'

'You can get a job in another shop, case it out, ingratiate yourself, and then immobilise the alarm.'

'This one time if you leave Charisa alone.'

'And miss her company? Her safety is in your hands, Billy Boy, you make the decision.'

'Okay, you've got me.'

'And don't tell the police. We will phone you in the next few days.'

The man sauntered out of the shop. Billy phoned his sister.

Chapter 17

Isaac met with Jeremy Brice. 'You're not getting anywhere on this,' Brice said. The two men were seated in a restaurant, not far from the radio station where he had made his scurrilous comments about the police investigation into the death of his daughter.

Isaac did not like the location, not because it was expensive, although Brice had said he was paying, but because every other person in the restaurant felt the need to stop by and say hello to the celebrity. Isaac was glad he was unknown. There had been a few times, as a result of a televised press conference, where he had been recognised for a few days afterwards. The first time it had happened, he had enjoyed the experience, but with Brice it was constant. 'Do you enjoy all that?' Isaac asked.

'Not really, but it comes with the job.'

After a suitable interval, when both men had ordered and the constant beeline to the table by the other patrons had diminished, the two men talked. 'You were hard on us the other day,' Isaac said.

'Is that why you're here? To calm me down?'

'Not at all. I wanted to lay out the facts. It may bring another insight into the investigation.'

'Commissioner Davies?'

'I've not heard from him.'

'Nor have I. I gave him a hard time when he phoned in that last time.'

'I heard a recording,' Isaac said.

'What did you reckon?'

'You were tough.'

'Davies wouldn't have liked it.'

'I suppose he wouldn't but he's not running the investigation, I am.'

'You don't like the man?' Brice said.

'He's the Commissioner of the London Metropolitan Police. It's not for me to either like or dislike him.'

'You've met him?'

'On one occasion.'

'How did it go?'

'He put across his point of view. It was an open and frank discussion.'

'DCI Cook, I know what open and frank means.'

'Very well,' Isaac conceded, 'he's not my kind of person.'

'You would have preferred Commissioner Shaw?'

'You knew him?'

'Very well. He did a good job. Confidentially, there's a move to unseat Davies,' Brice said.

'And your invective on your broadcast?'

'In part it's levelled against him; in part against you. It may be that you don't have the necessary support, office politics, that sort of thing.'

'We have the support we need,' Isaac said. He wasn't about to defend himself by apportioning blame when it wasn't correct.

'Goddard gives you what you want?'

'Yes, he does. I've known him for a long time.'

'That man knows how to play politics, though not so successfully with Davies in charge.'

'He knows that. And besides, you took us to task, not so much Davies.'

'I still need a conclusion to why Amelia was murdered.'

'And by whom.'

'Amelia had her faults, and sometimes she'd drive me crazy. Overindulged as a child, I'm afraid, and her mother was not a good role model.'

'There are no guarantees in bringing a child up. One of my school friends, good family, good parents, ended up knifed to death around the back of Paddington Station.'

'Was he a good adult?'

'He was a gang leader, no great loss to society. I grew up in a similar environment, and I ended up a policeman.'

'Even so, I still feel some guilt about Amelia.'

'There's no need for guilt. You've given us a pasting on the radio. What can you give us by way of recompense?' Isaac said.

'What else is there to tell you? There are no great secrets attached to me, and Amelia was old enough to choose her own life. If my daughter were shown to be less than respectable, it would not reflect on me, and besides, I'm reaching an age where I'm ready to give it away.'

'And do what?'

'They'll pay plenty for my life story, the classic rags to riches.'

'Was it rags?'

'Not really, but they'll gloss over that in the editing. I grew up middle class, but people don't want to hear that.'

'You've covered that up well,' Isaac said.

'I'm trusting you with a lot.'

'My confidence is guaranteed.'

'I've checked you out. You have some influential admirers. I'm surprised you're not a superintendent,' Brice said.

'So am I,' Isaac said.

'I could be the murderer.'

'You're not.'

'What do you mean?'

'The deaths were not amateur, which means someone paid for your daughter's and Christine Devon's murders. And then, we have Christine Devon's son being murdered, apparently because he cheated one of the gangs.'

'You believe there is a common thread tying all the murders together?'

'It's a thought. Samuel Devon was involved with the gangs before his mother was murdered, and Rasta Joe, another murder victim, was a villain.'

'What do you know about Quentin Waverley?' Brice asked. The two men were sitting back. A dessert had been declined, coffee was on its way.

'Amelia was frightened of him for some reason.'

'Quentin is an ambitious man, but I respect him enormously. I would never suspect him of anything untoward, but if Amelia were frightened of him, then it would have only been for her good. He'd not harm her.'

'Why?'

'Because he still loved her. If Gwen, her so-called friend, hadn't engineered the situation, he would have married Amelia.'

'You know this?'

'I observe, and besides, he told me.'

'When?'

'Whenever I see him. He loved both Gwen and Amelia, but Gwen made sure that he married her, and now he's in line to take over Happold's merchant bank.'

'What can you tell me about the father-in-law? We've not met him yet.'

'You don't want to.'

'Why do you say that?' The coffee had arrived, and Brice was pulling out his credit card.

'A charming man, charming to your face. He's the toughest banker I've ever come across. If he had chosen politics instead of banking, he'd have been prime minister. Mind you, he's made plenty of money, and he's in for a peerage in the next Honours List.'

'Could he have been involved in the murder of your daughter?'

'His reputation is all too important to become involved with crime.'

'As a merchant banker, he must have come across the occasional rogue.'

'No doubt, but Happold's always remained detached. Plenty will admit to a grudging respect for the man, but there are others who detest him.'

'Why detest him?'

'Those who've lost their money and then found out that Happold wasn't that accommodating. You know the adage, if you owe the bank a pound, you're in trouble; if you owe them a million, the bank's in trouble.'

'He takes advantage when you are down, is that it?'

'Not so crudely, but if you struck a deal with him, then you had to honour it. There are a few people in the city who are doing it tough because of him.'

'Any skeletons in Happold's cupboard?'

Brice put his credit card in his wallet and stood up. 'I'm on the television tonight. I must go.'

'Another diatribe about the police?'

'Not tonight. I'd suggest you meet with Happold, but don't expect too much. Personally, I don't think he's involved, although I'd not be sorry to see him go down.'

'You've had problems with him?'

'I've run close to the wind on a few occasions. Happold's not the sort of man to throw a rope to someone drowning.'

'His daughter?'

'Like father; like daughter. She was great friends with Amelia once: clubbing, getting drunk, but after the Quentin episode, I don't think they spoke again.'

'Did it upset Amelia?'

'It did, but she put on a brave face. Gwen wouldn't have cared.'

***

Isaac was aware that time was working against him and his team. Jeremy Brice may have been agreeable over a meal, even giving him some background information on one person they had not interviewed so far, but Isaac could see that Brice was a political animal, the same as Commissioner Davies, the same as DCS Goddard, and the man was opening up for a reason.

If, as Brice had alluded, the knives were out for the commissioner, why had he told him, a DCI? Did the man trust him, even after he had criticised the investigation into his daughter's death, and by default him, or did he throw in the commissioner as a diversionary tactic? It was a point that needed considering. On reflection, the lunch had been about others, not about Brice. Maybe that was what the man intended all along.

Back at Challis Street, DCS Goddard was in Isaac's office. 'How did it go?' the superintendent said.

'According to Brice, his broadcast was aimed indirectly at Davies, not at us.'

'Do you believe him?' Goddard asked. Isaac could see that the man was on edge.

'Not totally. He plays the game well.'

'What do you mean?'

'He'll sing your praises while at the same time holding a knife to your back. He confirmed that they're trying to get rid of Davies.'

'They?'

'The government is my assumption. He wasn't very specific.'

'They are, but Davies continues to get out from under. The man's fighting back, and we're the front line.'

'Again?'

'I've been summoned to the inner sanctum.'

'To Davies's office?'

'Today, and you're coming.'

'Why me?'

'Davies has asked for both of us.'

'I've a murder investigation to conduct,' Isaac said, knowing it was a futile protest.

'We leave within ten minutes. And the Isaac Cook charm is not going to work on this man. You'd better have some good answers.'

'Will he be listening?'

'Probably not, but so far we've kept him out of our business. Let's hope we can continue to, but you're no nearer to solving these murders.'

'We've charged two men with the murder of Rasta Joe.'

'What does that matter? Davies won't be interested in the murder of a criminal. He'll want to know about Amelia Brice and the other woman. It's their murders that are important, not some would-be Rastafarian who dealt in drugs and women. Men like him die all the time.'

'Ten minutes. I'll be ready,' Isaac said. Goddard left the office.

Isaac walked over to where Bridget was seated. 'Could you prepare a report on George Happold. I need to meet him.'

'Give me two hours,' Bridget said.

'If I'm still standing by then.'

'Tough day?'

'We're meeting with the commissioner.'

'I'll wish you the best of luck, sir.'

'Thanks.' Isaac left and went out of the office. Goddard was calling him from down the corridor.

***

Commissioner Alwyn Davies, a name that struck fear into many in the Met, especially DCS Goddard, was agreeable when Goddard and his DCI entered his office at Scotland Yard.

'I thought we should meet to discuss Jeremy Brice's radio programme,' Davies said. It was Isaac's first time in the office, but not for his DCS who had been there many times when Commissioner Shaw had been in charge.

Isaac and Goddard took seats on their side of Davies's desk. The man was methodical, Isaac could see, in that the desktop was clear apart from a laptop, and a pile of documents to one side. It was not often that inspectors were called into the commissioner's office for a discussion, and Davies's welcoming speech when he took on the position – about an open-door policy, just knock on my door – had been rhetoric. The man's usual manner was to be dismissive of anyone who could not help his career or could not show him the necessary deference.

Richard Goddard could, but Davies did not want it from him; Isaac could try, but he was not a natural, and on the occasion when Davies had entered Homicide in Challis Street, he'd had gone on the defensive, while Bridget had given the man tea.

'DCI Cook's met with Brice,' Goddard said.

'And what did he say?' Davies looked over at Isaac.

A truthful answer would have been to say that it was part of a plot to oust the man asking the question and to send him back to where he had come from. That, Isaac knew, would not have been wise. 'He said that it was a drive for ratings, the need to raise the heat on his target for the day,' he said instead.

'And we were it?'

'According to Brice, we were.'

'Chief Superintendent, if your people conduct their investigations as badly as they lie, then it explains why the murder rate in your part of London continues to rise.'

'But…' Goddard, unsure what to say, just mumbled.

'Now look here, Cook. I've just about had enough of you and your department,' Davies said. He was no longer sitting down but was standing up and leaning forward, his two hands firmly planted on his side of the desk. 'I've had to intervene with you before, and your DCS is unable to see the wood for the trees. I brought in one of my people once before. I'll do it again. And now I have this fool Brice making a fool of us, belittling the Met, and all because you can't find out who killed his daughter. I am not going to let my position and those of my people be undermined by you two.'

'Sir, this is grossly unfair,' Goddard said in a moment of terror. He had hoped that the visit would at least be cordial and that the commissioner would recognise that there were acceptable standards of behaviour.

'You've got a mouth. It took you long enough,' Davies said. 'You may have had your head up the rear end of Shaw, but it doesn't wash with me. I want results, the same as Brice. I don't need him sounding off against my team and me.'

'That is not what Brice said when I met with him,' Isaac said, attempting to deal with the situation. Goddard could only see an angry man trying a last-ditch attempt to rally support, to stack the Met with people who would help him to stay in his position.

'Did you hear my interview with him?' Davies said.

'We did, sir,' Goddard said.

'And what did you think?' The commissioner had resumed his seat.

'He was tough.'

'It was a setup. I walked into a trap set by others. Goddard, did you know this? Did you and your friend Lord Shaw feed Brice information to use against me?'

'Commissioner, Jeremy Brice has a research team behind him,' Isaac said.

'I know that, but he was baiting me with information that could not have come from them.'

'Was he, sir?' Isaac asked.If Davies were not the commissioner of the Met, Isaac would have said the man was paranoid. He wondered why he and his DCS were in the commissioner's office. If it was a reprimand, then why? And besides, that wasn't the commissioner's function. That would have been for a commander to deal with. And if it was to give him support, then it was a waste of time. Neither he nor his DCS had any respect for the man who had single-handedly diminished the respect of the general public for their police force; a man who had replaced key members in the senior hierarchy with his people through an adroit undermining of their positions.

'You'd like me out of here,' Davies said. 'Well, I'm not going to give you the satisfaction. I'm bringing in my team to take over. Firstly, Goddard, you're out. You can take leave if it makes you feel more comfortable, and as for you, DCI, you've got a new boss.'

'Who?' Isaac asked, knowing the answer already.

'Superintendent Caddick, a man who's attained his promotion through sheer professionalism, not through sucking up to his superiors.'

'You don't have the authority to remove me,' Goddard said.

'I'm the commissioner. I do what is necessary, and I'm not waiting for a committee to debate it or the time for you to ask your political friends to intervene. If they want to take me on, then I'm ready for the battle. Goddard, you've got one day to clear your office. Either you take extended leave while I figure out what to do with you, or there's a job down in Public Relations for you.'

'At least I'll have company,' Goddard said.

'Is that insubordination?' Davies said. Isaac could see that the man was pleased with himself. Isaac looked across at his DCS, could only see a defiant man. He knew that he'd be the better man for being unceremoniously dumped.

'Not from me, sir. I'll go quietly. DCI Cook will solve this case, and I'll make sure that he receives the credit. If you are intent on following this course, then it will be your responsibility if anything goes wrong.'

'That's a threat,' Davies said.

'It's not, sir. It's a reality. There are decisions in life which are key turning points. You, sir, have just made one of those. I hope that you are able to deal with the consequences.'

'Goddard, you'll roast in the fires of hell for this. And you, DCI Cook, mention one word of this outside of this office, and you'll be back out on the beat in uniform.'

'I will do my duty, sir. Seth Caddick will have no reason to complain about my policing. He will be welcomed with all the due deference that his position deserves.'

'Garbage. You'll be doing whatever you can to get him out of Goddard's chair.'

Both Isaac and Goddard sat quietly. Two minutes later, after a final blast of invective from the commissioner, they were both preparing to leave the building.

'Tough, sir,' Isaac said to his DCS.

'He's exceeded his authority,' Goddard said.

'You'll take action against him?'

'I'll register a case. In the meantime, find out who these murderers are.'

'And you'll be on leave.'

'Not me. I'll be down in Public Relations. This is the best thing that could have happened. The gloves are off. Once Davies stands up to move forward to strike the first blow, he'll realise that his opponent is twice the size of him.'

'He's already struck the first blow,' Isaac said.

'That wasn't the first blow. That was the verbal sparring at the weigh-in.'

Chapter 18

Isaac, smarting from Davies's drubbing but still the SIO of Challis Street Homicide, had only one option: wrap up the current investigation. His senior, Detective Chief Superintendent Richard Goddard, did not even have that luxury: he was out, and Caddick was in.

Both Isaac and Goddard knew that the man was a walking disaster, and his being in charge of Homicide was going to cause problems.

'Don't rile the man when he appears. Davies's days are numbered, he knows that,' Goddard said.

'But why, and why you?'

'I'm the conduit to Lord Shaw. Davies believes that if he isolates me, then he's secured extra time. And he's made a tactical error. I didn't feed anything to Brice; I barely know the man. It would have to be coming from someone higher than me.'

'Lord Shaw?'

'Not likely. He wouldn't sully his hands with such matters, and besides, the man's ethical. He'll play it by the book.'

'But if others do it?'

'Then he'll probably sit back and enjoy the ride.'

'And see the Met go down the drain?'

'It's not going down the drain; it's going through a period of change, that's all. Davies is an unfortunate consequence.'

'What will you do, sir?' Isaac asked.

'I'll go and clear my desk and report to Public Relations.'

'Are you still in line to take over Counter Terrorism Command?'

'That's the word. If it's going to be rough for a while, I'll just hang on tight. I suggest you do the same.'

The two men separated on their arrival at Challis Street – Goddard to his office to tidy up, although Isaac knew the man would finish his current work and ensure a comprehensive handover to his successor, and Isaac to his office to tell his team what was about to happen.

The team were in the office; Isaac had phoned ahead to ensure they would be there. Larry Hill, his DI, sat stunned, Wendy Gladstone, his sergeant, showed her disbelief, and Bridget Halloran, the office administrator par excellence, shed a tear.

'Whatever we do, we play this by the book: no insubordination, no dereliction of duty, and no attempts to act any other than totally professional. Are we clear on this?' Isaac said.

'You don't need to tell us, guv,' Larry said. 'We've been down this road before, but now to have Caddick as your senior, as well as ours. It smacks of stupidity.'

'It's not the first time, probably not the last, when the actions of our superiors make no sense. But, regardless, we've still got some murder investigations to wrap up.'

'Rasta Joe was my best contact,' Larry said. 'I've someone else, but he's not as reliable. According to him, Negril Bob's in the area somewhere, but those who know are not talking.'

'Scared?'

'Not of us. They're frightened of Negril Bob's reaction if anyone talks.'

'Did Rasta Joe?'

'He was speaking to me.'

'You were doing your duty. Rasta Joe must have known the risks.'

'Maybe he did, but I feel some guilt.'

'No point dwelling on it. People such as Rasta Joe have a short lifespan.'

'How do we find Negril Bob?' Wendy asked.

'He'll not stay hidden, and he's unlikely to stray far.'

'Why?' Bridget asked.

'Around here is his power base. If he goes anywhere else, what is he? Just give him a few weeks, and he'll turn up.'

'Billy and Charisa Devon?' Wendy asked.

'They're taking the normal precautions.'

***

George Happold, regarded as an astute banker, was not what Isaac expected. He and Larry were in the same building as where they had met Quentin Waverley before, but now they were in the chairman's office.

Isaac had expected to meet an upright man, greying at the temples, with a ready smile. The reality of the man standing in front of them was different: he had a pronounced stoop, his hair, what remained of it, was without colour, and there was no chance of a smile.

'You've been threatening my daughter,' Happold said.

'I don't believe that is correct, sir,' Isaac said. He and Larry were standing up; no chairs were nearby for them to sit. Happold, however, was leaning forward on his.

'My daughter is expecting another child. Your questioning is placing a lot of strain on her, on all of us. Amelia Brice was a cheap woman who slept with criminals. Why would you suspect my daughter?'

'We are conducting a murder investigation,' Isaac said.

'Then question those she slept with. There's plenty of suspects there.'

'We deal in facts, Mr Happold. Your daughter and your son-in-law knew her intimately.'

'In the past they did.'

'We are led to believe that your son-in-law has continued to see Amelia.'

'That is what my daughter suspects.'

'Do you believe your daughter?' Larry asked.

'Yes.'

'Do you know why Quentin Waverley was still seeing Amelia Brice?' Isaac asked.

'You'd better ask him.'

'We have. He denied it.'

'That's to be expected. He knows my views on such matters.'

'You're against any impropriety?'

'I believe in the sanctity of the family.'

'Are you aware of the circumstances when Quentin Waverley and Amelia Brice broke up?'

'He was willing to waste his time on the Brice woman.'

'Are you condoning your daughter's action?'

'She wanted Quentin. She did what was necessary.'

'Would that include murder?' Larry asked.

'What do you mean? My daughter took Quentin Waverley for herself. She did not kill Amelia Brice, if that is what you are implying.'

'You condone your daughter's action, yet you are critical of others,' Isaac said. He, like Larry, had seen the bank's website, the beaming face of the founder, his loyal team around him. In that office that day, no one was beaming, and as for loyal team members, the only two they had seen on the way up to the man's office had both had hangdog expressions, as though working for Happold was a chore, and loyalty was a one-way journey to oblivion. It was evident that Happold was loyal to his family but to no one else.

'My daughter is a driven woman, the same as I am. Do you think this bank is here because I was not?'

'I assume that you had to push hard,' Isaac said. There was no doubting George Happold's success in setting up the bank, and the wealth of the man was indicative of the drive that he must have applied to achieve it.

'Sixteen, seventeen hour days, seven days a week, for years. Gwen understands the value of hard work and determination, never accepting no for an answer, doing whatever is necessary to win through, and so does Quentin. He was a willing partner.'

'Do you mean that Amelia finding him and your daughter together was engineered?'

'If you must be so crude,' Happold said. Larry thought the man looked away at the thought of his daughter with another man. Isaac felt sure that Quentin Waverley was an innocent partner in the act, other than he was unfaithful to Amelia.

'We're police officers,' Isaac said. 'We deal in facts. Your daughter married Waverley, and Amelia Brice is murdered. We need to establish if there is any reason to connect the two.'

'Gwen is a determined woman, not a murderer, and besides, look at her. She's not in a condition to kill anyone.'

'But her husband is, and for whatever reason, he was in contact with Amelia Brice, and she was frightened of him.'

'What does he say?'

'He denies that he's been in contact with her,' Larry said.

'Then that's the end of the matter. Amelia used to go around with criminals. Why don't you check with them, instead of a respectable member of the community? A member who regards the prime minister as a personal friend.' Isaac recognised the veiled threat; it wasn't the first time either. One thing that Isaac knew: once they start making threats, it is proof that they are hiding something, but what?

Happold was right, his daughter could not have committed the murders of the two women. For one thing, she would not have had the strength to control Christine Devon. Gwen Waverley was slight in stature; Christine Devon had been a big woman, and there had been a struggle. And it was known that the same person had killed the two women.

'Mr Happold,' Isaac said, 'your influence will make no difference, or who you regard as friends. Someone is hiding something from us. You profess to be a moral man, yet you condone your daughter's actions. It is not something that most fathers would want to hear, that their daughter had used their promiscuity to achieve their aim.'

Steady on, Larry thought. He knew that Isaac was trying to break through, but implying that Happold's daughter was a tart was pushing it too far.

'DCI Cook, I am a strong believer in the basic structure of society, the importance of the family, not this modern fashion

148

for living together and having multiple partners. Gwen believes in this as well, and for a time she was living with Amelia Brice, the daughter of a man that I despise.'

'Why do you despise him?'

'Let me finish,' Happold said. 'My daughter for a brief period fell into Amelia's way of life.'

'Your daughter played around?'

'If that is a polite euphemism for sleeping around, then yes. She met Quentin through Amelia and decided that she wanted him. I checked him out, and he seemed suitable. Not only did he come from a good family, but he also had the right education and the skills to be brought into this bank.'

'It sounds mercenary,' Isaac said.

'It is realistic. My time at this bank is coming to a conclusion. Another five to ten years and I will be dead or no longer capable. My daughter, whom I love, is ambitious, but mathematically dyslexic. Quentin, if he was married to my daughter, would be the ideal compromise, and Gwen's children would be assured of a legacy.'

'Is Waverley worthy?'

'As my daughter's husband, yes. He will run this bank as I have run it, with my daughter's guidance.'

'To ensure that this bank survives, you were willing to dispense with your values,' Isaac said.

'This is the real world, DCI Cook. Not some childish vision of utopia. Gwen did what was necessary, and I respect her for it. Quentin may think that he is still his own man, but he is not. He will not give this life away.'

'A caged animal.'

'Except for him the door is always open, but each night he comes back.'

'Are you saying that if he were playing around with Amelia Brice, that would be alright?'

'That is not what I said. It is not alright, but the occasional indiscretion will not mean an automatic exclusion from this family. Waverley represents a significant investment on my part; an investment I intend to realise.'

'You've not explained the reason for your hatred of Jeremy Brice.'

'It is not only Brice, but he is the most contentious. The man, a so-called social commentator, revels in digging into the dirt of every successful person in this country, in making scurrilous remarks about leading politicians, even about me.'

'Have you met the man?'

'On many occasions.'

'Recently?'

'Not since the death of his daughter.'

'Is there any reason why not?'

'We do not make plans to meet. Our paths cross unintentionally, and when we meet, we are civil. Does that answer your questions for now? I am a busy man, as is Quentin, and I would appreciate it if you leave my daughter alone for now.'

'It's still a murder investigation,' Isaac said.

'My daughter's pregnancy is proving difficult, that is what I am saying.'

'We will take it into account.'

***

It had not been a good day for Wendy. Her investigation into Shirley Rourke and the ABC Cleaning company had come to fruition, which meant one thing: she'd have to arrest the woman.

It had been the Fraud team at Challis Street, investigating the insurance swindle, who had solved the crime, finding that the destroyed painting, long known to be a fake, had its twin, the original, on the wall of a house in the United States. An appraiser had been dispatched. The painting was checked, found to be genuine.

The cleaner who had switched the original for the fake, stealing the first, destroying the second, had also been found and had admitted to the theft and to her and her employer's involvement as well.

150

'I'm not guilty,' Shirley O'Rourke protested as Wendy arrested her at her house, although with some regret.

Once back at Challis Street, and in the interview room, Shirley O'Rourke, on legal advice, admitted to having known of the theft. The most she would get in prison would be two years, the maximum possible sentence avoided. Later, the woman confided to Wendy that it was a weight off her mind,, and on release she'd go and live somewhere warmer, which interested Wendy, as her arthritis was being aggravated by the weather.

Chapter 19

Negril Bob paced up and down in his room. He knew that he had been a man about town, a man to be feared, and now he was a nobody in a nowhere place. He also knew that the evidence against him for the death of Rasta Joe was flimsy.

Negril Bob had grown up in a culture of violence. His father, a stern man, fresh off the boat from Jamaica, had embraced crime and gangs. At home, the father would fluctuate from adoring father and loving husband to being violent and hateful. At those times, he'd use his fists to bring some sense to his children, his wife trying to hold him off, only to receive a fist herself. He still remembered the time when his father had hit his mother one too many times, and she had collapsed. And then the rush to the hospital, the pronouncement of death, his father taken into custody, pleading that it was an accident, only to receive fifteen years for murder. The last time he saw his father was when he had been convicted and sentenced. Negril Bob felt sad remembering back to then. He had only been eleven. There were the years after that in foster care as he degenerated into a criminal. He had been a good student, even wanted to be a doctor, and he would have made it, he knew that.

Negril Bob looked around the room; it was comfortable. He could even get a woman if he made a phone call, but what he wanted most of all was Charisa Devon. He had seen her before they had threatened her brother, the honest Billy, who now was the manager of the shop that he was meant to steal from. His sister had only been the threat, but he had watched her on several occasions after that: sometimes when she was walking home from her college, sometimes with a white man. She moved in a way that excited him. There was an innocence about her that he found irresistible; he knew he had to have her, and staying confined in a room looking out over the street in an unfamiliar city solved nothing.

He packed his case and walked to the nearest railway station. He phoned his lawyer and told him to prepare his defence.

'You'll not stand a chance. The case against you is tight.'

'Why, how?'

'There was a witness, and the other two admitted that you were involved, that you were the leader.'

'That's not proof, that's only an inconvenience.'

'I'm your lawyer, don't tell me.'

'And if the person who saw us changes his story?'

'Then the case against you would be weak.'

'An arrest?'

'Not for long, if there's no proof.'

Negril Bob ended the phone call, regretted staying out of sight for so long. There was a solution, and then he would deal with Billy and his sister. He was a man who did not forget, and Billy had reneged on their deal. It was time for him to pay up. The train pulled into the station, and he climbed aboard. It was four hours to London, long enough to formulate a plan, long enough to make a few phone calls to people who owed him a favour.

***

George Happold had not appreciated the visit by two detective inspectors. His elevation to the peerage was near, and this Amelia Brice business was starting to impact it; questions were being asked as to his suitability, and all because of the one person he loved, his daughter.

And why? After all, it had been him who had created the most significant merchant bank in the country, he who had bankrolled the government's latest election campaign, ensuring that it was financially sound. It had been touch and go at the last election, and the governing party were not likely to last long, eighteen months at most. If his peerage was not in the bag before then, he knew it would never come. The leader of the opposition and he did not see eye to eye after clashing at a Royal Commission investigating banking practices in the United Kingdom. The honourable leader of the opposition was all for stricter government control: more audits, the right to charge individuals who deviated from the rules laid down. Happold, a fervent believer in the need to maintain flexibility when deciding where to apply their funds, had argued with him.

It had been a battle that the leader of the opposition had won on political lines. Happold conceded privately to his daughter, his confidante in such matters, that the man had been right on a technicality. And now he had Waverley, the philandering son-in-law, causing trouble, and all because of a former flame. He was angry with his son-in-law, but his daughter was adamant that she wanted him, and that she could control him, which he knew she would.

After all, wasn't she a Happold, and they never failed, although his father, a punctilious snob, had. Life as a child for Happold had been a succession of schools, some exclusive, some not. Holidays on the continent, or at homes which varied in size and quality dependent on his father's latest business venture. The young George, mentally mature for his age, even if his body had been slow in developing, had seen it from his early teens. His father was a day-dreamer, the eternal optimist, believing that success was guaranteed if enough effort was applied. By the time of his nineteenth birthday, the young man's father had ceased to exist, as had the family fortune.

George Happold, as he reflected on the past, did the one thing he thought he would never do: he phoned Jeremy Brice.

***

Richard Goddard came into Homicide on his last day. There had been a plan for Challis Street Police Station to have a farewell party for the detective chief superintendent, but as he had told

Isaac, it was not goodbye, just au revoir. 'If this works out, I'll be back,' Goddard said. 'Although probably not here.'

'How long?' Isaac said, sorry to see this happen to the man who had guided his career, sometimes irritating him as well, a man who had been a good friend. Wendy had shed a tear when Goddard had come to say goodbye, even thrown her arms around him and kissed him on the cheek, which had embarrassed the normally formal DCS, although he should have expected it after Bridget had done the same. Larry Hill had shaken the man's hand firmly, holding it longer than he should, remembering that it was the DCS who had got him out of his previous police station and into Challis Street with Isaac. 'Sorry to see you go, sir,' he said.

'Just play the game, and it'll work out. That goes for all of you,' Goddard said. They all knew what he meant, although none were looking forward to the imminent arrival of Isaac's previous nemesis.

And then DCS Goddard was gone. Isaac could sense, as did the others in the department, the strangeness when something so familiar is no longer there. The unexpected visits, the pep talks – 'You've got five days to wrap this up', or 'I need an arrest soon', or 'It's only one murder. It won't take you long to find out who did it'.

Goddard had not answered Isaac's 'How long?'. Not because he had not heard him, but because he did not know. The demise of the Met's commissioner was not a simple process, and dependent on circumstances, he could last two weeks or two years. There'd be a reluctance to remove him without due process, which meant that Davies would need to agree to a face-saving exercise whereby he resigned or retired with the necessary fanfare, the accolades, even an acknowledgement in the Houses of Parliament. Meanwhile, behind the scenes, the daggers would have been drawn, the financial package agreed. There'd be those who would argue for no action, and that the man should be allowed to serve for another four years until his current contract was due for re-evaluation, but to Isaac, that was sheer madness.

Whatever happened, there'd be no public flaying of Commissioner Alwyn Davies – undermining the public's confidence in the office of the commissioner would serve no useful purpose.

Appointing Seth Caddick as Richard Goddard's replacement at Challis Street would only speed Davies's departure, or Isaac hoped it would, and then there he was, Superintendent Caddick in the doorway to Homicide. 'Has Goddard gone?' he said.

Isaac looked over at the man; he could see that his time sidelined back at his old police station had not mellowed the man, and now he was their superintendent. The thought of it scared Isaac.

'Good to see you. Welcome back,' Isaac said.

'A word in your office,' Caddick said. He made the rounds of the office, shaking everyone's hand, making the usual comments about how he would get himself settled before he made changes, and so on.

Inside Isaac's office, the door closed, the two adversaries sat down. 'DCI, let's be blunt here.'

'What do you mean?' Isaac said.

'You're Goddard's man. I don't blame you, but I'm here now. There'll be no telling him what's going on. I'm in charge now, and I expect total loyalty. Do I make myself clear?'

'That is abundantly clear.'

'And I'll not accept insubordination either. That comment was getting too close to the bone for me.'

'It was not intended.'

'You do not approve of me, and you certainly do not like me, but I'm the superintendent, you're not. You get on with your job, I'll get on with mine.'

'We are involved in several murders. Will you allow me to continue investigating without your involvement?'

'I've seen your investigating, and believe me I was not impressed. You've got four murders, and only one of those is possibly solved.'

'You've been reading the reports?'

'What did you expect me to do? To walk in here like a dummy. I know all about your cases, and how long it takes to solve them. From now on, I'll be keeping an eagle eye on this department, and if I see any incompetence, I'll be down on you like a ton of bricks. You may have been Goddard's pride and joy, you're not mine. Respect is earned, not given, and I've not seen proof that you deserve mine.'

'I appreciate your frankness,' Isaac said.

'I intend to ride you and this department. Do I make myself clear?'

'Yes.'

'And a daily report.'

'That's what we always do.'

'Good. I'll leave it to you while I go upstairs and sort out my office.'

Superintendent Seth Caddick left Isaac's office. Isaac sat back and put his hands behind his head in a sign of exasperation.

'What's up, guv?' Larry asked as he came in through the door. He was holding two cups of coffee, one for him, one for Isaac. 'You look as if you need a drink.'

'After that, thanks.'

'Difficult?'

'What did you expect?'

'It's going to be hard calling him "sir",' Larry said.

'You know the deal. No matter how difficult the man becomes, we don't attempt to destabilise him. And never give him cause to remove us from our positions.'

'He's got the authority.'

'Maybe he has, but he'll need to replace me first, and that's not so easy.'

'Why?'

'Our superintendent is the poisoned chalice. No one wants to sully their career by cosying up to him.'

'There are some, sir,' Larry said.

Chapter 20

The death of a homeless man on the street would not usually raise a comment. The weather had been unseasonably cold, and those who slept rough invariably succumbed if they were weak or aged.

Gordon Windsor had been on the scene within two hours of the body being found under a bridge. 'Dead by natural causes,' he said. 'Which doesn't help you, does it?'

'Not at all. He was our witness to Rasta Joe's killing.'

'Would he have had credibility?'

'Not a lot, but with the confessions of two of Negril Bob's gang, we'd have secured a conviction.'

'And now?'

'If those in custody change their story, we've got problems. Are you sure of the natural causes?'

'There's no sign of violence. Although it wouldn't have taken much to suffocate him.'

'That means our case against Negril Bob will go against us.'

'I can only report the facts,' Windsor said.

Isaac left the scene, despondent. In the past, he would have informed Richard Goddard of the latest developments, but now there was another man in charge. Isaac wasn't sure how to proceed. If he did not tell Caddick, and he found out through another channel, then he, as the SIO, would have been negligent in his duty. If, on the other hand, he told the new superintendent, then the man would be on the phone to Commissioner Davies. Isaac could see that he was between a rock and a hard place.

Isaac chose the only option possible. At the far end of the top floor corridor in Challis Street, the sign on the door prominently displayed: Superintendent Caddick. Inside, the man sat at his desk. Isaac saw that the bookcase had been moved, and the desk no longer sat in front of the large window; it was now to one side. 'What is it, DCI?' Caddick said.

'Our primary witness to the murder of Rasta Joe is dead,' Isaac said. He was standing, no invite to take a seat.

'Murdered?'

'The evidence points to the cause of death as being natural.'

'What does this mean? Caddick asked. Isaac could only reflect as he stood there that behind the desk was a man less experienced than him, less educated, less professional, and now he was answering to him, following his orders if they were given.

'It means that our case against Negril Bob is substantially weakened.'

'Does that mean you cannot arrest him now?' Caddick said. Isaac could see the man enjoying himself.

'If those two we've arrested stick to their story, then we can.'

'How likely is that?'

'The word will soon get to them.'

'In prison?'

'Someone will have a phone. They probably know already.'

'So what are you going to do, or do you need me to deal with it?'

'I came to inform you. We don't need assistance.'

'You've charged two people with murder, and now you're telling me the evidence is flimsy. What kind of policing is that?'

'It's good policing. Negril Bob is guilty of the murders of Rasta Joe and Samuel Devon.'

'And you can't prove either?'

'There is no evidence for either murder that will hold up.'

'And there are two other murders. That's four in total, and you've not got a firm conviction against any of them.'

'That is correct, sir,' Isaac said. He realised that it grated on his nerves when he had to acknowledge his senior's status. Once outside Caddick's office, he phoned Richard Goddard.

'Three months maximum. That's all I can give you,' Isaac said.

'It's not possible to put a time against this. There's not much I can do here in Public Relations.'

***

Jeremy Brice was not sure why he had agreed to meet George Happold. He knew one thing about the man: he did not like him. He knew it to be mutual from Happold's side as well.

'Why are we meeting?' Brice asked. It was early evening in an upmarket restaurant in Mayfair.

'I've been visited by the police,' Happold said. The two men had shaken hands on meeting. Brice had asked for financial assistance from him once in the past when he had considered buying the radio station where he broadcast every Tuesday and Thursday. Happold had refused.

The reasons were unclear, but Brice found out the truth in time; the man was advising a rival bid, providing financial support as necessary. In fact, Happold had done him a service in refusing, as the radio station continued to haemorrhage money, not on account of his programme, but because the advertising revenue generated was now being diverted online.

'Gwen was friends with Amelia, as was Quentin. What did you expect?' Brice said.

'What have you told them? The truth?'

'What they need to know. My daughter's been murdered. Are you implicated?'

'Brice, I've asked you here to discuss the matter, not to listen to your accusations. What would I gain from her death?'

'You're a private man, and Gwen and Amelia would talk. What if Gwen said something untoward, indiscreet? How far would you go to protect your bank, your family name, your peerage?'

'Not as far as murder, that's for sure.'

'Happold, you'll not convince me. You're a wolf clothed in sheep's clothing.'

160

'And that's the way it will stay. Better than being a sheep in wolf's clothing.'

'Touché,' Brice said.

The two men ordered their meal, a vintage red wine to complement it.

'Amelia was frightened of Quentin,' Brice said. The two men, dissimilar in many ways, alike in others, clinked their glasses before drinking.

'Amelia was always dramatic,' Happold said. 'Are you sure, or was she exaggerating?'

'I'll grant you that she could gild the lily, not like Gwen, straight up and down with her.'

'Both women had their faults, but I'll not allow anything to be said about my daughter,' Happold said.

Brice was aware of Happold's unswerving belief in his daughter. He knew it to be well-founded. He had always enjoyed Gwen's company, an articulate and smart woman, whereas Amelia was whimsical and carefree. Their friendship was a consternation to many people, but the two women were as thick as thieves for many years.

'Nor against mine,' Brice said. 'What's the real reason for our meeting tonight?'

'I will require your confidence,' Happold said. He poured himself another glass of wine, topped up Brice's glass.

'You have it.' After so many years of dealing with politicians and his influence with them, Brice had heard many secrets, knew of a few too many indiscretions, whether financial or sexual. Not once had he used that knowledge to his financial advantage, although some would have paid handsomely for his information, and never once had he mentioned anything to a third party, and especially to those who listened and watched him every week on the radio and the television.

'Good man,' Happold said. The meal was finished, the plates were taken away. Both men had a glass of port in their hands. 'I'm an ambitious man, and this ongoing concern over Amelia's death is affecting the possibility of my peerage.'

'It may prevent it.'

'You've heard something?'

'I hear a lot of things, but yes, I've heard.'

'I'm sorry to raise your daughter's death. It must be difficult for you.'

'It is, but Amelia was a reflection of her mother. Delightful but fickle, loving but always looking elsewhere. Quentin was the rock in her life. I was the rock in my wife's life.'

'What happened, if you don't mind me asking?'

'My wife was at home with Amelia, and as she started to grow up, wanting to exercise her independence, my wife started to stray.'

'Stray?'

'Other men. And in time she met a younger man. One day I come home, and she's gone.'

'Where is she now?'

'You know the answer. Why are you asking?'

'It's your story.'

'She died overseas in an accident. I went out there with Amelia and brought the body back. We buried her in the local churchyard. It was sad at the time, but we move on. Amelia, unfortunately, was tarred with the same brush. Eventually, her life would have followed the same route: the wrong men, the wrong decisions, the inevitable regrets.'

'Quentin concerns me,' Happold said. 'Was he seeing Amelia?'

'I don't know. I had not seen Amelia for some time before she died, maybe six to eight weeks.'

'Any reason?'

'Her behaviour was becoming more irrational, and she was messing around with the criminal class.'

'The gangs?'

'Some of them. I only knew about it. I never saw any of them.'

'Who do you believe murdered your daughter?' Happold asked.

'You know the answer.'

'Gwen?'

'Not her personally, but she's a strong woman, a woman who doesn't like to lose.'

'That's what I worry about,' Happold said.

'Have you spoken to her about it?'

'No. She would only deny it.'

'And Quentin?'

'He has disappointed me.'

'Competent to take over the bank?'

'Competent to run it. Gwen will always be the controlling partner. Men such as Quentin can never be trusted totally.'

'Why are we here?' Brice asked.

'I need to protect Gwen and Quentin.'

'Then why ask me? I only want the murderer of my daughter to be found.'

'What do you have hidden? What dark secrets are there that could be revealed?'

'Are you accusing me of having my own daughter murdered?' Brice replied. He was indignant and insulted.

'Let's be honest, Brice. You're a man who has risen to the top of your profession. treading on other people's toes, committing the occasional misdemeanour, even turning a blind eye when it was necessary.'

'Both of us are equally guilty of some things we are not proud of.'

'Not me,' Happold said. 'There is nothing that I have done or would do that would cause me any sleepless nights.'

'Including murder?'

'If it was for my family.'

'Did you kill Amelia because she had something on Gwen, because she was involved with Quentin?'

'Not Amelia. I am only giving you a generalisation as to the extent men like ourselves will go to achieve our aims.'

'That would also extend to Gwen and Quentin.'

'Precisely. I will do whatever is necessary to protect my daughter and her life,' Happold said.

'You'd protect her and Quentin even if they were guilty of murder?'

'I would prefer them not to be involved, but if they are, believe me, I will do what I must.'

'That sounds like a threat.'

'It's not a threat; just a notification of intent.'

'Then let me tell you. If either of those two killed my daughter, I'd pursue them through the police, and if they fail to act, then I will deal with it myself.'

'That sounds like a threat to me,' Happold said. 'I believe we have made our positions clear. Let us hope that my daughter and her husband are innocent.'

'And if they are not?'

'I will do whatever is necessary.'

'Including having me killed?'

'I have made my position clear,' Happold said.

'Crystal clear,' Brice replied.

***

Negril Bob's return to the area was not welcomed by some people, least of all the team in Challis Street Homicide. As expected, once his two incarcerated gang members had heard that the only witness to the murder of Rasta Joe had died, they had changed their tune and denied their involvement, and with the poor quality finger and shoe, the case against them was unsustainable. As for the knife wounds, no knife had been found.

A brash individual, Negril Bob's first act had been to march into the Westbourne pub to announce that he was back.

Larry Hill was out in the area testing the mood on the return of the violent gang leader. Not only was there a general level of fear, but there was also the need for revenge. Rasta Joe had had a gang, and with them, it was tit for tat, kill one of ours, we'll kill one of yours.

Isaac could see the odds increasing in favour of the gang war that had not yet eventuated. Society would not miss any that would die, but if it was intense, then the chance of it spilling into the general populace was possible.

'Another stuff-up,' Caddick said when he had hauled Isaac up to his office. 'What is it with you and your department? Can't you get anything right?'

Isaac wanted to say that he had solved more murders than his superior, his track record was unblemished, and to just back off and leave him to it. But he did not. He had the measure of Caddick, a man who rode his staff hard but did not remove them until just before the case came to a conclusion, so he could take all the credit.

'It's a setback,' Isaac said.

'It's a stuff-up. Goddard may have gone easy on you. I've no intention of doing so. I'll need regular updates, a list of the day's activities, and a reason why if any were not completed, and those that you did, what was achieved.'

Isaac had heard it all before, straight out of the mouth of Commissioner Davies. Caddick should have still been a sergeant, possibly a junior inspector, but the man was already a superintendent. It had only been a few years since Isaac had seen the possibility of becoming the commissioner of the Met, but his approach was through competency, not through sycophancy.

'We've four murders, one suspicious death; I don't have time for what you want,' Isaac said.

'What I want, I get. That's the way to get results. One day, Cook, you might learn, but I doubt it, and as for your Goddard, this sweet arrangement you had with him is over. From now on, we do it my way. Is that clear?'

'It's clear. I will put it in writing to you that the direction you are asking us to take is contrary to good policing,' Isaac said.

'Covering your back, is it? Lily-livered, hoping that when this investigation comes crashing down on your head, you'll be able to wave a piece of paper to abrogate responsibility.'

The voices of the two men were elevated. Isaac knew that his career prospects were dashed, but there was no way that he was going to lick the man's boot.

A message on Isaac's phone. He looked at it. *Don't bait Caddick.*

It was clear that someone outside the office had heard the voices and had SMSd Richard Goddard, who in turn had SMSd Isaac.

'Very well. I'll comply with your request,' Isaac said. 'And we will solve these murders.'

'Don't be surprised if you see me in Homicide on a regular basis,' Caddick said.

Chapter 21

Charisa Devon's visit to Challis Street was not unexpected. Negril Bob was back, and even though he was in Homicide's field of view, there was not much they could do about him. Isaac knew the man to be smart, and he would not incriminate himself in the interview room. It seemed better for him to be out on the street and visible. In time, Isaac was convinced, the man would make an error, and he'd be arrested.

'Billy's been threatened again,' Charisa said.

'When?'

'A few days ago.'

'Why didn't you tell us about this before?'

'I only found out from him today. He didn't want to worry me as I had exams.'

'He could have told us,' Isaac said.

'They had told him not to.'

'They?'

'It wasn't anyone he knew. A man came into the shop and threatened him, not long before Negril Bob returned. Billy was frightened. He's doing well at the shop. He doesn't want to steal from there again.'

'Are you part of the deal if he doesn't pay?'

'Yes.'

'How long does he have?'

'Five days, and now they want all the interest that's been accumulating.'

'How much?' Isaac asked.

'Forty-six thousand pounds. If he doesn't pay, they'll take me.'

'What protection do you have?'

'None. After Negril Bob disappeared, we'd assumed it was all over, but now he's around.'

'Have you seen him?'

'Yes. Once when I was walking home from college.'

'What did he do?'

'He was on the other side of the street. He made a suggestive sign.'

'Describe it.'

'You know it,' Charisa said.

'Thumb and forefinger of one hand, the forefinger of the other,' Larry said.

'That's the one.'

It was clear that the situation was dangerous. 'Charisa, you've got to get away,' Isaac said.

'I've still got exams. I can't afford to miss them.'

'These people are murderers. They probably killed your mother, and your exams are more important!'

'I need a visa for America. It's dependent on my passing these exams.'

'You know what will happen if they take you?'

'I prefer not to think about it,' Charisa said.

'You must. They'll drug you, no doubt rape you. Are you prepared for this? Is America that important? And then there's Billy. We can't protect you and your brother if you're both stubborn.'

'We'll not be intimidated by then.'

'These are vicious men.'

'I know, but I'm staying.'

'Billy?'

'He'll not let down Mr Loeb.'

'I can deal with Loeb,' Isaac said, 'but I can't protect you and Billy from Negril Bob.'

Isaac could see in Billy Devon a decent young man, and in Charisa, the sister he never had. He could see the goodness in her that could easily be destroyed, and Negril Bob was a man of few morals.

Negril Bob was around the same age as Isaac, but he had not come across him before. Larry said that was because he had grown up to the east of the city, and he was known there as a tough individual.

Isaac phoned Billy two hours later and had a brief conversation with him. He confirmed what Charisa was saying, but was initially angry that she had put herself at risk.

Isaac phoned Larry who had since left the office. 'What's the latest on Negril Bob?'

'The man's visible, treating everyone to drinks at the pub, no doubt bragging about how he beat the police.'

'Where are you?'

'Notting Hill, trying to get an angle on the death of Samuel Devon.'

'Any luck?'

'Not really. Those who knew him said he was full of himself. Nobody, it appears, has a good word to say about him, not even his school teacher who called him an obnoxious little punk.'

Isaac looked over at Charisa who was still in the office. 'He was,' she said.

'Sorry about that,' Larry said. 'I'd have been more discreet if I'd known you had company.'

'Don't apologise, Inspector. Samuel was only fifteen. Young enough to grow out of it,' Charisa said.

'Maybe,' Larry said. 'Most times, they're into gangs by the time they're twelve or thirteen. Petty crime then, but Samuel was playing with the grown-ups. He wasn't the first one to come to a sticky end, won't be the last either. What's important, Charisa, is that you and Billy make it through, make your mother proud of the both of you.'

'That's what we intend to do.'

Isaac ended the phone call and turned to Charisa. 'You've got to make yourself scarce.'

'I can't.'

'Your boyfriend?'

'We're living together.'

'You're both young, maybe too young to be living together.'

'That's what my mother would have said, and if she were still alive, then I wouldn't be. Troy's a very moral person, but my life, as well as Billy's, is not normal, is it?'

'I've seen too much to form an opinion of what is normal now,' Isaac said.

'Samuel, was that normal? I remember how he looked after his death, how I felt.'

'I've seen worse. And time heals, you know that.'

Isaac could see that the young woman wanted to stay at the police station with him, but he had work to do, and a superintendent who wanted to be kept informed. On the other hand, he worried that at any time she could be snatched off the street, even if she was taking care to watch out who was around her. In the end, he asked Bridget to drop her off at Troy's place.

Free of anyone in his office, Isaac opened his laptop, saw ten emails, six from Caddick. He let out a long sigh, almost felt like swearing, but checked himself.

It was clear that Caddick's demands were designed to deflect Isaac away from the investigation, with the inevitability of one of Caddick's people coming in to wrap it up. Isaac knew that he had to play the man tactically. If he abided by his dictates, he was finished; if he didn't, then he had a good chance of wrapping up the investigations.

Isaac knew that a successful outcome would remove any pressure on him from Caddick. He leant back in his chair, put his hands on the back of his head and weighed up the pros and cons for a few minutes. In the end, he sat up straight, nominally filled in the reports, and left the office. He knew there'd be trouble.

***

Negril Bob enjoyed the notoriety. He had beaten the system, as far as he could see it. The police had wanted to arrest him for murder, yet he had evaded them, and now they couldn't pin anything on him, not even a parking ticket. Larry had observed

170

him from the other side of the pub; an opportunity for him to have a couple of drinks. At one stage, Negril Bob had looked his way, another of his gang letting him know that there was a police officer in the pub. A couple of women were draped around Negril Bob's neck. Larry knew one of them, knew her to be a prostitute who hawked her wares from a small house not far from the pub; the other woman he did not recognise, other than noting she was the prettier of the two.

Larry knew that he should not have been there on his own, but he had seen the man highest on Homicide's radar entering the pub. It had been several weeks since he had started following his wife's instruction on sensible eating and drinking; three days since he had had a beer. He had wondered at first if he was an alcoholic but decided he wasn't, although he sure missed it. And now, a pub and Negril Bob; the need to enter and to order a pint was irresistible, and if his wife complained, not that she did as much as before when his weight had been piling on, he could say that it was in the line of duty.

As he sat there, not talking to anyone, pretending to check his emails on his phone, occasionally glancing around the pub, he could see that not much had changed since Rasta Joe's death. The amorous couple in the corner who should find a room before it became embarrassing, the old man sitting on a chair in the corner, the assorted businessmen, the local villains, black and white, some English-born, some recently arrived in the country.

Larry ordered another pint, took the opportunity to buy himself a pub lunch, a juicy steak. He'd had enough salads at home to last him a lifetime, and a pint and a steak were as close as he was going to get to heaven that day. Another two pints and he would be sleeping on the sofa with only a cat for company. For once, he was going to take the risk and to indulge himself.

'Spying on me, is that it?' a voice said.

Larry looked up, saw the ominous presence of Negril Bob. 'Not me. I often come in here for a pint,' Larry said. He knew that he was compromised. The pub was full, but no one would be coming to his rescue. He was not ashamed to admit that he felt a little frightened. The man who sat opposite him was an imposing figure: jet-black with pearly white teeth, the scalp clean-shaven, his muscles apparent under the shirt he wore. Negril Bob was a good-looking man, no one had ever denied it. Rasta Joe with his dreadlocks and the faint odour of ganja, had not been. And now Negril Bob was threatening him.

'Look here, Hill, I'm a law-abiding man. I mind my business, I suggest you mind yours.'

'Can't a man have a pint without being disturbed?' Larry said by way of a weak defence.

'You know who I am. I'm a tough man, not afraid to mix it with the locals, not willing to let anyone say anything against me or get in my way.'

'Is that a threat?'

'Not from me, it isn't. I mind my own business, I suggest you mind yours, as well.'

'There's still a case against some of your people.'

'Who's to say it was them.'

'There was a witness to Rasta Joe's murder.'

'Your drinking pal. I'm surprised you bothered with the toad of a man, although he was no doubt keeping you informed. Did he ever mention me?' Negril Bob said. To Larry, it looked as though he intended to stay and harangue him.

'Rasta Joe never mentioned you. He was a cautious man, careful in what he said, and besides, who are you? Should he have mentioned you? Have you done anything that the police should be concerned about?'

'Not me,' Negril Bob said. He was looking at Larry, attempting to get the measure of the man, attempting to ascertain how far he could push him.

'Then how do you make a living?'

'Honest graft, that's all. Has anyone told you different?'

'We rely on our own investigations. As far as we are concerned, you're a criminal, unproven bar a few minor offences.'

'And that's the way it'll stay. Do I make myself clear?'

'Now that's a threat.'

'It's not a threat, but if I find you hanging around me, I'll get my lawyer to issue a writ against you for police harassment, and that goes for Isaac Cook as well.'

'You know him?'

'By sight, no more. I've broken no law.'

Larry knew that he had been threatened, and with a man as violent as Negril Bob, he knew he needed to be careful. The man would not be averse to threatening his family if there was a court case pending. Larry also knew that there was no proveable crime against the man. He needed something solid on him, but from whom?

Negril Bob left Larry where he was sitting and went back to his gang. Larry sat still for five minutes, taking the opportunity to message Isaac. After that, he left the pub. Outside was quiet as he walked to his car. He opened the door and sat in the driver's seat. On the windscreen, someone had thrown paint. It was probably local hooligans recognising a police car, but he couldn't be sure if it were more sinister. Not wanting to linger, Larry left the area and drove to Challis Street.

Chapter 22

Isaac, as expected, was in front of his laptop typing when Larry walked in after his encounter with Negril Bob. It was ten in the evening, and Homicide was dark apart from the light in Isaac's office. Isaac could smell the beer on Larry's breath.

'Not ready to face the music at home?' Isaac said, more by way of jest than criticism. Isaac wasn't a drinker, but sometimes he had drunk more than his fair share if it was work-related. However, Isaac knew that for him it was work, but for Larry it was a pleasure.

'He's keeping you busy,' Larry said. There was no need to say who the 'he' was. Neither of the two men liked the new superintendent, yet Larry was more adept at concealing his disdain for the man who had breezed in through the main entrance of Challis Street a few days earlier.

Isaac had submitted his report, not spending too much time on the detail, aware that there would be words from his superintendent. It had been the wrong tactic, he knew that now, in that Caddick had taken note that Detective Chief Inspector Isaac Cook was not acting correctly towards a senior. It was Richard Goddard who had phoned him up after the latest confrontation between the two men. 'If you show any opposition to his rule, then it will be marked in your official record,' he said.

'There is a murder investigation,' Isaac said in his defence. 'I can't be expected to lose focus.'

'Sorry, but that's the way it is. If you continue to defy the man, you'll be up on disciplinary charges, and you know what will happen?'

'Caddick and Davies will make sure I'm found guilty.'

'Caddick's already got a man lined up for your position.'

'Has he?'

'A snivelling weed of a man from what I've been told. He's currently a detective inspector dealing in homicides, to the north of London.'

'Your description?' Isaac said.

'That's what I've been told. I've looked up his service record, and it's sound. Of course, that may be because he and Davies go back a long way, but I believe that the man may be capable.'

'One of Davies's stooges and competent? That's not something we've come across before.'

'Maybe, but if Caddick gets you out, then it's not going to be so easy to come back.'

'How do you suggest I proceed?' Isaac said.

'Play the game. If Caddick wants reports, you give him reports. If he wants you to jump on the spot, you jump.'

'It's not my style.'

'Style or not, that's what Caddick hopes you'll not do. The man's baiting you, don't let him catch you.'

'How's Public Relations?' Isaac said, to talk about something else.

'If they want me to jump, I'll jump.'

'Is this what we've become, performing animals?'

'Unfortunately, it is.'

***

With Isaac busy, Larry sat down at his desk. He realised that he had drunk more than he should have, and he still had to go home. He helped himself to a cup of coffee, black, and checked his emails.

So far, Caddick had not annoyed him, only shaken him by the hand and patted him on the back. Larry knew that the man was looking for allies, and he, as a detective inspector, could not afford to burn bridges. He did not have a mentor as his senior did in DCS Goddard. All he had was Isaac, and it was hardly a mentoring role. His senior had brought him into the department as a detective inspector, and that's what he still was, and there was no mention of promotion. With Caddick, assuming he survived, there was always the possibility.

Larry knew that now was not the time for sucking up, and he didn't want to, but he was a realist. Success was about power and compromise, diligence and honesty, subtlety combined with reality and sycophancy.

In the office, he could see Isaac slaving at his laptop, the top button of his shirt undone, the tie off to one side. Larry picked up the phone and made a phone call. 'I met Negril Bob,' he said.

Wendy yawned on being woken up. 'What did he have to say?'

'He made it clear that our continued investigation would be met with action on his part.'

'Violence?'

'Not him. He threatened to contact his lawyer.'

'What good will that do?'

'Not a lot, I suppose.'

Wendy, realising that Larry wanted to talk, got out of her bed and went into the other room. One of her cats followed her. 'Why were you near to Negril Bob?'

'I followed him into the pub. I was thirsty; it seemed a good opportunity.'

'And you were checking him out?'

'I'm entitled to a pint.'

'You were stalking him.'

'What can we do to wrap up this case?' Larry said. 'What do we have?'

'You pick a fine time of the night to talk,' Wendy said.

'We can talk later.'

'I'm awake now.'

'Samuel Devon, where do we stand on this?'

'Nowhere.'

'We know the gangs; we have a fair idea who killed him.'

'Where's the proof?'

'Do you have any contacts?' Larry said.

'Shirley O'Rourke, but she's in jail, pending a trial for insurance fraud.'

'Is she a woman who'd have her ear to the ground?'

'I'd say so. Not that she's been involved with the gangs, but she'd know who they were.'

'Tomorrow, you and I will meet with her.'

'Great, now can I get back to bed?' Wendy said.

'Sleep tight. I'll go and talk to our DCI.'

***

Larry could see an increasingly frustrated man in Isaac's office. He went and organised a cup of coffee for him. 'Here you are, guv,' he said as he placed it on Isaac's desk. It was way past midnight, the clock in the corner of the office clearly visible.

Outside in the street, it was quiet apart from the occasional car, a couple of drunks arguing.

'I've nearly finished. What were you saying before?' Isaac said. 'Just let me send this report to the man.'

'He's hardly likely to read it tonight.'

'Whether he does or not is not my concern. I've followed instructions, that's all. Most of it is padding anyway. He's flexing his muscle, aiming to see how far I'll bend before I react.'

'How far will that be?'

'I'm not there yet.'

'You were busy before, so I didn't mention it.'

'Mention what?'

'I've met Negril Bob.'

'Where?'

'At the pub. I was there at the same time.'

'Did you follow him?'

'I saw him going in. It's a public place.'

'On your own, that's dangerous.'

'There was no one else that I could have called to join me, you know that.'

'Certainly not me. I'm known in the area. There are some there who dislike me more than you.'

'I know that, and Negril Bob knew you by name.'

'What did he say about me?'

'Just to let you know that he did not appreciate you or anyone else prying into his business.'

'Threatening?'

'Intimidating. It was a busy place, although I was careful when I left.'

'You shouldn't have followed him in. It was reckless.'

'It was necessary. I needed to get the measure of the man.'

'What do you reckon?'

'Smart, careful in what he says. There was no mention of overt violence, only implied.'

***

George Happold paced in his office. The situation with his son-in-law was intolerable. Now the man was accusing his daughter of being involved in Amelia Brice's death.

Happold, someone who had always been careful in what he said, did not understand Quentin Waverley. The man had only needed to wait for another few years, and he'd be in effective control of the bank. Now his chances were looking slim.

Discretion and a careful manner were what was required when you were dealing with billions of pounds. The bank could not be entrusted to a man who openly accused his wife of murder, had been carrying on an affair with his ex-lover, and showed a tendency to uncontrolled anger where the tongue moved faster than the brain. Happold knew he could not continue forever; he was seventy-eight and feeling it, and the mind, once so sharp, was starting to wander. He hoped it wasn't what he thought it was.

He made a phone call. 'Quentin, my office in five minutes.'

Six minutes later, Happold's personal assistant, a woman in her sixties who had been with him for nearly forty years, showed Waverley in.

'Yes, George. You wanted to see me,' Waverley said. He could see that the man facing him was not in a good mood. He remembered when he had first moved in with Gwen, Happold's daughter. The man had been stand-offish, almost dismissive of his daughter's choice. Waverley recalled the grilling he had received the next day, the checks into his background. Happold had even paid for private investigators to check him out; they had found out about the girl he had got pregnant in school, the miscarriage, the consternation of his parents, the anger of hers.

The investigators had also found out about other romances, the dangerous driving, even his alcohol and drug intake in his youth. Quentin had mentioned it to Gwen at the time, her only comment was, 'Don't worry. He's my father, he cares about me, and besides, he's checking you out, see if you'll stand up to the governance required of the bank. Don't worry, you'll pass. I'll make sure of that.'

And then Happold was shaking his hand. 'There are some skeletons there, but you were only young. Just remember, you're joining the Happold family. We play by a different set of rules, and whatever happens, whenever one of us strays, we look after each other, and if you ever upset my daughter, then be prepared.'

At the time, Waverley had dismissed it as the standard speech of a father about to pass over his daughter to another man, but now, standing in front of Happold, he was not so sure.

'Amelia's upset, and if she is, some am I,' Happold said.

'She's pregnant, emotional.'

'That's as maybe, but you've not been staying on the line. Some of your decisions in this bank have been less than satisfactory.'

'I've not heard any complaints.'

'You are now.'

'Is this because of Gwen? Are you aiming to sideline me?'

'Quentin, you're a Happold now. We look after our own. I will not sideline you, nor will I remove you from your position as the chairman-presumptive of this bank. But just remember, if it's a decision between you and Gwen, it will always be her. She's blood, you're not.'

Waverley could see what the old man was saying: he was serving notice. Quentin Waverley, an astute man, had seen the benefit of transferring his affections to Gwen from Amelia, even though he had preferred Brice's daughter. And Jeremy, her father, was an educated man with a biting tongue but retained the willingness to enjoy himself, to have a drink, even a joke. With George Happold, there was no biting tongue, no enjoyment, and no humour.

To Waverley, Happold was a killjoy, and the man's only pleasure was in seeing the bank's financial statements. He couldn't see him staying retired for too long. Away from the bank, the man would sit in his library at home, a seventeenth-century mansion, reading books on finance, nothing else. He certainly didn't go fishing or play golf, regarding both of those as pursuits of the idle mind. And now the man was giving him a lecture.

As Waverley stood there listening to the father, he could see no way out, and he knew that in the future, once he was the chairman and his wife had the controlling stake, it would be her giving him the third degree. Waverley knew he could not tolerate the situation. Back in his office, he considered the possibilities.

Chapter 23

Larry Hill sensed it at a café in Portobello Road. It was the day after his encounter with Negril Bob. Before, everyone had been civil, whether they were honest or not, but now there was a tension in the air. It was still early, and he had managed to avoid the wrath of his wife the night before, the few hours in the office with Isaac had dealt with that problem.

'The usual?' the waitress asked, although it was not necessary. There was always just the one reason for him entering the café and taking a seat close to the window; it was the full English breakfast, the tomatoes, the bacon, the two eggs, the toast, and then a pot of tea.

'Why not?' Larry said to the woman. 'It's quiet in here,' even though eight people were sitting at the other tables.

The woman bent low, low enough for Larry to smell her perfume. 'The word's out.'

'What word?'

'You're closing in on Negril Bob. Nobody wants to be too close, just in case.'

'Just in case of what?'

'You know.'

'I'm sorry. Maybe it's because it's early or I'm slow on the uptake. What is it with me?'

'Negril Bob's put out the word that anyone who assists the police will be on the wrong side of him.'

'And people are frightened of him?'

'Around here they are.'

'And you?'

'The man kills for pleasure, what do you think?'

'But you're talking to me.'

'I'm serving you breakfast,' the waitress said. Larry looked at her as she walked away. He picked up his phone and called Isaac.

'We'll not get much out of anyone around here, at least, not for a few days,' Larry said.

'Why's that?' Isaac replied.

'The people are frightened of Negril Bob.'

'What kind of leverage does he have over these people?'

''Fear is a powerful lever. We know that he killed Rasta Joe because he talked to me; these people must know this, as well.'

'If they do, maybe there's further proof."

'We only had the one witness.'

'There may be others, but they'll not talk either. How do we move forward?'

'We can't. If this is the mood where I am, then those who might have spoken to me are going to be tight-lipped.'

***

Charisa Devon could not agree with her brother. He was convinced that their only protection was for him to acquiesce to the threats and to give Negril Bob what he wanted. He had been angry when Isaac Cook had phoned him up in the shop, angrier when he heard that his sister had refused to leave the area.

'You'll not understand,' Charisa said. 'No qualifications and I can't go to America with Troy.'

'And what will you be over there – the black wife of a white man? They're racist, you know.'

It was the first time that Charisa had heard her brother talk that way. It was if he was starting to believe the gangs' distorted view of life.

Charisa knew that she had never felt that. Sure, there was the occasional abuse, but she was educated, she could handle herself, whereas Billy was not. She worried about him, so much so that she considered not going with Troy to America. But she knew that she was not a nursemaid.

'Billy, you can't stay here. You must leave the area,' Charisa said.

'These are my people.'

'No, they're not; they're criminals.'

'It is only a result of the system, the prejudice in society.'

'Why this change?'

'I've been speaking to my friends. They're doing well, got a good set of wheels.'

'And no doubt a few women dangling after them.'

'And why not? Why should I work in a shop for minimum wage when I can make a bundle out there?'

'They killed Samuel, don't you remember? Your friends may be fine now, but they could be dead tomorrow.'

'I don't forget, but Samuel, he was a child.'

'And what are you? At nineteen, you're a man, is that it? An education, that's the answer.'

'You sound like our mother.'

'That's what I am now to you. You're supposed to be the man of the house, even though it's only the two of us, but you're acting like the child. Stand up and be counted.'

Charisa realised the conversation was going nowhere. She changed tack. 'They want their money within a few days, what are you going to do?'

'I will make a deal with them to protect you,' Billy said.

Charisa knew that Billy loved her, the way she loved him. Even if his actions were dishonourable, his intent was not. She knew she had to protect him from his own folly. She ended the phone conversation and made another phone call. 'It's Billy,' she said.

'What about him?' Isaac said. Charisa knew that her approach had an element of risk. If Billy committed an illegal activity, or if he did in the future, she was giving the police early notice of her brother's decline from decency to dishonesty.

'He's planning to do something wrong,' Charisa said. She was waiting to enter the exam room, and her mind was not focussing. She knew that it would be a disaster to take the exam and a failure would mean a wait of six months before she could sit for it again.

'I thought he was not going to,' Isaac said.

'I'm not sure if he believes in what they do, or whether he's trying to protect me.'

'Assuming he is, what can he do? It's forty-six thousand pounds this time. There's no way he'll be able to get that sort of money out of the shop and sold on the street.'

'Maybe you can talk to him?'

'I'll bring him in, subject him to the third degree. And you've got to disappear, exam or no exam.'

'I'll phone Troy. He'll have to understand.'

'Will he?'

'Yes, I know he will. I can't leave England while Billy is wavering. He's all I've got left after Mum and Samuel died.'

'When will you disappear?'

'I need to go home, collect some clothes. Later today.'

'It needs to be now. I'll send over Sergeant Gladstone to your college. She'll stay with you until you're safe,' Isaac said. Wendy had been listening to the conversation; she nodded her head.

'Tell her ten minutes,' Wendy said.

***

Larry had spent a day working his contacts, seeing if there was any further evidence that could link Negril Bob and his gang to three deaths, those of Samuel Devon, Rasta Joe, and a homeless man. It was dark, and he still had one more possibility. The homeless man had a friend who went by the name of Dave. The man had not been seen for a few days, though there was nothing unusual in that as he was also homeless, and he moved around the area, sometimes sleeping here, sometimes there. He had heard from another homeless man that Dave could be found around the back of a local hardware store, sleeping in the back entrance doorway.

Larry parked his car at the end of the street. The rain had started to fall, and it was miserable. He would just talk to this man, find out what he had to say, and then be off home. His wife, by way of a treat for him losing weight, had promised to make him a good meal for once, steak and kidney pie, followed by apple crumble and an early night.

Up ahead, Larry could see a man huddled in a doorway. 'Dave?' Larry said.

'What do you want? This is my place so you can bugger off.'

'Detective Inspector Larry Hill, Challis Street Police Station.'

'I've done nothing wrong.'

'I know that. I've a few questions for you, nothing more.'

'You don't have a bottle of something, do you?'

'I'm afraid not, although I could give you some money if you want.'

'Fifty pounds.'

'Fair enough. You had a friend, he was a witness to someone dying.'

'Where is my money?'

Larry pulled out his wallet, removed the fifty pounds and gave it to the man, standing to one side to avoid the smell.

'He told me about it,' Dave said.

'Were you there?'

'I don't get involved, it's safer that way.'

'Are you saying you were there, or you weren't?'

'I mind my own business. They killed him, you know?'

'Who?'

'Gappy, my friend, the one you're referring to.'

'Why Gappy?'

'He had no teeth, not at the front anyway.'

Dave, were you there when they beat the man to death?'

'I need another fifty pounds. I need to buy myself some food.'

Larry complied, opening his wallet. The homeless man took the money and stuffed it inside the old coat that he wore. Larry knew that it was not food that Dave would be buying.

'I was there, but no one saw me, and Gappy, he knew I'd not say anything.'

'You are now.'

'Here, not in your police station, and not in any court.'

'Why's that?'

'I spent time in prison, long time ago. I don't intend to go back.'

'You're a witness, not a criminal. That won't happen.'

'It did last time.'

Larry realised that the man was probably confused, and an unreliable witness. 'Did you hear any names mentioned?'

'Only Rasta Joe and Negril Bob.'

'Rasta Joe was the man who was killed.'

'I know that. I'm not stupid. It was Negril Bob who was hitting him.'

'How do you know this. Gappy said it was dark and he only heard voices.'

'His eyesight wasn't so good. It was Negril Bob; I know him well enough.'

'Will you testify against him?'

'Not a chance. I've told you what happened, but don't take me down to your police station.'

'If I do, you'll change your story.'

'That's it.'

Larry knew that Dave would not stand up in court to testify and that the defence would devalue his testimony, even if he gave it, as the man was a homeless alcoholic.

Larry left the man and walked back down the street. As he approached his car, a heavy object hit him in the back; he collapsed to the ground, a bag placed over his head. He remembered little after that, other than men hitting him in the chest as he was pinned up against a wall, the fists to his face, the sound and the weight of a baseball bat or similar slamming into his legs, causing him to collapse. Barely conscious once the

186

beating had ceased, he removed the bag from his head. He picked up his phone; it was smashed. With no more energy he propped himself up against the side of his car.

Isaac first heard of the attack when he received a phone call from the hospital. He went straight over there; it was eleven in the evening. At the hospital, Larry's wife waited. 'He's going to be alright,' she said. Isaac could see the worry on her face.

'What do you know?'

'He's in a bad way; no broken bones, thankfully.'

A doctor entered the room where Larry was lying, semi-conscious and sedated. 'He'll pull through,' he said. 'We've taken x-rays.'

A uniformed officer stood outside the treatment room. Isaac left Larry's wife with her husband and went to speak to him.

'A brief report,' Isaac said.

'We found him next to his car. At the time, we didn't know he was a police officer. We phoned for an ambulance, and it brought him here.'

'You didn't think to look in his wallet, in his car.'

'No, sir. We had a man in need of hospitalisation, another one further up the street.'

'Another one?'

'A homeless man.'

'His condition?'

'He's dead. There was a knife in him. I phoned back to the station; I assume they phoned you.'

'Not yet. We'll deal with that oversight later. What can you tell me?'

'Not a lot. We found DI Hill, followed procedure. The other man, not that we knew him, was clearly dead. My colleague, he stayed with the body. I came here.'

Isaac phoned Gordon Windsor. 'You've heard about Larry?' he said.

'I've dispatched my team. What happened? We seem to have lost valuable time here,' Windsor said.

'I don't know. We'll worry about it later. Larry's going to pull through; the other man isn't. See if you can put a name to the perpetrators this time.'

'We'll do our best, but attacking a police officer, that's over the top.'

'They're arrogant, believe themselves to be invincible, and Larry was pushing.'

Isaac ended his phone call with the station's crime scene examiner and went back to check on Larry. He was lying on his back, his wife holding his hand. 'How are you?' Isaac said. The look on his DI's wife's face showed that she would have preferred it if he had let her husband rest.

'It only hurts when I laugh,' Larry said.

'At least your sense of humour's fine.'

'Dave, he was there when Negril Bob killed Rasta Joe. You need to talk to him.'

'Unfortunately, he didn't fare as well as you.'

'Dead?'

'Yes.'

'We're back to square one,' Larry said.

'Windsor's out there with his people. Anything you remember?'

'No idea who it was, although it was definitely more than one person. No one spoke, just beat me up.'

'A warning?'

'There's a few who don't like me, but if they've killed Dave, they're worried.'

'Then we know who.'

'You can't prove it.'

'Let's see what the CSIs come up with.'

A nurse walked in, administered an injection. 'It's a sedative. He needs to rest,' she said.

Chapter 24

Caddick was on the phone. 'You're one man down,' he said. 'You'll need additional resources.'

'DI Hill's fine,' Isaac said, knowing full well that the supercilious superintendent wasn't interested.

'Yes, sure. I was going to ask,' Caddick said.

'We don't need help at this present time. Dependent on Larry's condition, he'll be back with us in a couple of days.'

'Don't try to palm me off, DCI. The man's taken a severe beating; he's not likely to be up and about for a week, and then he'll only be on light duties.'

'How do you know his condition?' Isaac asked. 'I've only just found out myself.'

A clearing of the throat on the other end of the phone. 'I've just checked with the hospital.'

'There was a delay in contacting me,' Isaac said. 'Did you know that?'

'Are you accusing me?'

Isaac smelt a rat. 'Not me.'

'It's sir to you,' Caddick said. The man was pleased, his DCI was rising to the bait. He knew that if he dangled it even more, DCI Isaac Cook would say something that he'd regret. Accusing a senior officer was a disciplinary charge, and he had Cook's replacement lined up and ready.

Isaac could feel the tension in his body, the need to make a comment, but then he remembered Richard Goddard's advice: 'Don't bait Caddick.'

'We've got the crime scene investigators checking. They could well give us the breakthrough we want,' Isaac said.

'Very well. I'll need a full report.'

*****

Isaac was anxious to get out to the crime scene, although fully aware that it was one in the morning, he had barely slept, and he had been in the office until late the previous night. As he left the hospital, his phone rang again. 'DI Hill, how is he?' DCS Goddard asked.

'He'll be fine,' Isaac said, aware that Goddard was genuine in his concern for Larry.

'I was told that it was a severe beating.'

'He should be up and about in a few days. How about Caddick?' Isaac asked.

'He wants to bring in a replacement for you. Just ignore the man and get on with it. I'll do what I can, but it won't be much.'

Once free of the phone calls and the hospital, Isaac made his way out to the crime scene. The small lane at the back of the hardware store had been closed to traffic. Come daylight, Isaac knew, there'd be trouble with the delivery trucks when they were denied access. Isaac parked his car and walked up to where the dead body was, passing by Larry's car, a group of investigators checking it.

In the doorway was the dead man, his head drooped forward, almost as if he was sleeping. 'Another one,' Windsor, the CSE, said. The area was bathed in light, a floodlight to the rear of the two men.

'Anything you can tell me?' Isaac asked.

'Male, approximate age fifty to sixty. His general health, his teeth, would indicate that he's been living rough for a long time.'

'The cause of death?'

'A knife to the heart. It doesn't look professional.'

'Why?'

'It looks hurried. As if they had decided at the last moment to kill him. I'd say they were after Larry first, then saw the man up here, realised that they may have been talking.'

'Then why not kill Larry?'

'I'll leave that up to you,' Windsor said. 'I can only give you the facts.'

Isaac walked back down to Larry's car. Grant Meston, Windsor's deputy, was checking it.'

'Anything, Grant?'

'Two men, not very strong.'

'Why do you say that?'

'Judging by the reports from the hospital, and from what we can see here, Larry should have been dead, or at least seriously concussed with some broken bones. I just phoned the hospital, the man's back up on his feet.'

'We breed them tough in Homicide,' Isaac said. 'What else can you tell me?'

'We've found some fingerprints on the car.'

' In our database?'

'The two you initially arrested for the murder of Rasta Joe, but this time the prints are clearer.'

'Negril Bob?'

'Not him, but his colleagues.'

Isaac instinctively picked up his phone to call Larry, before realising that he was in the hospital. Instead, he phoned Caddick to get him off his back. 'We've got proof this time,' Isaac said. The reply from his superintendent was not congratulatory, not that Isaac cared.

Back at Challis Street, Isaac organised a couple of police cars and an armed response team. The addresses of the two men that they wanted to arrest were known. One location, not far from where Christine Devon had been murdered, was vacant. The second place, a third-floor flat close to Paddington Station, was occupied. Negril Bob's car was parked in the street. One of the police cars was parked in front of it to prevent it being used if anyone attempted to escape. Two armed response men stood outside the door to the flat, another held a battering ram in case the door did not open. Outside, in the floor's passageway, a group of people started to gather. The flats were upmarket and the residents were not used to seeing the police. Isaac shuffled them back, as did the uniforms. Downstairs, another police officer waited in case the men inside the flat got that far.

'This is the police. Come out with your hands in the air,' one of the armed response officers shouted. Isaac stood to one side, wearing a bullet-proof vest.

'We've done nothing wrong,' a voice said from inside the flat.

'Open this door.'

The door opened. 'Cook, good to see you,' Negril Bob said. He was dressed casually: an open-necked shirt, a pair of shorts. Inside the flat, Isaac could see women.

'We are here to arrest Morris Beckford and Marcus Roots,' Isaac said.

'They've done nothing wrong.'

'We can prove that they were at a crime scene earlier.'

'You've got nothing on them. Leave us alone.'

'Are they here?'

'They're busy. We're having a party. Ditch your friends and come and have some fun. There are enough women to go around,' Negril Bob taunted.

'Morris Beckford and Marcus Roots,' Isaac said again.

'Give them five minutes to finish up.'

'With what?'

'You know what they're busy with.'

Isaac knew, but it did not alter the fact that the men were wanted for murder. One of the armed response men, sensing activity in the flat, pushed past Negril Bob. Two other armed response team members followed straight after. Outside in the passageway stood another two officers, their weapons raised.

'You bastards,' Negril Bob shouted.

Inside the flat, the first door had been flung open, a naked woman jumping from the bed, a semi-clothed man attempting to follow her, only to be roughly held by a police officer. The man was flung down on the bed, his hands clasped behind his back as the handcuffs were applied. In the other room, a man hurriedly dressed, a gun in his hand. He fired, the bullet only just missing one of the armed response team and lodging

192

itself in the wall next to the kitchen. 'Stand back,' the lead officer shouted. 'The man is armed and hostile.'

At the entrance to the flat, Isaac stood with Negril Bob. 'You bastard, your own people,' the gang leader said.

'My people are law-abiding,' Isaac said.

Inside the flat, another shot. 'Man down,' an armed response officer shouted.

Two minutes later came the all clear. Isaac entered the flat, with Negril Bob now in handcuffs. Morris Beckford was sitting in a chair in the living room; two women were near to him, although unrestrained. Another two women sat on the other side of the room, one that Isaac knew by sight.

In the second bedroom lay the body of a man, his face visible. 'He's only wounded,' one of the officers said. 'He took a shot.'

'I thought you'd shoot to kill,' Isaac said.

'It was a judgement call. There was a woman in there with him. If he had shot again, then I would have killed him. There's an ambulance on the way.'

Wendy was on the way over; she'd deal with the statements from the women. Isaac took hold of Morris Beckford, read him his rights, and then escorted him out of the flat, handing him over to a uniform outside. 'Take him to Challis Street. He's charged with murder, so keep a watch on him.'

Inside, Marcus Roots had moved to one side of the bed, attempting to sit up, blood visible on his arm. 'I had to aim for his arm to make him drop the gun,' an officer said.

It was a good shot, Isaac could see that. 'Marcus Roots, do you understand me?' Isaac said as he stood next to the wounded man.

'Yes, I understand.'

'You attempted to shoot a police officer. That's a serious crime.'

'I thought it was someone else.'

'We had announced ourselves at the door before entering.'

'I didn't hear anything. I was busy.'

Phillip Strang

'Marcus Roots, you're under arrest for murder, do you understand?'

'I'm innocent.'

Isaac did not intend to labour the point with a man who was in pain. Once he had been treated, he'd be transferred to Challis Street Police Station and formally charged. Negril Bob, even though there was no case against him for the murder, would also be taken to the police station. The man had protested, but he had been in the company of two men who were charged with murder; he was a witness and regarded as hostile.

***

Seth Caddick realised yet again that Isaac Cook was outsmarting him. With the arrest of two men for murder, the chance to sideways promote him was no longer possible. That would be a blow to the aspirations of another detective inspector who had been waiting for the opportunity to take Isaac's office.

Isaac called Richard Goddard, Caddick phoned Commissioner Davies: one phone conversation was congratulatory, the other was not.

Morris Beckford, short, not a very bright individual, judging by his poor English, was led into the interview room. Isaac waited for ninety minutes while Wendy concluded her interviews at the flat. Upon her return, she told Isaac that the women were not significant, only rented by the hour.

'Morris Beckford, you've been charged with murder. How do you plead?' Isaac said. He had followed the procedure, informed the man of his rights.

The man shifted uneasily on his seat, attempted to avoid eye contact. Adam Galbraith, his lawyer, another old school friend of Isaac's, was representing him.

'I've killed no one,' Beckford said, looking over to his lawyer for support.

'My client is innocent of all charges,' Galbraith said.

'We have proof that you, Morris Beckford, were responsible for the death of a homeless man, who has since been

194

identified as Dave Dallimore. Your fingerprints were discovered at the scene. We have them on file from our investigation into the murder of Joe Brown, commonly known as Rasta Joe. We've also found proof that Marcus Roots was at the crime scene as well. Once his injuries have been dealt with, he will be brought to this station. He will then be interviewed in this room. Any discrepancies will point to the guilt of the other. Also, Detective Inspector Larry Hill was severely beaten.'

'I've killed no one,' Beckford said again.

'No admission of guilt will go against you in your trial.'

'I would request twenty minutes with my client,' Galbraith said.

'Twenty minutes, fine. I'll send in refreshments,' Isaac said.

Outside the interview room, Caddick was waiting. 'Is this watertight?'

'Yes.'

'Very well, carry on. A full report before you go home tonight.'

'It's more likely to be tomorrow,' Isaac said. 'We're wrapping up the loose ends now.'

Caddick mumbled some words of encouragement and walked away.

'He's not happy,' Wendy said.

'Does it worry you?' Isaac said.

'Not at all, but that man's dangerous.'

Back in the interview room, Beckford's lawyer spoke. 'My client wishes me to read a statement.'

'Please proceed,' Isaac said. He looked over at Morris Beckford, realised that the man was, if not illiterate, probably not capable of writing a statement and then reading it.

Galbraith placed a sheet of paper in front of him and spoke. 'I, Morris Beckford, was present at the death of the man known as Dave Dallimore. We had seen him speaking to Detective Inspector Hill, who we had been following. The attack on the detective inspector was committed by Marcus Roots. I did

195

not take part. After he had attacked the detective inspector, we walked up the road and confronted the homeless man. We did not know his name at that time. We asked him what he had been talking to the police officer about. He said nothing; we thought he was drunk. Marcus pushed him to make him talk, but he just told us to go away. Marcus became angry and hit him. I stood back. Eventually, the man swore at us. We made a phone call for advice; Marcus followed instructions and stabbed the man. That is the end of my statement. I am not guilty of murder.'

'Who did you call?'

'I don't know his name.'

'Negril Bob?'

'Not him.

Isaac realised that Beckford feared the man more than he feared a lengthy prison sentence.

'Thank you,' Isaac said. 'Some facts have not been given correctly.'

'My client has made a full disclosure.'

'The knife had your client's fingerprints on the handle. I am afraid that your client is guilty of murder and we have the proof,' Isaac said.

'I had to do it,' Beckford said, jumping up from his seat.

'Sit down and be quiet,' his lawyer said.

'But why a knife and why in such a visible place?'

'There was someone in one of the buildings nearby. We could see his shadow. We were frightened, not sure what to do.'

'So you killed him?'

'He had seen Marcus kill Rasta Joe. He was there that night.'

'All three of you killed him. We know there was more than one person involved.'

'I was there, but I didn't take part. I was keeping a watch for anyone coming up the lane. That's the honest truth.'

'We'll be talking to Marcus Roots later today. Will he corroborate your story?'

'Corroborate?'

'Agree with your story.'

'He'll try to blame me, but I'm innocent.'

'Not with your fingerprints on the knife's handle, you're not.'

The lawyer sat back, knowing full well that he had no defence to offer.

'We will check your statement with his.'

'Don't, please. He'll kill me.'

'What was the celebration at the flat for – payment for a job well done, is that it?'

'It was someone's birthday.'

'Whose?'

'One of the women.'

'If you continue to lie, it will not go well for you. The women were rentals, that's all. Did Negril Bob put on the party by way of thanks?'

'Thanks for what? It was just a party.'

Isaac could see that the man was going to keep to his story. He knew it was pointless to contradict him anymore, and besides, Homicide had the evidence.

The interview concluded, and Isaac took the opportunity to phone Larry. His wife answered. 'He's much better. He wants to talk to you.'

'Larry here, what's the latest?'

'We've proof against one of Negril Bob's gang. His fingerprints were on the knife that killed Dave Dallimore.'

'Who?'

'The homeless man up from where you were found.'

'Dave. He was there when they killed Rasta Joe,' Larry said.

'Morris Beckford told us. He's back in the cells; we're about to interview Negril Bob.'

'I wish I was there.'

'Not this time. What's the doctor saying?'

'My wife's scowling at me, but she understands. I'll be in the office in two days, light duties only.'

'Hopefully, we'll have sewn up Rasta Joe's death by then.'

'Samuel Devon?'

'Beckford's not admitting to his murder. Mind you, the man's not too bright. He could change his story at any time. His defence will use the man's low intellect as a defence.'

Wendy took the opportunity to go across the road and bring back some sandwiches. After she and Isaac had eaten, they reentered the interview room. Negril Bob was waiting. He was using the same lawyer as Beckford.

'Robert Gosling, also known as Negril Bob. Is that correct?' Isaac asked.

'That's correct,' Negril Bob said. He had a scowl on his face. 'I've not done anything wrong. If Beckford and Roots have done something stupid, then it's not my problem.'

'We cannot prove that you were present when Dallimore was killed or when DI Hill was severely beaten.'

'Then why am I here?'

'Morris Beckford and Marcus Roots are colleagues of yours, is that true?'

'You know it is. We're friends if you like. Beckford's not too bright, but Roots is okay.'

'You're obviously smarter.'

'Galbraith, you're the lawyer, get me out of here.'

'I suggest you stay for the time being,' Galbraith said.

'Mr Gosling.'

'Everyone calls me Negril Bob.'

'Morris Beckford spoke to you by phone. Beckford tried to pass the knifing of the man onto Marcus Roots, but we know that not to be true. Beckford acted on instructions, your instructions. Is that correct?'

'Not me. If Beckford killed him, then he's to blame. Don't try to smart-arse me into a confession. I'm guilty of no more than being a hard case.'

'And if Marcus Roots corroborates Beckford's story?'

'You're putting words into my client's mouth,' the lawyer said. 'May I remind you that in English justice, a person is innocent until proven otherwise.'

'I'm aware of the law,' Isaac said. Wendy sat to one side, not sure what to say.

Isaac knew that the connection between the death of Dave Dallimore and Negril Bob was tenuous. He had not been at the murder scene; he had never met the murdered man, and the phone number that Beckford had phoned for advice was no longer operating.

'We will have a corroborating statement from Marcus Roots.'

'Two men, guilty of murder, wanting to strike a deal with the police for a lighter sentence. Galbraith will destroy their evidence against me.'

'DCI Cook,' Galbraith said, 'your evidence against my client is circumstantial.'

Isaac knew that it was. So far, all of it was hearsay, and there was no connection between Negril Bob and Samuel Devon, only the word of Rasta Joe that there was. The only charges against him were minor, and if he were charged, then he'd be granted bail. Isaac chose to leave the man free, knowing that his luck would eventually run out, and his support base was weakening.

Negril Bob walked out of the police station later in the evening. He looked back at Isaac as he left, and smiled. Isaac knew that to him it was personal. He phoned up Ann, Phillip Loeb's PA. It would have to be another weekend before they met.

Chapter 25

Five days after Negril Bob walked out of Challis Street Police Station, three things happened: Gwen Waverley gave birth to a son, Larry Hill reported for duty, and George Happold died.

Another child for the Waverleys further cemented Quentin's position within the Happold bank, and he knew it. It came with some regrets, namely that Amelia was not there, even though she had become difficult, threatening to disrupt his plans. He had spoken to her about it on several occasions, tried to convince her to wait and to lay off the men and the drugs. The last two times that he had seen her, it had been a case of 'you do what I say or else', although he had never known what the 'else' was.

Each and every time that he had seen her, he had wanted to sleep with her, but he had resisted, even if she had been willing. He was not the paragon of virtue that he pretended to be with Gwen's father, a man who would send you to the poor house without compunction, yet set high standards for his family, even for him, the son-in-law. Quentin Waverley knew one thing: he had hated the man, and now the man was dead and he was running the bank. The compromises were acceptable, and if that meant Gwen, then he would not complain. The side benefits, the occasional dalliance, the obligatory mistress as befitted a man of status, would suffice.

Larry, the effects of the savage beating still feeling sore in places, walked into the police station. It had been longer than the two days he had initially said. He received a hug from Wendy which hurt, another from Bridget which hurt even more, and a firm handshake from Isaac. 'Our man is still here?' Larry said.

'He's not that easy to shift,' Isaac replied. 'He'll outlast me at this rate. We've got no one in custody for four of the five murders.'

'It's not our fault. If there's no evidence, what can we do?'

'Are you up to winding up the heat?'

'I'm ready. Mind you, I don't think I want to get involved in any violence for a while.'

'Your wife?'

'She's worried. I can't blame her. I could have ended up dead.'

'Why didn't they kill you? It didn't seem logical to leave you alive.'

'The two you arrested, they're not very bright. They follow instructions.'

'Are you saying that Negril Bob told them to leave you alive?'

'Why not? He knew what would happen if a police officer was killed in the line of duty.'

The news of George Happold's death became public later in the day. According to reports, he had visited his daughter and his new grandchild in the hospital in the morning, and then, as he was leaving, he had collapsed with a heart attack, and had died not more than fifty feet from where his daughter had given birth.

Isaac and Larry made their way over to the hospital on receiving the news. Outside were two reporters that neither of the men wanted to talk to. George Happold was an influential man; his death was newsworthy, not the same as a celebrity, but he would get a mention on the news broadcasts for that day.

Quentin Waverley was inside. Isaac and Larry spoke to him, offered their condolences, their congratulations when told about the birth. 'A brilliant man,' Waverley said.

'You weren't fond of him,' Isaac said.

'I could admire him.'

'Your wife?'

'She's fine.'

'And what now for you?' Isaac asked.

'I'll take over the bank.'

'A day of change.'

'As you say.'

Isaac and Larry realised that there was no more to be gained at the hospital. George Happold was elderly and not in good health. His death was not suspicious, although its timing was unexpected.

Back at Challis Street, Caddick was on the warpath. Isaac could see him as he entered the building. 'Where have you been? I've been trying to phone you,' he said.

'My phone is never switched off. George Happold died.'

'Who?'

Isaac could see that Caddick had not been reading his reports.

'The merchant banker, the father of Amelia Brice's former friend, the father-in-law of her former lover.'

'Yes, I remember.'

'What did you want me for?' Isaac said once Larry had moved away.

'Commissioner Davies wants these murders wrapped up.'

'So do we,' Isaac said.

'You're taking too long. He wants me to become involved.'

'I'm the SIO, not you,' Isaac said before remembering what DCS Goddard had said about riling the man.'

'I'll need twice-daily reports, that's all. I don't intend to come down here and do your job for you.'

Isaac left the man and walked up to Homicide. He was still shaking his head in disbelief. He thought to phone Richard Goddard but decided against it. Davies was either raising the heat through his lackey to protect his position, or it was a further effort to bring his man into Homicide. Neither made any difference as to how Isaac would handle the case.

***

Jeremy Brice was in a good mood that day. George Happold had died, and his secret was safe. The secret that he had slept with Gwen before she had married Quentin; the secret that Happold would not forgive. Gwen had regretted sleeping with Amelia's father, she had often said that to him since then, but she had been drunk, so had he, but Amelia was not in the house, and one thing led to another.

Amelia knew the truth, so did Quentin, but neither of them was concerned at the time. Amelia was with Quentin, and Gwen was a free agent. Brice remembered that Amelia had teased him about it, not that he appreciated it. Sober, he had felt guilty, but not enough for him to stop sleeping with Gwen on an infrequent basis. And now, with Happold's death, the truth would never be revealed, and if it was, then so what. An older man with a younger woman did not have the negative connotations of earlier generations, and there had been no coercion by either party, just the occasional coupling when the house was quiet.

It had not concerned Gwen, although her father, a man who had no issues when it was a tactical seduction, would not have understood why she had chosen Jeremy Brice. Gwen would have told her father that it was because she liked him and she needed a man.

***

Negril Bob's reputation had only been singed by the police, not burnt entirely, but those who had shown him respect, even bought him pints of beer in the pub, were holding back. He had phoned one of the women who would generally come round, but she was busy; he knew she wasn't.

He looked out of the window of his car as he drove past the college and there she was. He knew there would be trouble, but what did it matter? In two days time, he would board a flight to Jamaica, but till then, he would enjoy himself.

He waited for Charisa to walk around the block from the college, using a shortcut down an alley that she often took on her way back to Troy's. Negril Bob came up from behind her, covered her mouth with a scarf and tied it, then bundled her into the boot of the car and drove off. After five minutes, he stopped in an isolated area and released her from the confined space, only to tie her hands and feet. Charisa was in fear for her life. 'Don't worry,' Negril Bob said. 'I'll not harm you.'

He then set off again, having first made sure that Charisa was restrained in the back seat of the car. He drove to a small house outside London that he had rented for a couple of days. Charisa was led into the house and placed in a comfy chair. Negril Bob, a man who had killed in the past, inflicted torture, even occasionally raped a woman when he had been fighting for his country, felt no remorse.

Billy, Charisa's brother, had not followed orders. He had known the penalty for disobedience, and now he would pay. Charisa focussed on her surroundings. 'Where am I?' she said.

'You're in the country with me.'

'But why? What have I done to you?'

'Nothing yet. You knew the penalty, yet you and your brother chose to ignore me.'

'I will not let you touch me,' Charisa said.

'Do you think I care? If your brother does not pay me, then I'll take my payment another way.'

'It is wrong what you're doing.'

'So is murder, but I have done that. Taking you by force will not worry me.'

Charisa made a move towards the door; Negril Bob grabbed her roughly and threw her into the corner. Too frightened to move, she sat still. Her phone was in her handbag; it was not more than ten feet from her. She leant over and grabbed it with her tied hands. Inside she found her phone. Her captor had gone into the other room. Even though it was difficult, she managed to dial Troy. 'I'm being held captive by Negril Bob,' she said. At that moment, the man returned. He took the phone from her and smashed it on the floor, breaking it into several pieces.

'I will not take you by force,' he said. 'But tonight we will make love.'

'Never.'

'You're a beautiful woman, and I'm a good-looking man. What is the harm? One night and the debt with Billy is free. Isn't he worth that?'

Charisa faced a dilemma, she knew that. Could she trust this man, a man known for violence, but not for deceit.

***

Troy, Charisa's boyfriend, phoned Isaac; his speech was garbled. 'What is it?' Isaac said.

'It's Charisa. Negril Bob's taken her.'

'When? How do you know?'

'She phoned.'

'What did she say?'

'Nothing more, only that Negril Bob had her.'

Isaac called over to Bridget. 'Charisa Devon, instigate a search on her phone, a call in the last five minutes. See if you can give us a location.'

Billy Devon was notified; a police car would pick him up and bring him to Challis Street. Troy Hall would find his own way. Larry was on his phone checking with his contacts, and Wendy was preparing to get out and do the legwork once Bridget had pinpointed the general search area.

Superintendent Caddick had been notified; Isaac had phoned him. The man said little in response. Isaac was worried. Charisa Devon was eighteen and bright and in the clutches of a known killer. If she did not play her cards right, the man could act irrationally, maybe kill her, but not before he had satisfied his lust. Isaac felt sorry for the Devon family. They had come to England looking for a better life, and now the mother was dead, the younger son also, and the daughter had been kidnapped. Within that one family, more than several lifetimes of sadness.

Bridget came into the office. 'A village in Kent. I can only be precise to within one hundred feet.'

'That'll do,' Isaac said.

Wendy was standing at the door. 'I've got a team of ten already. We'll leave within the next six minutes.'

'Okay, keep us updated, and remember, Negril Bob is dangerous, possibly armed. Make sure you don't approach without armed response.'

'We won't.'

Larry was out of the office and meeting up with his contacts. With Negril Bob no longer exerting the same level of fear, they were more willing to talk. His first contact he met in a café, not the one where he usually enjoyed an English breakfast, although this one would have made him one as well, even though it was late afternoon. For once, he did not feel the need; maybe it was after his wife continually being at his side in the hospital, fussing over him, but perhaps it was because he was feeling much better because of his reduced weight. 'What can you tell me?' he said. Across from him sat Jimmy, one of Rasta Joe's men.

'He's not around here.'

'We know that. It's somewhere out of London.'

'Nobody has a clue. Kidnapping Charisa Devon is not a good move.'

'It'll only bring focus onto all the gangs.'

'That's why we're looking for him as well.'

For once, Larry could see, the police and the gangs were united. Charisa was an innocent, so was Billy, and Rasta Joe had been a friend of the family. His gang would assist, but how? If Negril Bob was not in London, there was not a lot they could do.

'Samuel Devon?' Larry asked.

'It was Negril Bob.'

'Proof?'

'There is none.'

***

Quentin Waverley left his wife and child at the hospital and drove over to his bank. He assembled all the staff and made an announcement that mother and child were doing well, although the founder of the bank, the man who had guided it from its humble beginnings to where it was now, was dead. Everyone had already heard by the time Waverley told them. However, there was still a sense of sorrow amongst the assembled people. George Happold hadn't been an admired leader, but for a lot of people he had formed part of their lives for many years.

After making the announcement, Waverley made his way up to Happold's office. The old man's PA was there for him, as she had been for his predecessor. 'I've moved some of your things in already,' she said.

Waverley opened the door, savoured the magnificence. He moved to the other side of Happold's desk and sat down. He leant back and closed his eyes. For once, his mind was at rest. It had been a long battle to reach this point in his life, and now he knew it had been worth it.

The personal assistant came in. Waverley looked at her; she had been with Happold from when the bank had been no more than two offices above a high street shop. It was time for her retirement.

Chapter 26

Charisa could tell that Negril Bob, apart from making sure that she could not leave, did not intend to force himself on her.

If she acquiesced to his demands, would Billy be safe? If she did not, would he let her go free? She didn't know.

Whatever happened, it was clear that she was in danger. Outside of the house where she was confined, she could see open fields, another house in the distance, but what if she made a run for it? Would Billy be safe, or would Negril Bob get there first? She believed that the man holding her had killed one of her brothers; she didn't want to be responsible for the other one's death.

It was late in the evening, four hours since she had briefly spoken to Troy. She knew he would have contacted DCI Cook; she knew they would not let her down. Negril Bob, surprisingly for a violent man, appeared to be besotted with her. Her best defence was to pretend to enjoy his company without allowing it to go too far.

'Did you kill my brother?' Charisa asked.

'Not me,' Negril Bob said. Charisa did not believe him, and she saw him divert his eyes when he replied.

Apart from that, their conversation was limited. The two of them were sitting in the living room of the house. There were books on a bookcase, but Charisa did not want to read, and Negril Bob kept looking at her in a manner that made her feel uncomfortable. But then, she wondered, why had he brought her to the house? His intention must have been dishonourable, but he made no move. She knew she was in the company of a murderer, but she could not be afraid of the man.

'Why do this? You intended to rape me, didn't you?'

'Yes. That was the deal with Billy.'

'But you're not going to.'

'You are safe with me. I'm just glad of the company.'

'Then release my bindings. I will not attempt to escape.'

'Why would you stay?'

'If you leave here, the police will capture you.'

'You'll testify against me?'

'Not me, as you haven't done anything.' Charisa did not know why she felt sorry for the man. Maybe it was because she could see some decency in him.

Negril Bob came over and sat next to her. He removed the cable ties holding her hands together. 'You remind me of my youngest sister. She's your age, doing well at school.'

'Where is she?'

'Back home in Jamaica. I intended to take you by force when I grabbed you, but now, I can't.'

Charisa shed a tear, realising that in a moment of contrition the man felt sorrow for the life he had led, the acts of violence he had committed, the anguish he had caused others by his actions. The two people, so different in many ways, shared a moment of mutual trust. She felt as though she wanted to kiss him on the cheek, the same way she would with an older brother, the same as she would with Billy.

Outside the house it was dark, the quiet of the evening disturbed by a barking dog. Negril Bob stood up from where he had been sitting and walked to the window. He looked to the left and the right. 'I'll take you home,' he said.

'Thank you,' Charisa said.

Negril Bob walked out of the front door of the house and towards a garage on one side. He bent down to pull up the roller door. On the other side of the road, a police officer trained his weapon. 'I've got a clear shot,' he said to his superior. 'There is no chance of collateral damage.'

'Take the shot,' the command was given.

Charisa sat in the house, oblivious to what was happening outside. If anyone asked her, she'd say it was not kidnapping and that she had come with him voluntarily. She did not know why she would, but she could not feel the hatred for the man that she had before.

Wendy was on the phone to Isaac, updating him as to what was happening. It had not taken them long to find the house as most of the others within the triangulated location were either empty or had been checked by the police.

There was the sound of a shot, the impact of the bullet, and Negril Bob collapsed to the ground. Inside the house, Charisa heard the noise. She came running out, only to see her kidnapper lying on the ground. 'Charisa, stay back,' Wendy shouted. 'It's Sergeant Gladstone. He's not dead.'

Charisa, not sure whether to check on Negril Bob or to retreat into the house, stood still. Two armed officers came rushing forward. One of them levelled his gun at the injured man; the other bent down to check his condition. 'He'll live,' he said.

'It's all clear,' one of the officers said. 'He's taken a bullet to the shoulder.'

Negril Bob moved slightly. Charisa walked over to him. 'He was going to take me home,' she said.

'That's as maybe,' one of the officers said. 'Our instructions were to immobilise him, shoot to kill if necessary.'

Wendy came down the driveway, put her arms around Charisa. 'I'm glad you're okay.'

'He didn't do anything. We just talked,' Charisa said. 'Have you told Troy and Billy that I'm fine?'

'They know. They're with DCI Cook at Challis Street.'

'I want to go to the hospital with Negril Bob.'

'He's under arrest for kidnapping. He's also a suspect in the murder of two people, one of them being your brother.'

'He said I reminded him of his sister,' Charisa said.

Wendy could see that the traumatic events had left her confused. 'We'll follow the ambulance in my car if you like. Troy and Billy can meet us at the hospital.'

'Thank you.'

***

Larry met Jimmy, his best contact with the gangs in the area. Jimmy was not a drinker, or, at least, not to the extent of Rasta Joe. There was no longer an excuse for Larry to drink as much as before, and for that, he was pleased. 'You've heard about Negril Bob?' Larry said.

'A lot of people were frightened of him around here.'

'He's not coming back. If we can't get him for murder, then we'll get him for kidnapping.'

'What do you want to know?' Jimmy said.

'You've always been careful before in what you said.'

'Before there was a Negril Bob to worry about. If we must, we'll tell you what you need to know.'

'We?'

'The other gangs. You're being here all the time is not wanted.'

'There'll always be a police presence looking into gang activity.'

'But it won't be you. It's you and DCI Cook they don't like.'

'Why's that?'

'You two are persistent. You keep looking for dirt.'

Larry wasn't sure if that was a compliment, or whether some members of the police were taking bribes to look the other way.

'Rasta Joe? Was Negril Bob there?'

'Yes.'

'Can we prove it?'

'Not without Morris Beckford and Marcus Roots.'

'They've already been charged with one murder; they're not likely to admit to another.'

'That's your problem. Beckford's not that smart; he tends to talk too much sometimes.'

'Samuel Devon?'

'Beckford and Roots, probably Negril Bob.'

'Probably?'

'Devon was trying to be smart. Most times, it's a severe beating, maybe a knife wound, but they don't normally kill someone for their first offence,' Jimmy said. So far, he had kept to one pint, the same as Larry.

'Then why was he thrown into the river?'

'Beckford had a temper. And Samuel Devon had a big mouth.'

'You think he upset him?'

'It's possible, but Beckford and Roots wouldn't have done it without Negril Bob giving them the order.'

'But it can't be proven?'

'Not a chance.'

Even the beating up of Billy Devon was unproven. Beckford and Roots were the keys; reduced sentences a possibility for providing testimony against their former leader.

***

Negril Bob's shoulder wound was minor. The armed officer's intensive training had ensured no lasting damage, but if the man had not collapsed to the ground, he would have fired another shot. One thing was certain as Negril Bob walked out of the front door of the house: he wasn't going back. Wendy had expected the worst, was relieved that nothing had happened.

At the hospital, Charisa was reunited with Troy and Billy in the reception area. Inside, in one of the rooms, Negril Bob sat up in his bed. His shoulder had been bandaged, the bullet having passed through it. Outside his room were two uniformed police officers.

The doctor had warned about taxing the man; Isaac, cognisant of the need to respect the doctor's advice but desperate to wrap up the current investigations, sat to one side of Negril Bob's bed.

'You've been charged with kidnapping,' Isaac said.

'Charisa will tell you it was a misunderstanding.'

'We know that, but we have proof that she was locked in the boot of your car, and then the back seat, and that restraint was used. That's a clear conviction for us. The prison term is at the discretion of a judge.'

'In my case, a long time, then?'

'That depends on you.'

'What do you mean?'

'Samuel Devon, Rasta Joe, and Dave Dallimore.'

'What about them?'

'We know that you were with Beckford and Roots when Rasta Joe was killed.'

'Where's your proof?'

'Dave Dallimore was our proof, but you had him killed,' Larry said.

'I've never heard of him,' Negril Bob said.

'He was a homeless man that I had found. Beckford and Roots had followed me.'

'This is the first time I've heard of this.'

'You're a liar,' Isaac said. 'We know you weren't there when Dallimore was killed, but we know it was you who gave the order. That's still conspiracy to murder.'

'My lawyer will have it thrown out.'

Isaac knew that he probably would. A phone call at the approximate time was insufficient evidence.

'Samuel Devon,' Isaac said.

'What about him?'

'Beckford and Roots will talk.'

'Why would they do that? If, as you say, you've got them for one murder, they're hardly likely to admit to another.'

'Beckford might. He's not too bright.'

Both Isaac and Larry knew they had their man, but the proof was uncertain. There was no way that Beckford and Roots would be advised by their lawyer to admit to an additional murder. The kidnapping charge could be proved, and if Charisa kept to her story that the man had behaved impeccably, then his sentence was not likely to be too long.

Outside the ward, Charisa waited to see Negril Bob. Troy was understandably not pleased with the situation, although Billy was relieved that he was off the hook. He would have done anything to have saved his sister, but in the end, it had been the gang leader who had provided the solution.

***

With some resolution to three murders, Isaac and Larry returned to Challis Street. 'It's not very satisfactory, is it, guv?' Larry said.

'We'll have the man off the street, but you're right. There's not much more we can do.'

Caddick walked into the office. 'You've had some luck,' he said to Isaac.

'Luck?'

'Finding the woman. Rape her, did he?'

Isaac glared at the man. 'Don't you check your messages?'

'Why? Should I?'

'I messaged you from the hospital. The woman was untouched.'

'Good, good,' Caddick said. Isaac could see that he revelled in the salacious and that his mind was in the gutter. 'Convictions for the murders?'

'We can prove Dave Dallimore's murder.'

'Who?'

'The homeless man in my reports. The ones I sit in this office until late at night preparing.'

'I don't have time to read them. I'm too busy.'

'Then why am I preparing them?'

'I'll read them in future,' Caddick said. Isaac knew he wouldn't.

There had been another terrorist attack in the city, two people killed. The rumour was that Davies's hold on his position as commissioner was in question again. Caddick was looking for brownie points to impress whoever he was sucking up to. Isaac had no intention of giving him anything other than the facts.

'We'll not prove Samuel Devon's murder, probably not Rasta Joe's,' Isaac said.

'But you know who killed them?'

'Unless they confess we'll not get a conviction. We'll secure a conviction against two of them for the murder of Dave Dallimore. The other one will serve time for kidnapping.'

'It's not much to report,' Caddick said. Isaac felt like telling the man to get off his back. Sure, it wasn't the result they wanted, but it was a result.

Caddick left before he could irritate them anymore.

'You'll take his job when they move him out,' Larry said.

Isaac did not comment. There were still two murders to solve.

Chapter 27

Gwen Waverley watched the news on the television at home. At her side, the newborn infant. Her husband was still in his office at the bank. She wondered whether he was checking the figures, or he was with his personal assistant, having sent her father's PA on extended leave while they figured out her retirement package.

Her father, she knew, had been having an affair with his PA for thirty-five of the forty odd years that she had worked for him. The discretion of both of them had been absolute, and Gwen had only become aware of it when she was in her mid-twenties. Her father, a kindred spirit, had confided in her, knowing that her reaction would not be one of shock, only of acceptance. And if her father could sleep with his PA, then so could Quentin, her husband.

Gwen looked over at the baby and realised that life was as it should be: two healthy children, a loving husband, even if he strayed occasionally. She switched off the television and picked up her child. She knew that Quentin would be looking for ways to secure the controlling interest in the bank, but she would never allow it. Men such as her husband were to be admired for their resolute desire to succeed at any cost, and without any compunction about who they trod on or hurt on the way, although there was no way that her husband would ever get the better of her.

She put her child back into its bassinet and went and poured herself a drink. She then phoned her husband.

'I'm busy,' Quentin Waverley replied. He omitted to say that it was busy with his PA, busy cementing their relationship in George Happold's old office, now his.

'I just want to let you know that we make a good team and that you'll do a good job looking after the bank,' Gwen said.

It was rare for his wife to phone him, even more unusual for her to comment positively on their relationship, but then, he had noticed her predilection for drinking more than she should in recent months, and with her father recently dead and a new child, he thought it understandable. Her timing could not have been worse.

His PA, a younger woman than Gwen, and very capable professionally, as well as personally, took advantage of her elevated position in the bank. No longer the mistress of a senior director, she was now the mistress of the chairman. It was a life she chose for herself, and Quentin Waverley was not difficult to manipulate, especially for a beguiling female intent on seduction. She knew about him and Gwen, and before that, Amelia. She did not want the involvement of a marriage or children, she wanted the life of a liberated woman, and the new chairman had ensured that for the last year, and she knew he would in the future. She also knew that some of his financial dealings had not been altogether legal and that he had been syphoning bank funds into a separate account overseas. She admired the man that she had taken as her lover. And on the phone was his wife, pretending to care about her husband when she did not.

She had observed Gwen Waverley since before she had married Quentin. It took a woman to know a woman, and she had seen it from the start, that she and Gwen were the same, although one was the daughter of a bank chairman, the other the daughter of an accountant.

There was begrudging respect from each woman for the other, she knew that, but also a battle for dominance. She knew who would win if she could only keep her boss under control, and she had the goods.

When Gwen Waverley's phone call ended, the PA focussed back on the chairman. After the lovemaking in the office had concluded, and he was sitting back in his chair, a smile on his face, she went back to her room outside. She switched on her laptop and looked for an upmarket flat, the type that befitted the mistress of a merchant bank's chairman. Mayfair, or maybe

Park Lane, and there was a nice little Audi that appealed. She knew they would be hers.

***

Superintendent Caddick realised that his DCI knew more about how to run a police investigation than he did. And now, in his office, he was confronted by additional responsibilities: the need to deal with staffing levels, the demands of preparing an annual budget, the need to make a presentation at Scotland Yard to his superiors. He was not nervous of standing up in front of a group, but now he had to stand in front of those who would ask questions which he would not be able to answer.

He phoned the one person who could help him. 'Commissioner, I have to present an updated report on the department. I'm not sure what to do,' Caddick admitted.

Commissioner Alwyn Davies did not want to hear from members of his team, and especially not Caddick. He knew the deficiencies of the man, but had only put him in Goddard's place because he did not like the former head of Homicide.

Davies knew that Isaac Cook was competent, although he would not admit it, and that Seth Caddick, apart from his loyalty, was not, and now the man was in trouble, as was he. Too many terrorist attacks in the city and the man he had put in charge of Counter Terrorism Command was struggling, the same as Caddick, the same as he was.

He had studied his contract, knew that if he could hold out for another thirteen months, he would be able to resign with a sixty per cent retention of his pension, but he did not know if even that was possible.

Davies knew the forces were gathering, and Caddick was about to go down the tube. As for terrorism, he didn't know what to do. He wished that he had let sleeping dogs lie, and had left competent people in their places rather than bringing in his team. And what did they give? Not a lot when he had to deal with senior politicians who were baying for his blood.

'I can't help you,' Davies said.

218

Caddick, isolated in his office, could see no way out. He looked through the previous reports presented by Goddard: meticulous, full of detail. He took the template and filled in what he could, which was not sufficient. Panicking, he knew that a solution to the murder of Amelia Brice would give him some breathing space, but how to achieve it? His DCI was in charge, and wouldn't allow him to become involved, but he was the superintendent, he could do what he wanted. He closed the report and left his office.

***

Wendy Gladstone met up with Shirley O'Rourke. The woman had been released on her own surety; her trial was in six weeks' time.

'There's a good chance I'll get off,' Shirley O'Rourke said.

The two women met in a restaurant close to Challis Street. 'Your business?' Wendy asked. She had to admit that the woman who sat next to her looked better than previously.

'I've closed it, sold my house.'

'I thought you liked that house?'

'I did, but mounting a good defence costs money.'

'I'm sorry about that.'

'There's nothing to be sorry about. I committed the offence, I'll admit to it, but I'll state extenuating circumstances: recent divorce, family tragedy.'

'Are they true?'

'In part. I'll leave it up to my lawyer. And if I serve time, I've still enough money to live well. It's strange, when I was there in that office, all that I wanted was money. Greed, I suppose, but now a comfortable life, free of worry, will do me.'

Wendy felt some kindness for the woman. A waiter came over, the two women ordered.

'And what about you, Sergeant Gladstone?' Shirley O'Rourke said.

'Another few more years, and then I'll take it easy.'

'The same as me.'

'You were ruthless in business. You did not always treat your employees well.'

'I'll not deny it. Business is tough, and I was tougher than most. Maybe I regret some of it, but not much. It was fun while it lasted.'

'We've still not solved the murders of Amelia Brice and Christine Devon.'

'You've had some success. I read about it in the newspaper.'

'The murder of one man.'

'And the others?'

'Innocent until proven guilty. We'll put those responsible in prison, but for other crimes.'

'Amelia used to go around with some rough men.'

'Rasta Joe, did you know him?'

'Not really. I used to see most of the gang members from time to time. They were always civil to me.'

'Violent men.'

'Not with me. I never had any trouble with them.'

'Why do you think Amelia liked them?'

'Amelia was rich, spoilt, never worked a day in her life, or not seriously anyway. She was looking for the thrill, the chance to walk on the wild side.'

'Anyone she preferred in particular?'

'I wasn't taking any notice. I knew her, of course. We'd say hello, nothing more. What she got up to wasn't my business.'

'But you were friendly with her father?'

'He never asked me to keep a watch out for her.'

'He must have been disturbed by her behaviour. Did he ever mention it?'

'Only once.'

'Did you ever see Amelia leave the pub with anyone in particular?'

'Not me. I'd leave early. I saw her there once with another woman.'

'Who?'

220

'The one that she shared the house with.'

'Gwen Waverley?'

'Gwen, yes, her. I never knew her surname.'

'When was this?'

'One year, maybe longer. The woman didn't stay long.'

'According to our information, they were no longer friends then.'

'I don't think they were when I saw them. The other woman, she wasn't into the Rasta men, not like Amelia, and Amelia looked angry.'

'You've not mentioned this before.'

'It was a long time before her death.'

'It's relevant,' Wendy said. 'Anything else you've not told us?'

'No, that's it. I just saw the woman that one time.'

The two women ate their meals. They shared a bottle of wine, chatted like old friends. Wendy was anxious to finish the meal and to get back to Challis Street with what to her was vital information; Shirley O'Rourke was happy to take her time.

It was two hours later when the two women parted with a brief hug. Wendy had arrested the other woman, but there was no lasting animosity.

***

Superintendent Caddick came looking for a friend. Isaac knew that he would only offer him civility. The presence of the man, agitated and looking lost, in his office had come as something of a surprise to Isaac. Usually the man's visits had been those of a blustering senior attempting to throw his weight around, but not this time.

'DCI, Isaac, we need to wrap up these investigations.'

'We're working as hard as we can.'

'What do you have that I can pass on?'

'Pass on to who?'

'I have people to report to, the same as you.'

Isaac did not feel inclined to talk. Wendy's brief message had intrigued him, and she was due in the office in five minutes. He wanted to see her, not his superintendent.

'We are doing our best,' Isaac said.

'Do you need my help?' Caddick said. Isaac knew that something was wrong, but he did not know what. He had been told of Caddick from other stations, even seen it himself in the past, but the man's behaviour was out of character.

'This department needs a free hand, and I need to be more actively involved,' Isaac said. Whatever he said to the man, he, at least, intended to act professionally.

'You have a free hand.'

'Not with these reports that I have to submit.'

'Okay, forget the detail for the time being,' Caddick said. Isaac sensed a minor victory, but not because of his persuasive argument.

'Thank you. We have a development. I will be pursuing this with my team. I will keep you informed.'

Caddick sat still, unsure how to proceed. Upstairs, in his office, he had a presentation to prepare: full of facts, short on hyperbole. And downstairs, he got straight answers to straight questions, but nothing that would help him. He felt trapped, and not for the first time in his career. Sometimes, before, there had been a breakthrough at the right time, and he had been able to take the credit and to sideline the person who should have received it. Isaac Cook, he knew, was well-connected; a man who could not be moved easily. If the commissioner was not behind his superintendent, he was trapped. Caddick reacted in the way that a trapped animal does; he went on the attack.

'DCI, I need results. I've let you off the reports, vital as they are, but I need something in return. You've got two days to wrap up this case.'

'And then?' Isaac saw the change, knew that something was happening.

'I'll bring in another man.'

'You've not got the authority to remove me at such short notice. I will need a warning, and then there'll need to be a handover.'

'You can stay and assist.'

'I'm due for some leave. It may be a good time,' Isaac said, knowing full well that he did not intend to take leave, had no need to. But he had to see how far Caddick could be pushed.

'You're subject to regulations. Deserting a murder investigation at a crucial juncture will not be seen favourably.'

'And what do you think changing out the SIO will be seen as? Superintendent, you're in trouble, and you want me to help you out.'

'I need support, not hostility,' Caddick said, his voice raised.

'There is no hostility here. We have shown respect for your title.'

'But not for me.'

'Respect is earned, not given.'

Caddick realised that he was indulging in an argument he could not win. He retreated from the office as Wendy came in. She acknowledged the man; he nodded his head in return.

Chapter 28

Gwen Waverley, aware of another visit from the Challis Street Homicide Department, had attempted to put them off. When her lawyer had questioned Isaac about why it was so important, considering that the woman's father had just died, his reply was only to say vital new evidence.

Isaac felt, as did Wendy, that Gwen Waverley and Amelia Brice meeting was significant, and if Shirley O'Rourke's timing was correct, then Gwen was already married to the other's former lover.

The door at the Waverley house was opened reluctantly. Ushered into the living room, Isaac and Wendy were given tea. They sat patiently waiting.

After a few minutes, the sliding door from the dining room opened, and Gwen Waverley came through. 'We can do it here or in the dining room,' she said.

'Here will be fine,' Isaac said.

Another man came in. 'This is my lawyer, Bruce Bamford,' Gwen said. Isaac and Wendy shook the man's hand. Isaac had not met him before.

'I believe that you've questioned my client excessively,' Bamford said.

'My apologies, but this is a murder enquiry,' Isaac said.

'Very well. Could you please ask your questions and leave.'

'Mrs Waverley,' Isaac turned to face the woman. 'We have confirmed that on one occasion you met with Amelia Brice.'

'Not since she caught me with Quentin.'

'According to a reliable source, you met her at the Westbourne pub in Bayswater about one year ago. At that time, you would have been married to your husband. Our witness will testify in court that this is correct.'

'Do you have a date?' Bamford asked.

'We are obtaining more precise information, but no. At this present time, our statement is correct, the date is to be confirmed.'

'Then it's not admissible.'

'It's alright,' Gwen said. 'I did meet her one time.'

'But you've always denied it,' Isaac said.

'I had hoped to conceal the fact about my husband and Amelia.'

'Did you confront her?'

'At the pub, yes. It was the only time, that's the truth. I knew she was going up there of a night, and I needed to tell her to back off.'

Wendy could see the woman was flustered.

'Do you believe that your husband was having an affair with Amelia Brice?' Isaac said.

'He was still sleeping with her, I know that.'

'Your husband has always denied it.'

'My husband is a liar. The man can't help himself.'

'You're husband is the Q that is mentioned in Amelia Brice's diary?'

'I believe so.'

'You've denied this in the past. In fact, Mrs Waverley, you have a habit of contradicting yourself. If your husband was having an affair with her, why was she so frightened of him?'

'That's Amelia. She was always a little strange.'

'Tell us about that night at the pub.'

'I found her there. It was early in the evening, too early for the men she liked to have come in. I went and sat down next to her.'

'What was her reaction?'

'She was shocked to see me there. She said nothing at first.'

'And then after?'

'For a while, we were old friends again, laughing and joking. Eventually, we got around to Quentin and how I'd stolen him away from her, and how he wanted to go back to her. That's according to Amelia.'

'Is it true?'

'Which part?'

'Both.'

'I didn't steal him. Their romance was on the rocks. I wanted Quentin, always did, so I made sure he was mine. You know the story, so don't ask me to repeat it.'

'Did your husband want to go back to her?'

'She thought so, and no doubt, in the heat of passion, he would have said what she wanted to hear. My husband, DCI Cook, is a philanderer.'

'And you do not object?' Wendy said.

'Of course I object, but men such as Quentin have large egos that need to be fed. He'll stay with me and be a good father to our children.'

'But your husband continued to see her. According to her diary, up until just before she died. Mrs Waverley, why did Amelia Brice die? Why did Christine Devon die? What did they know?'

'This questioning is unacceptable,' Gwen Waverley's lawyer said.

'It's either here or at Challis Street today. The reason for the two women's deaths is in this house,' Isaac said. 'It's either Mrs Waverley or her husband, and I don't know which of the two, if either, is telling the truth.'

Wendy thought that her DCI was pushing hard, a tactic he had used in the past. Rapid-fire questions, trying to break the slow and reasoned answers of the other person, but she knew that Gwen Waverley was unlikely to make a mistake.

It was clear that the woman was uncomfortable with the situation. She looked over at her lawyer, hoping that he could help her. She had nothing to answer to; on the contrary, she was innocent of all charges, bar the one of being ambitious and driven. Gwen Waverley looked over at the two questioning her: one, a woman in her fifties, her accent indicative of her background, the other, a smart, attractive man, not English heritage. She felt that she should be judged and questioned by her peers, not those that she deemed inferior. She thought back to that night in the pub with Amelia, the fascination that her former friend had for the men that came in. The place had repulsed her. It hadn't in the past, but she had moved on from being rebellious and an easy lay.

To her, Quentin Waverley had been the ideal subject for her to snare: well-educated, well-spoken, a good family, good breeding stock. The fact that he was a man who could lead her father's bank when he was gone was a benefit. She remembered how she had snared him, knowing that he loved Amelia, but then, how could he not. Gwen knew that Amelia was a woman that men found attractive, a willowy blonde with an approachable personality, whereas she was not.

The two women had met at boarding school: one, the child of an abrasive media personality, the other, the child of a punctilious banker. They should not have been friends, but they bonded from day one. After that, at school and after they had left, where one was, so was the other. When one was getting drunk, or making out with a boy or, in later years, a man, so was the other, and then Quentin came into Amelia's life, and her friend started to change.

And then the bond that had made Amelia and her almost like sisters was broken.

Gwen had never felt such loneliness, she knew that. Her father was a cold man; a man who would indulge her every whim, but not a man who was capable of showing affection, not even to her mother, who had remained steadfastly in the family home, rarely venturing out, until she had succumbed in her late sixties to cancer.

Her father had battled on, sorry that she had gone, but then he had his personal assistant. Not that it shocked or concerned Gwen, as that was what powerful men did.

After Amelia had spent time with Quentin, even moving in with him, Gwen had confided in her father about her love for the man, the possibility that he may be the solution to the lack of a male heir to take over the bank. Her father would have let her have the chairmanship, but she did not have the necessary financial acumen. It wasn't a major issue, and it was not enough to prevent her passing her exams at school, even obtaining a degree in English, but it was enough to make it impossible for her to consider taking on the bank. That needed a genius-level understanding of finance and the law.

Quentin Waverley had all the right attributes; her father had checked him out, even met his parents. In the end, George and Gwen Happold had put in place a plan, a plan that would upset Amelia, but as her father had said, you can't make an omelette without breaking an egg. But it was her friend, and she was going to steal her man away from her.

'Mrs Waverley,' Wendy said, 'is it a fact that your treatment of Amelia led to her disruptive behaviour?'

'Yes, I believe that, but I can't be expected to shoulder the blame for her death. People fall in love, fall out of love, move on, but she couldn't. She remained committed to Quentin, and he was back there, sniffing around.'

'But she was frightened of him, you know that. Do you know why?'

'No, even assuming he is the Q.'

'We are convinced that he is,' Isaac said. 'Why would she be frightened? You say your husband was sleeping with the woman. We are certain that you, Mrs Waverley, know the truth, the same as your father always knew the truth.'

'Okay, Amelia knew that I had been sleeping with her father.'

'Jeremy Brice?'

'That's the only father she's got.'

'Even if it sounds bizarre, why is that a problem?'

'It's not now.'

'What do you mean?'

'It was before I married Quentin. I was young, promiscuous, and Jeremy, he was there a lot of the time. One thing led to another, and we ended up sleeping together. Satisfied now?'

'Why is it not a problem now?'

'My father detested the man; Jeremy detested him. It goes back some time, and if my father had known about Jeremy and me, he would have probably changed his will.'

'To what?'

'I don't know. He could have even considered not leaving me the fifty-one per cent share of the bank. He could have set up a consortium to run it, maybe even sold it.'

'His anger would have been that severe?'

'My father was no saint, but my sleeping with an older man would have been enough.'

'Even after you were married?'

'Don't get me wrong. He wouldn't have left me penniless, but I wouldn't have the bank.'

'It's that important?'

'To me it is.'

'And Quentin knew about this?'

'Amelia, whenever he saw him, she'd bring it up, and how she was going to tell my father about my sleeping with hers.'

'Are you now telling us that you knew about your husband and Amelia?'

'I knew. He was still in love with her, and with me. He was confused, that's all.'

'And you removed that confusion by having her killed? But why Christine Devon? Did she know about you and Jeremy Brice?'

'You're leading my client,' Bamford said. ' Mrs Waverley will not answer any more questions today.'

Isaac realised that he had pushed more than he should, but now there was a motive. It seemed weak in itself, but, if, as the woman had indicated, her father may not have ensured the handover of the bank to her, then she had a reason to want Amelia dead.

'A devious woman,' Wendy said on the drive back to London.

'Capable of murder?' Isaac asked.

'Hell hath no fury like a woman scorned.'

'Was she scorned?'

'She was, or she thought it was possible. Her husband is back on with Amelia; he's screwing his PA, and whoever else. His wife collects possessions, men included. She does not give them away.'

'She couldn't have killed Amelia Brice and Christine Devon,' Isaac said.

'Nor could Quentin Waverley.'

'Why not?'

'He's not a professional killer, we know that, but there's a more important consideration.'

'And that is?'

'You've been to Christine Devon's flat. What do you reckon?'

'Unless he was good at disguise, he'd never get through.'

'Even with a disguise, the area is a no-go for anyone white, unless they're carrying a badge.'

'Even the uniforms don't go there unless they're in threes.'

'Which means?

'Gwen or Quentin Waverley could have organised someone else to commit the murders.'

'Either or both.'

'They'll do anything to protect their lives,' Isaac said.

***

Gwen Waverley sat with her lawyer after Isaac and Wendy left. 'Are you involved? he asked.

'With murder? Why do you ask? You've known me since I was a child.'

'That's why I'm asking. I handle your father's legal matters, as well.'

'I'm not sorry that Amelia's dead.'

'That's what I thought. Nor am I,' Bamford said.

'Why you? What's it got to do with you?'

'Your father paid me to make problems go away.'

230

'What sort of problems?'

'Any that could threaten him.'

'Were there any?'

'An influential man such as your father, what do you think?'

'Over the years there must have been someone or other who got in the way, but murder? That's something else.'

'I can only advise if you level with me. Gwen, you're your father's daughter. You would have no problems with taking the appropriate action if you and your children were threatened, would you?'

'No, but I did not kill Amelia.'

'But you know who did?'

'I know people who would have been capable.'

'If you're innocent, then say no more for now. If you aren't, then tell me, or if steps need to be taken to protect the truth, then I must know. My discretion is assured.'

Chapter 29

Quentin Waverley had been forewarned by Gwen about what had happened when she met DCI Cook. He had not expected the man to be in his office with his sergeant within hours of leaving his wife.

'DCI Cook, I'm a busy man,' Waverley said.

'So are we. Your wife had told us facts that we never knew before. Facts which give you and your wife a motive.'

'I knew about Gwen and Jeremy. It was before Gwen and me.'

'Did you know at the time?'

'I suspected something. Gwen confirmed it a few months back. She had lost her temper, started talking irrationally. She let it slip.'

'Then why were you threatening Amelia?'

'Amelia had met with Gwen in the pub sometime before. Their meeting didn't go well, and Amelia accused Gwen of stealing her man and her father.'

'Amelia knew from before?'

'Even when I was with her, she knew, but she never told me. Amelia worshipped her father, although he didn't always reciprocate, and I don't think she ever approved of him and Gwen.'

'What was your reaction when you found out?'

'What do you think? My wife's past life included sleeping with the father of my former girlfriend. I was shocked at first, then angry. I may have called Gwen a whore.'

'May?'

'I did. Not that she liked it, but that's what she was, still is.'

'It's hardly the basis for a long-lasting marriage,' Wendy said. She had seen the personal assistant outside, noticed that she was attractive and knew how to smile at her DCI, look down her nose at his sergeant. Wendy knew a tart when she saw one.

'What do you want me to say? You've met Gwen, you met her father. Both of them were without shame. Her father, pretending to be a beacon of decency, allowing his daughter to cheapen herself by getting me in her bed.'

'It takes two,' Wendy said.

'I know that, and I can't say I'd act differently, even now.'

'We know about you and your personal assistant.

'Gwen?'

'She told us.'

'I've no intention of apologising for my actions. You're here because of Amelia and the other woman, and besides, your opinion of me, good or bad, does not interest me. I've assumed the chairmanship of this bank, and I intend to succeed. Now, if you don't have anything more to discuss, I'll bid you goodbye.'

'I'm sorry, Mr Waverley, but it doesn't work like that. We can either discuss this here or down at Challis Street. The decision is yours.'

'Ten minutes, that's all I can give you.'

'Do you want your lawyer to be present?' Isaac asked.

'No. I don't intend to compromise myself, and you've no evidence against me.'

'Should there be some?'

'Get on with your questions, please,' Waverley said. Isaac could see the man becoming annoyed.

'We know now that you are the Q mentioned in Amelia's diary. According to her, she was frightened of you, even considered ending her life because of it.'

'Amelia had flights of fancy. You can't believe all that she wrote.'

'Unfortunately, Mr Waverley, we do. It is clear that Amelia, increasingly irrational, not necessarily because of you, was threatening to reveal the fact that your wife and Jeremy Brice had been sleeping together. And we know from your wife what your father-in-law's reaction would have been. The man had some old-fashioned ideas, not that it stopped him keeping his mistress as his PA for all those years, even when his wife was ill.'

'It's not stopping you either, Mr Waverley,' Wendy said.

'As you say. I'll not deny it, why should I?'

'Mr Waverley, have you no shame? Your wife sleeps with Amelia's father, you carry on a friendship with the man, even after you know, and then on the one hand, you're sleeping with Amelia, and on the other, you're threatening her to keep quiet or else.'

'You make it sound sordid,' Waverley said.

'It is sordid,' Wendy said.

'It may be according to your proletarian values, not ours,' Waverley said. Isaac had wondered how long it would be before the personal insults started. Now he knew he had Waverley on the ropes.

'Mr Waverley, I put it to you that you murdered Amelia and then you travelled the short distance to Christine Devon's flat and killed her. How do you plead? Guilty?'

'You've got it all wrong. Amelia liked Christine Devon; told her once her life story. It was dynamite. Gwen, the daughter of George Happold, and Jeremy Brice in a love triangle with Brice's daughter's lover. There would have been a media frenzy. The Devon woman had no money; she could have sold the story. And if it were out in the open, George Happold would be forced to defend the honour of his daughter. It would have affected the value of the bank, confidence in the chairman would have been lost. It's all to do with perception. Happold, he treasured his reputation, and now it was about to go south. Christine Devon was the key, not Amelia. If one died, they both had to die.'

'Christine Devon would never have told anyone. You killed her for no reason.'

'I didn't kill her.'

'You've just confessed.'

'No, I haven't.'

'Then what have you just said?'

'I've told you what happened, but I've not told you who gave the instruction and who committed the crime.'

'Mr Waverley, you've allowed us to question you here without a lawyer, knowing full well that you intended to tell us the truth. Will you allow your wife to be charged with murder? Was this your intention all along?'

'It's a hard world. George Happold taught me well, so did Gwen.'

The two police officers sat still for twenty seconds, allowing all that had been said to sink in.

In their careers, they had met rogues and villains of all shapes and colours, but none so deceitful and callous as the man who sat in front of them, a smug look on his face.

'Was it all worth it?' Isaac said.

'Whatever happens, I will hold all of Gwen's assets in trust for our children until they turn twenty-one. By that time, I will have brought this bank into the twenty-first century and made plenty of money for myself. I may even try for a peerage.

'Mr Waverley, you are a despicable human being,' Wendy said.

'The truth belongs to the victor,' Waverley said. 'Your opinions of me count for little. And now, I'll bid you goodbye.'

Outside the building, Isaac and Wendy sat on a bench. 'The foulest man I've ever met,' Wendy said.

'I'd agree, and legally he's not answerable for any crime, other than withholding evidence' Isaac said.

'What's next?'

'Gwen Waverley, and this time at Challis Street.'

***

Gwen Waverley arrived at Challis Street Police Station at seven in the evening. Bruce Bamford, her lawyer, was with her. Isaac and Wendy were to conduct the interview; Larry would listen in from the other room. Seth Caddick, somehow surviving the presentation at Scotland Yard, was with Larry.

Isaac went through the formalities. It was nearly 8 p.m. 'Mrs Waverley, we have a clear statement from your husband that it was you who organised the murders of Amelia Brice and Christine Devon, with the sole purpose of preventing your affair with Jeremy Brice from becoming public knowledge.'

'Quentin said that?'

'He did. We will access all your phone records, bank statements.'

'Are you charging my client?' Bamford said.

'Based on the statement from Quentin Waverley, we have enough to hold Mrs Waverley.'

'Quentin, he finally wised up,' Gwen said. 'I thought he didn't have it in him.'

'Did you expect to get away with this?' Wendy said.

'Where's the proof? I couldn't have committed the murders, neither could Quentin.'

'Based on your husband's statement, there is a case to answer.'

'DCI Cook, I request a break to confer with my client,' Bamford said.

'Twenty-five minutes. We'll reconvene at 9 p.m. Is that acceptable?'

'Yes. We will be ready.'

Isaac and Wendy went in the other room where Larry and Caddick were. 'A conviction this time?' the superintendent asked.

'We're hopeful,' Isaac replied. He noticed that their senior was relaxed.

'She didn't kill the women,' Larry said.

'We know that, but her husband is willing to give evidence that she is behind the women's murders.'

'What kind of bastard would do that?'

'The Waverley kind,' Larry said. 'They're each as bad as the other.'

'And you all thought I was,' Caddick said. It was the first time that the man had spoken civilly to his Homicide team. Isaac didn't like it, as if he was starting to feel comfortable, as if he was going to stay.

After the agreed period, Isaac and Wendy reentered the interview room.

236

'My client has a statement,' Bamford said.

'Very well,' Isaac said.

'I, Gwen Waverley, wish to state that the accusations made by my husband are scurrilous and untrue, and I will defend myself against all charges. I did know about my husband and his ongoing relationship with Amelia Brice, and the threats levelled against her to not tell my father about my relationship with Jeremy Brice. My husband has subsequently found a loophole in my father's will that will give him effective control of all my assets if I am convicted of a criminal offence. This is why he is making these accusations.

'He is my husband. I love him. I do not understand why he is doing this. That is the end of my statement.'

Wendy could see that the woman had been crying, although she could feel no sadness for her.

'DCI Cook, it's husband against wife,' Bamford said. 'Whose word are you going to believe?'

'Both are lying,' Isaac said. 'We have been conducting investigations into the financial dealings of both Quentin and Gwen Waverley. Certain anomalies need explaining. Mrs Waverley, you are innocent of the murders of Amelia Brice and Christine Devon.'

'But...'

'That does not, however, excuse you from the consequences of your actions. Two women have died because of you and your husband's shameless greed. Unfortunately, you two will not be together for a very long period of time. Thirty minutes ago, your husband was arrested. We have proof that he paid for their deaths. You are free to go, and I hope that your conscience allows you to sleep, knowing full well that the father of your children will be in jail.'

***

Quentin Waverley sat in another interview room as his wife left the police station. Wendy watched her go and turned to Isaac.

'There's more hatred and greed in that woman than anyone we've ever dealt with.'

'She will have a lifetime to reflect; a lifetime to figure out what to tell her children about their father.'

'Let's deal with the man now,' Isaac said.

Larry stood in the room adjoining where the interview was to be conducted. Superintendent Caddick was not there. Larry assumed he was on the phone to Commissioner Davies, attempting to gain early credit for solving the murders.

'Quentin Waverley, you will be formally charged with conspiracy to murder of Amelia Brice and Christine Devon,' Isaac said. Bamford remained in the police station, as Waverley and his wife used the same lawyer.

'How, why?'

'You were concerned, as was your wife, that George Happold would change his will, as well as prevent the handover of the bank, if it were revealed that his daughter was involved with Jeremy Brice. There was always the risk that if Christine Devon died, Amelia would speak to George Happold. It may be that your wife is complicit in this.'

'Why did I tell you it was my wife?'

'You knew that if she were tried, she'd be acquitted due to lack of evidence. And by then, time would have moved on, and the original investigation would be given to another team of police officers, and you'd be in the clear. However, you made one error.'

'What's that?'

'Rasta Joe.'

'Who's he?'

'He is a gang leader who was killed by Negril Bob and his people. He was killed for two reasons: one, he was friendly with Detective Inspector Larry Hill, and two, he had seen you and Negril Bob together. It has been a considered possibility for some time that Negril Bob was involved, but until he was arrested for kidnapping, nobody had been willing to tell us everything about him. It was one of Rasta Joe's gang who identified you after we had arrested Negril Bob. Up until then, neither Rasta Joe nor his gang was willing to discuss Negril Bob, such was the fear of the man in the community.'

'Negril Bob, who's he?'

'Negril Bob, his real name is Robert Gosling, is a known killer. He was a professional soldier, former SAS. We are not sure how you connected with him, but we know that you were seen with him on one occasion and we have evidence, recently unearthed, that a sum of two hundred thousand pounds was deposited into his account.'

'It was Gwen's idea,' Waverley said. It was not the first time that Isaac had seen it. The link was not yet made, and would probably be difficult to make, but presented with unassailable facts, the guilty often admit to the crime, almost as if they are attending confession and asking for the priest's blessing.

'We will check, and your wife may have been capable, but it is you, Mr Waverley, who is guilty. We will require a full written confession, duly signed by yourself.'

'You'd better do what he says,' Bamford said.

Isaac turned to Larry. 'Arrange for Negril Bob to be brought to Challis Street. We need to charge him with the murders of Amelia Brice and Christine Devon.'

Isaac left the interview room and made some phone calls. The first he made was to Charisa Devon, the second to her brother, the third to Richard Goddard, the fourth to Superintendent Caddick. The fifth, the most important to him that day, to Ann, the PA of Phillip Loeb. This weekend he was free, and he intended to book a hotel close to Brighton; he knew she'd come.

The End.

ALSO BY THE AUTHOR

Death and the Lucky Man – A DI Tremayne Thriller

Sixty-eight million pounds and dead.

Hardly the outcome expected for the luckiest man in England the day his lottery ticket was drawn out of the barrel.

But then, Alan Winters' rags-to-riches story had never been conventional, and there were those who had benefited, but others who hadn't.

Death and the Assassin's Blade – A DI Tremayne Thriller

It was meant to be high drama, not murder, but someone's switched the daggers. The man's death took place in plain view of two serving police officers.

He was not meant to die; the daggers were only theatrical props, plastic and harmless. A summer's night, a production of Julius Caesar amongst the ruins of an Anglo-Saxon fort. Detective Inspector Tremayne is there with his sergeant, Clare Yarwood. In the assassination scene, Caesar collapses to the ground. Brutus defends his actions; Mark Antony rebukes him.

They're a disparate group, the amateur actors. One's an estate agent, another an accountant. And then there is the teenage school student, the gay man, the funeral director. And what about the women? They could be involved.

They've each got a secret, but which of those on the stage wanted Gordon Mason, the actor who had portrayed Caesar, dead?

Murder is the Only Option – A DCI Cook Thriller

A man, thought to be long dead, returns to exact revenge against those who had blighted his life. His only concern is to protect his wife and daughter. He will stop at nothing to achieve his aim.

'Big Greg, I never expected to see you around here at this time of night.'

'I've told you enough times.'

'I've no idea what you're talking about,' Robertson replied. He looked up at the man, only to see a metal pole coming down at him. Robertson fell down, cracking his head against a concrete kerb.

The two vagrants, no more than twenty feet away, did not stir and did not even look in the direction of the noise. If they had, they would have seen a dead body, another man walking away.

Death Unholy – A DI Tremayne Thriller

All that remained were the man's two legs and a chair full of greasy and fetid ash. Little did DI Keith Tremayne know that it was the beginning of a journey into the murky world of paganism and its ancient rituals. And it was going to get very dangerous.

'Do you believe in spontaneous human combustion?' Detective Inspector Keith Tremayne asked.

'Not me. I've read about it. Who hasn't?' Sergeant Clare Yarwood answered.

I haven't,' Tremayne replied, which did not surprise his young sergeant. In the months they had been working together, she had come to realise that he was a man who had little interest in the world. When he had a cigarette in his mouth, a beer in his hand, and a murder to solve he was about the happiest she ever saw him. He could hardly be regarded as one of life's sociable people. And as for reading? The most he managed was an occasional police report or an early morning newspaper, turning first to the back pages for the racing results.

Murder in Little Venice – A DCI Cook Thriller

A dismembered corpse floats in the canal in Little Venice, an upmarket tourist haven in London. Its identity is unknown, but what is its significance?

DCI Isaac Cook is baffled about why it's there. Is it gang-related, or is it something more?

Whatever the reason, it's clearly a warning, and Isaac and his team are sure it's not the last body that they'll have to deal with.

Murder is only a Number – A DCI Cook Thriller

Before she left she carved a number in blood on his chest. But why the number 2, if this was her first murder?

The woman prowls the streets of London. Her targets are men who have wronged her. Or have they? And why is she keeping count?

DCI Cook and his team finally know who she is, but not before she's murdered four men. The whole team are looking for her, but the woman keeps disappearing in plain sight. The pressure's on to stop her, but she's always one step ahead.

And this time, DCS Goddard can't protect his protégé, Isaac Cook, from the wrath of the new commissioner at the Met.

Murder House – A DCI Cook Thriller

A corpse in the fireplace of an old house. It's been there for thirty years, but who is it?

It's clearly murder, but who is the victim and what connection does the body have to the previous owners of the house. What is the motive? And why is the body in a fireplace? It was bound to be discovered eventually but was that what the murderer wanted? The main suspects are all old and dying, or already dead.

Isaac Cook and his team have their work cut out trying to put the pieces together. Those who know are not talking because of an old-fashioned belief that a family's dirty laundry should not be aired in public, and certainly not to a policeman – even if that means the murderer is never brought to justice!

Murder is a Tricky Business – A DCI Cook Thriller

A television actress is missing, and DCI Isaac Cook, the Senior Investigation Officer of the Murder Investigation Team at Challis Street Police Station in London, is searching for her.

Why has he been taken away from more important crimes to search for the woman? It's not the first time she's gone missing, so why does everyone assume she's been murdered?

There's a secret, that much is certain, but who knows it? The missing woman? The executive producer? His eavesdropping assistant? Or the actor who portrayed her fictional brother in the TV soap opera?

Murder Without Reason – A DCI Cook Thriller

DCI Cook faces his greatest challenge. The Islamic State is waging war in England, and they are winning.

Not only does Isaac Cook have to contend with finding the perpetrators, but he is also being forced to commit actions contrary to his mandate as a police officer.

And then there is Anne Argento, the prime minister's deputy. The prime minister has shown himself to be a pacifist and is not up to the task. She needs to take his job if the country is to fight back against the Islamists.

Vane and Martin have provided the solution. Will DCI Cook and Anne Argento be willing to follow it through? Are they able to act for the good of England, knowing that a criminal and murderous action is about to take place? Do they have any option?

The Haberman Virus

A remote and isolated village in the Hindu Kush mountain range in North Eastern Afghanistan is wiped out by a virus unlike any seen before.

A mysterious visitor clad in a space suit checks his handiwork, a female American doctor succumbs to the disease, and the woman sent to trap the person responsible falls in love with him – the man who would cause the deaths of millions.

Hostage of Islam

Three are to die at the Mission in Nigeria: the pastor and his wife in a blazing chapel; another gunned down while trying to defend them from the Islamist fighters.

Kate McDonald, an American, grieving over her boyfriend's death and Helen Campbell, whose life had been troubled by drugs and prostitution, are taken by the attackers.

Kate is sold to a slave trader who intends to sell her virginity to an Arab Prince. Helen, to ensure their survival, gives herself to the murderer of her friends.

Malika's Revenge

Malika, a drug-addicted prostitute, waits in a smugglers' village for the next Afghan tribesman or Tajik gangster to pay her price, a few scraps of heroin.

Yusup Baroyev, a drug lord, enjoys a lifestyle many would envy. An Afghan warlord sees the resurgence of the Taliban. A Russian white-collar criminal portrays himself as a good and honest citizen in Moscow.

All of them are linked in an audacious plan to increase the quantity of heroin shipped out of Afghanistan and into Russia and ultimately the West.

Some will succeed, some will die, some will be rescued from their plight and others will rue the day they became involved.

ABOUT THE AUTHOR

Phillip Strang was born in England in the late forties, during the post-war baby boom. He had a comfortable middle-class upbringing, spending his childhood years in a small town to the west of London.

An avid reader of science fiction in his teenage years: Isaac Asimov, Frank Herbert, the masters of the genre. Much of what they and others mentioned has now become a reality. Science fiction has now become science fact. Still an avid reader, the author now mainly reads thrillers.

In his early twenties, the author, with a degree in electronics engineering and a desire to see the world, left England for Sydney, Australia. Now, forty years later, he still resides in Australia, although many intervening years were spent in a myriad of countries, some calm and safe, others no more than war zones.

Printed in Great Britain
by Amazon

55078282R00149